Doct___
N___

Richard Gordon

HEINEMANN : LONDON

William Heinemann Ltd
15 Queen Street, Mayfair, London W1X 8BE
LONDON   MELBOURNE   TORONTO
JOHANNESBURG   AUCKLAND

First published 1979
© Richard Gordon Ltd 1979

SBN 434 30254 6

Printed in Great Britain by
Cox & Wyman Ltd
London, Fakenham and Reading

I

As a virtuous surgeon and unswerving patriot, Sir Lancelot Spratt kept faith with the British National Health service until the morning his operating theatre ceiling collapsed. It had already been a dreadful day.

At six a.m., his bedside telephone had rung.

'Spratt here.' His brain was instantly scalpel-sharp, tempered by a lifetime of arousal to impending surgical catastrophe.

'Sir Lancelot? Good morning,' came a pleasant male voice. 'What's the weather like?'

Sir Lancelot's eye turned appraisingly to his bedroom window. 'I should say clear, with some patchy high cloud. Temperature, about fifteen degrees Centigrade. There appears every possibility of a fine June day.' He roared into the mouthpiece, 'If you want a prognosis on the weather, you necrotic little nuisance, whoever you may be, dial the Meteorological Office instead of breaking into the valuable sleep of an expensive consultant surgeon.'

'This is Chipps, sir. Pip Chipps.'

Sir Lancelot's groan rang across the bedroom.

'Where I am, sir, it's dreadfully hot.'

Sir Lancelot's face brightened. Was it possible, through the tantalizing mysteries of extrasensory perception, to communicate with the afterlife? 'Where are you?' he asked hopefully.

'In Nairobi.'

'And what, pray, grips you with an impulse to telephone me from darkest Africa at six in the morning?'

'Six? Oh, sorry, sir. I'd forgotten the time-change.

We've just finished our paw-paws. Auntie Florrie suggested that I got in touch with you.'

Sir Lancelot's groan rang across four thousand miles. Auntie Florrie had been matron of the St Swithin's private patients' wing. During the past year, she had won charge of St Sepulchre's Hospital, a subsidiary of St Swithin's, where its patients could be diverted and its students taught, some ten miles away in the London suburbs. She burnt with a passion for Sir Lancelot which she believed to be secret, but was as familiar to the staff of both institutions as the items on the canteen menu. He would inevitably be facing her within the next four hours.

'I'm coming home, sir,' Dr Phillip Chipps announced cheerfully on the telephone.

'You're bloody not,' Sir Lancelot told him vigorously. 'You remember perfectly well our bargain over your surgery finals. I'd pass you, if you'd take yourself instantly to some clinical St Helena. I regarded your permanent exile precisely like Napoleon's, essential for the health of Europe.'

'Only on leave, sir,' Pip explained quickly. 'We're arriving on Monday week. You've never met the wife—'

'Of course I've met her, you fool. I distinctly remember thinking her much too good for you. I was invited to dine in that little flat of yours behind the St Swithin's laundry – moussaka, and you might have done better than that half-bottle of Hungarian Riesling. Hello? Hello? Still there, Nairobi?'

There was a long silence. 'Er—yes, sir.'

'I'm delighted to hear that you are shortly to enjoy a refreshing holiday, Chipps. But I fail to see why you could not have announced the event with a picture-postcard, instead of imparting it at such expense.'

'The point is, sir,' he continued awkwardly, 'auntie thought you might be able to fix me up with some lucrative and not over-worked locum job for a month. You know, standing in for some family doctor who's off on his own summer hols. I rather would like somewhere pleasant,' Pip enlarged. 'The Cotswolds, perhaps? The seaside? The Highlands of Scotland would suit nicely. Oh, and somewhere where my wife and I can live over the shop. You see, I don't earn enough out here in Kenya to save up for expensive holidays. My work is reward enough in itself. Or is supposed to be.'

'I am not a blasted medical temps' bureau. And if I were, I wouldn't offer you a job doctoring tom-cats.'

Pip said pleadingly, 'But Auntie Florrie told me that you rather enjoyed putting yourself out to help your former students.'

'Not a student of such ignorance, ineptitude and indolence that he stood out even in a place like St Swithin's.'

'Auntie Florrie—'

'Your Aunt Florence incites in me a peculiar reflex. Every time she opens her mouth, she gives me a pain in the arse. Good morning.'

Sir Lancelot replaced the telephone.

He lay thoughtfully in his striped pyjamas, hands clasped over the dome of his belly. In his massive oak four-poster bed, his father had breathed his last and he himself his first. He too would probably die in it. Sir Lancelot saw himself as a traditionalist. In the less patient glance of others, he was a hideous old fogey.

A breeze stirred the net curtain of his first-floor bedroom. His narrow terrace house looked across a cramped walled back-garden, its roses standing in ranks and its lawn clipped as tidily as a marine's haircut. Beyond towered the new white buildings of St Swithin's itself, which had first treated the sick on the same spot in the unruly times of King Stephen.

He noticed lights shining, forgotten. Hospital night was turning officially to morning. Crumpled nurses would be replaced by crisp day-staff, the patients shaken

3

awake with a heartening cup of tea. A hospital is like the army, Sir Lancelot reflected. The consultants were the remote generals, unflaggingly busy and professionally infallible – what was the point in patients or privates thinking otherwise, when no one else held the threads of their lives? The registrars and housemen were the officers, the nurses the brisk NCOs, the backbone of the force. The patients were the poor bloody infantry, trying to cheer each other up as they crouched under the surgical shellfire. Unfortunately, it was now the unionized NAAFI assistants who could bring the battle to an instant halt.

It was too bright to sleep, too early to rise. He reached for a thick paperback from his bedside table. Its plain glossy white cover said in stark black –

SHRINK
AMELIA
WITHERSPOON.

It was not Sir Lancelot's usual reading, but like all successful men of action he knew the value of diligent homework.

Within an hour he rose, bathed, shaved, donned the dark suit and white shirt which he felt befitted his profession, and went downstairs with the foreboding which clouded the sunniest mornings increasingly thickly.

The french windows of his small, square dining-room stood open to the walled garden. He was sitting sipping coffee at the circular table when the door opened.

'Aye, noo, and what's this? Ye no care for your smokie, then?' Miss MacNish, the housekeeper who shared Sir Lancelot's home, took his plate of uneaten fish as though it were a personal insult.

'That yellow-dyed, deep-frozen, machine-filleted haddock bears as little relation to a real finnan haddie as catfood to caviar.'

'Ye dinna eat your haggis wi' bashed tatties I did specially for you last night,' she continued accusingly.

'I regard Scottish cuisine, consisting as it does largely of oatmeal and offal, interesting only in accounting for the poor physique and worse teeth of many Scotsmen.'

Miss MacNish was short, pale, slight and gingery. She had arrived in London with a Scottish accent as pure and sweet as Edinburgh rock. Now she achieved the glottal obscurity of a Glasgow Rangers' supporter on a Saturday night. Many Scots doctors were similarly affected, Sir Lancelot recalled resignedly. Perhaps they imagined that the accent breathed heather-scented, Presbyterian wholesomeness through the sickly London air. Or perhaps it was something to do with the television shows. Miss MacNish drew herself up in the doorway like a piece of elastic. 'Very well, Sir Lancelot,' she told him. 'If you are not satisfied with my cooking, with my housekeeping, in short with my devoting my life to you—'

'My dear Miss MacNish!' He always found himself plunging into humility, like a shot grouse into the gorse. He could not live without Miss MacNish. He would have to wash his own socks and boil his own eggs, a drudgery he had abandoned as gratefully as replenishing the midnight oil when ceasing to be a student. It was ludicrous, but a man of his importance and effectiveness could be reduced to baffled immobilization in the morning by the lack of a shirt-sleeve button. 'I assure you that I meant to be neither unappreciative nor uncivil—'

'I shall be *perfectly* happy to quit this house, Sir Lancelot. For ever. Before lunchtime.'

'Possibly I am a little tetchy this morning,' he grovelled. 'I was woken at six, by some idiot raving at me from Nairobi.'

'Ye need a good hot meal inside you, afore ye go to do your surgery,' she said, glaring at the cold haddock.

'As I am constantly advising others about their diets,'

he protested mildly, 'might I perhaps be trusted with my own?'

'Och, it needs a woman to tell such things.'

'Indeed, yes. I know you have only my welfare at heart, Miss MacNish. May I promise that I have yours?' He hesitated. All women presented personality problems, which unfortunately he could not solve by the practical methods of Henry the Eighth. 'It might be advantageous if I arranged for you to see a colleague at St Swithin's.'

'Why? I'm as fit as a wee flea.'

'One must not overlook the onset of the menopause—'

'How *dare* you!' She looked as though he had uttered some filthy expression. To Sir Lancelot's relief, the door-bell rang. She slammed down the plate. She took a carefully folded white linen handkerchief from the pocket of her green overall, and holding it to her eyes strode to the front door. 'Sir Lionel Loftus,' she announced. Sir Lancelot gave his loudest groan of the morning.

'Lovers' tiff, eh?' asked the dean of St Swithin's, twinkling as the dining-room door closed behind him.

'Your innuendo trips with the delicacy of the Abominable Snowman. Miss MacNish is simply traversing the time of life when women become emotionally unstable.'

'Oh, no need to protest so much,' the dean said lightly. 'The whole hospital takes your relationship for granted.'

He sat at the breakfast-table. The dean was a small man with a pointed bald head and large ears, resembling a garden gnome on which a pair of oversized eyebrows expressed his rapidly-fleeting emotions like two over-excited hairy caterpillars.

'You know perfectly well the stout door which guards Miss MacNish's self-contained flat and honour on the top floor,' Sir Lancelot told him gruffly. 'I can assure you that were she separated from me by nothing more solid than a see-through nightie, I should remain untempted.'

'We think you're rather a good match. She's one of the

6

few women you can't treat like a bulldozer in a flowerbed. Mind if I have some coffee? Mine was cold at home. Awfully convenient, isn't it, our occupying neighbouring houses on St Swithin's property?'

'Particularly if you are the dean, and live rent-free.'

'I suppose you've read the paper?' asked the dean, ignoring the remark and nodding towards the folded *Times*, while absent-mindedly breaking and buttering one of Sir Lancelot's breakfast baps.

'Only the cricket. That was all the late Lord Attlee read in the papers, while running a normally quarrelsome Labour Cabinet. I am beginning to appreciate how he kept his coolness, if not sanity.'

The dean looked offended. 'I happen to be in the news this morning.'

'Pinched for speeding again? A man of your age shouldn't drive a Lotus.'

'I have joined a new consortium,' announced the dean proudly. 'Headed by Hamilton Tosker. Remarkable man!'

'You mean Ned Kelly's little brother?' asked Sir Lancelot with curiosity.

'He is a very great Australian,' the dean corrected him expansively. 'It is petty jealousy, resenting his activities in this country. Not only is he the builder of anything from highways and heliports to hotels and hospitals, but he is a businessman of great enterprise. He has quietly taken over several manufacturers of medical equipment for a brilliant new plan. We are going to sell ready-made hospitals to the Arabs. A package-deal, the building, fully-furnished wards and completely equipped operating-theatres, oxygen-tents, blood-banks, X-rays, electron-microscopes, the lot.'

'What about the doctors and nurses?' objected Sir Lancelot.

'No problem.' The dean tapped his chest. 'That's my

job. Everyone I recruit will walk into a brand-new hospital in the sunshine, pick up scalpel or stethoscope and start work. At about ten times NHS salary. A wonderful export effort. A great humanitarian service towards underdeveloped nations,' he added solemnly.

'What's Tosker paying you?'

'Mind your own business.'

'If you choose to spend your spare time at that sort of thing, it's up to you. Personally, I prefer fly-fishing.'

'Ah, but the world it opens! Power, finance, politics ... It's all a matter of contacts, you know. A man like Hamilton Tosker can pick up the telephone and get through to Downing Street any time he feels like it. Sometimes I think that – had I not decided to dedicate my life to humanity—' The dean gazed at the ceiling with eyebrows speculatively arched. 'I could have been a millionaire, too. There honestly doesn't seem much to it.'

'And how does this square with your employment by the National Health Service?' Sir Lancelot gave him a narrow look. 'And your membership of an Area Health Authority?'

'No conflict of interest whatever,' the dean told him airily. 'Really, Lancelot, you can be depressingly straitlaced. A touch of the buccaneering spirit made this country great. Look at Raleigh, Drake, Clive of India, those sort of chaps. I have a very important business lunch today with Hamilton Tosker, to settle our strategy. Which reminds me, I must cancel my three o'clock lecture on the kidney. These business lunches open up all sort of discussions on the ongoing aspects, you know. Liable to occupy much of the afternoon. Don't you want your fish?'

'You're welcome to it, if you care to risk a case of botulism.'

The dean rose, brushing crusty crumbs from his light grey suit. 'I must get along to Harley Street. Thursday is your day for St Sepulchre's, isn't it? A very salutary experience for you, I'm sure. Thank God none of my patients are ever incarcerated there. I'd rather be camp doctor in Siberia.'

'Today I have a companion.' Sir Lancelot stood up. 'Ms—as I understand she prefers to be called – Amelia Witherspoon from Boston. She wrote an exhaustive investigative book called *Shrink*.'

The dean frowned. 'About laundries?'

'Psychiatrists. The Americans refer to them as head-shrinkers. As our army doctors were once called prick-farriers,' he added helpfully. 'Though I gather from the book that the most noticeable, and indeed drastic, effect of psychiatric treatment in the United States is upon the patient's bank balance rather than his mental one. She is now studying systems of health care round the world. Which naturally includes our National Health Service.'

'You *are* a dog for the ladies, aren't you, Lancelot?'

'If I am, I can only reply that Ms Witherspoon, from her printed word, displays the single-mindedness of an out-of-season bitch unearthing its favourite bone. I think I'll slip out quietly with you,' Sir Lancelot added, peeping warily round the dining-room door. 'I have suffered enough Celtic umbrage for one morning.'

2

Sir Lancelot drove his ancient Rolls-Royce towards the West End. His weather forecast to Nairobi seemed accurate. They had suffered, to quote his more accustomed bedside author, 'The usual nipping inclemency of May,' a month which in England has kindled more poetic imaginations than warmed fingers. The early days of June had languished shivering prisoners in winter's dungeon, but that week the sun had repossessed a sky of Wedgwood blue, and the air of summer bestowed upon the rheumy citizens its reviving, light-fingered caress.

He parked outside Bunter's Hotel in Mayfair. This was small, red-brick, tucked-away, its inside all plush curtains and plum carpets, offering the hushed opulence of an Edwardian nobleman's house during the London season. Sir Lancelot entered the gold-and-cream walled lobby where no voice was ever raised, no footsteps hurried, and visitors were paged with such solemnity they might have been dead. No Briton had been able to afford to stay there for several years.

He asked the young man in the tailcoat behind the mahogany desk for Ms Witherspoon.

'Sir Lancelot?' came a voice in his ear. 'There – I didn't call you "Sir Spratt". And I've never met a real knight before.'

He turned, startled. From the pages of *Shrink* he imagined Ms Witherspoon one of those flinty women from whom the friction of the world continually strikes sparks of blinding indignation. The sort who become consumers' crusaders, and the noisy leaders of worthy but boring causes. Instead, he saw a slight, slim blonde, with a mouth that intrigued him because it looked too big for her face. Her eyes were water-blue, but her glance suggested dangerous reefs under the surface. She wore a cream dress with white gloves and a white handbag, as though off to a Buckingham Palace garden party. He wondered how old she was. Anywhere between thirty and fifty. No one would ever tell, he decided, until she hit senility.

'Do all knights look as fearsome as you?' she asked amiably. 'Though I'm sure you're not, really. Do you want me to curtsy, or will a handshake do?'

He bowed. 'At your service.'

'Isn't it a lovely day? You know, I've never been to Britain before. I was brought up believing London to be invisible all the year round, in pea-soup fog.'

'Charles Dickens was as self-indulgent a caricaturist of our weather as of our people.' He led her towards the front door. 'May I express the hope that you will retain no unflattering preconceived notions about the weather, or anything else, here?'

He had prepared for the encounter with his usual profundity. He could remember the days when the British patronized the Americans. Now the Americans unthinkingly patronized the British. It all seemed to do with the dollar exchange-rate. He was old enough to recall the Empire running like a red carpet across the world. He was loyally determined to present his country in an equally rosy glow, even if the reality was a stormy sunset.

'Possibly you imagine us as a stuffy, quarrelsome nation?' he said with a soft chuckle. 'A people of stiff upper lips, cold shoulders and tight—er, sphincters. But we are warm, jolly, tolerant, cheerful and unfailingly courteous. Our sense of humour is, of course, world-famous.'

'Oh, you have a nice Queen and much to admire,' she said agreeably. 'It's a pity you're so broke.'

'At least we don't put ice in our whisky,' he said more sharply. 'I mean—er, here's my car.'

'Yours, is it?' A scrawny woman in black-and-yellow uniform fixed him with an eye as cold as a slice of jellied eel.

'Your eagerness is commendable, but may I point out that it is not yet eight-thirty?'

'And may *I* point out that you're on a double yellow line? Which means no parking, not at any time. Right?'

Sir Lancelot's beard elevated to the firing position. 'I am a doctor.'

It was the armour-piercing shot in his locker. It missed.

'Listen, mate, I don't care if you're a doctor or a docker. The whole world's one to me, when it parks on my yellow lines.'

'My dear good woman!' Sir Lancelot exploded. 'Do be reasonable—'

'Don't you "good woman" me,' the traffic warden said sourly. 'There's your ticket. Now take your daughter and leave some space for other people.'

Sir Lancelot twisted his face into a grin. 'These females tend to grow somewhat touchy.' He opened the car door for Amelia. 'Which is perfectly understandable, when the whole world continually insists that they are in the wrong. Cassandra must have felt exactly the same.'

'May I ask where we're going?'

He edged into the thickening traffic. 'St Sepulchre's Hospital.'

'An inspired name,' she reflected. 'It hardly stiffens morale, being wheeled in under *that* in big gold letters.'

'It is an ancient and not uncommon name for our churches. A fine example stands opposite St John's College in Cambridge. I operate at St Sepulchre's every Thursday. I gathered from the Department of Health that you wished first to study some typical small unit of the National Health Service, rather than a clinical showpiece like St Swithin's.'

'All hospitals fascinate me.'

'They all frighten me to death. And that's before I've set eyes on the doctors. You bloody fool,' he roared through the open window. 'If you want to commit suicide, chuck yourself off Westminster Bridge, but don't dent my expensive coachwork.'

'What language,' murmured Amelia admiringly, as the pedestrian shook both fists and passed observations on his sexual proclivities.

Sir Lancelot gave an oily smile. 'Doubtless from Billingsgate. The luridity of the speech there is traditional.'

'Mind if I smoke?'

'Yes, very much,' he snapped. 'I mean, my dear Ms Witherspoon, I strongly disapprove of the habit, but do entirely as you please.'

She obediently replaced the cigarettes in her handbag. They had come to a halt, jammed between two panting lorries. 'Why have the traffic signals all gone out?'

He explained airily, 'The men who keep them going happen to be working to rule.'

'What rule?'

'The British worker is subject to many strict rules. These are to prevent him working too hard. Which might be dangerous to health, or even life itself. But our employees are so zealous, that they simply break them.'

'You mean everyone in Britain works harder than they're legally permitted to?' she asked wonderingly.

'The rules are often quaintly archaic. I believe that, strictly legally, I should have a man with a red flag walking in front.'

'But if the rules are that ancient, why don't these enthusiastic workers of yours scrap them?'

'Ah! Then they couldn't demand payment for obliging their bosses by breaking them.'

She gave a brief sigh. 'Britain would seem a very complicated society.'

'It is. The only man in our history who really under-stood it was Sir William Gilbert.'

'A prime minister?'

'No. He wrote comic operas. We are a simple people to fathom, if you have a strong enough sense of the ridicu-lous. After all, we are so ludicrous, that in 1940 we didn't even recognize that we were beaten.'

'Where is this hospital of the happy name?'

'Spratt's Bottom.'

'Any relation?'

'As it happens, yes. I come from a family of squires, who farmed there over a hundred years ago. Now it is just another suburb. Without shape, character or discoverable identity. Simply a place where people go to sleep and shop. No more of a community than a seaside holiday-camp.'

'It's the same the world over. There's only one com-pelling argument for the suburbs. Most people live in them, and the rest all want to.' She noticed Sir Lancelot's lips moving noiselessly, as he glared at the immobile tail-lights of the lorry ahead. 'As we're going to be stuck here quite a while, tell me about yourself. Married?'

'Widower.'

'Oh, I'm sorry. You live alone?'

'I have a Scots housekeeper.'

'Domestic or euphemistic?'

'Her performances in the kitchen are sufficiently unin-spiring to quash any curiosity over those in the bed-chamber.'

'I see. Well, I'm divorced. Again. Just. The title "Ms" covers a multitude of sins. Or mistakes, which are by and large less enjoyable. You enjoyed *Shrink*?'

He nodded. 'It made me proud, Ms Witherspoon, that the science of psychiatry was invented by the grandfather of a British Liberal MP with a fixation on dog-food.'

This remark mystified her. 'Why not call me Amelia?'

'Because I distrust the modern habit of instant intimacy.'

'Lancelot's an attractive name,' she mused. 'You know, the Round Table, the Holy Grail, Lady of the Lake. Is your scalpel ever referred to as Excalibur?'

'No, but I am sometimes called "The Knight of the Long Knives".'

'Perhaps you've some little pet-name, which you'd prefer?'

'I have. But as it's Pooh-Bear, I should not prefer.'

She laughed. They began to crawl forward. 'Did you know that in Britain you spend 5.2 per cent of your gross national product on health, of which 4.6 per cent is public money?' she asked.

'I did not.'

'And that the comparable figures for the United States are 7.4 and 3.0 per cent?'

'Indeed?'

'That the average British doctor's income is 2.7 per cent of the average British labourer's?'

'I can well understand it.'

'Compared with 5.6 in the United States?'

'Lucky chaps.'

'Your average Briton's life expectancy at the age of 30 is 41.7 years – are you very interested in all this?'

'Not in the slightest.'

'Then what shall we talk about?'

'Cricket?'

'Cricket!' She looked shocked. 'That's only a game.'

'It most certainly is not,' he told her warmly. 'It is an enduring social cement. According to the historian Trevelyan, if the French aristocrats had played cricket with their peasants in 1789, their châteaux would never have been burnt. It is an activity enjoyed equally by dumper-drivers and dukes, one of whom quite recently made the successful manager of an English team.'

'I just can't see one of the Kennedys or the Rockefellers managing the New York Mets,' she said thoughtfully. 'You know – you're already teaching me something which gives hope for the British.'

'Which is?'

'You don't mind being crazy, when the rest of the world is sending itself mad trying to keep sane.'

They were suddenly loosed from the tangled traffic. Sir Lancelot drove quickly to Spratt's Bottom against the incoming commuter tide. The original village of the jovial, ruddy-faced Spratts had clustered against the manor house of the Lords Cherrymore, round a Norman church, an Elizabethan inn and a smithy which had shod Cromwell's horses. When the Spratts sold their birthright – for a sharp profit, they foresaw the railway as a contrivance here to stay – the hamlet had spread as haphazardly and uncontrollably as weeds on a compost-heap.

It first grew an outwork of red-brick castles, battlemented and turreted, to which Victorian merchants puffed each evening along the newly-cut lines from their solid desks in the City. After the Kaiser's war, main roads spread their ribbons across the fields, on their verges houses growing in the style of Anne Hathaway's cottage, all enjoying the permanent architectural copulation of semi-detachment. After Hitler's war, fascinatingly variegated dwellings sprawled over the remaining spaces – pink-washed Andalucian villas, plastic Wild West ranch-houses, neatly functional split-level human-hutches. They crawled up little creaks of roadway. They were jammed into corners by architectural contortionists. They grew in the gardens, and over the foundations, of the first massive houses which had scurried with servants like mice.

'We're here,' announced Sir Lancelot, nodding through the windscreen. 'That's the golf club.'

It was the only open space left in Spratt's Bottom.

Stockaded behind poplars and beeches, its lush fairways were already speckled with magnificently equipped players, its tennis courts already joyous with leaping brown-legged housewives in last year's Wimbledon fashions.

'It looks kinda Californian,' observed Amelia.

'Yes, the place represents a hiccup in local history. It was built in the 1930s by one of the Hungarian producers who so enlivened the British film industry. Like all Hungarian film producers, his overriding ambition was to become an unnoticeable English country gentleman. But he made so many lavishly successful films he went bankrupt. His herds of prize cattle, flocks of pedigree sheep, stables of horses and packs of hounds were auctioned along with his Chippendale and Hepplewhite, his Gainsboroughs and Romneys. Meanwhile, many young women had dutifully frozen blue beside his open-air swimming pool, the producer suffering a fixed belief that the climate of Spratt's Bottom should resemble that of Santa Barbara.

'It billeted an anti-aircraft battery during the war,' Sir Lancelot explained. 'And I believe has since passed through the rapacious fingers of many property owners.' He was driving along a broad, well-paved, tree-pierced, officially dog-constipating middle-class road. 'We're taking the short cut,' he said turning a corner.

The whim of the speculative builder was suddenly replaced by the severity of the municipal mind. Rows of russet-brick, red-roofed council houses stretched across the gently undulating land, all as indistinguishable as the teeth of a comb.

'Who lives here?' Amelia asked.

'The workers.'

'All together?'

'They were unthinkingly condemned to social apartheid by Mr Herbert Morrison's kindly London County

Council. You see how they are obliged to keep their cars in the gutters, through an undiagnosed official blindness to the honest wage-earner ever moving himself except with the noble humility of the bicycle. I do not care to decry socialism – to which half of my fellow-countrymen subscribe – but it is conducted on the two depressing principles that the poor will always be with us and nobody can be trusted to spend his own money.'

'What's Spratt's Bottom politically? Socialist or capitalist?'

'Remarkably balanced. Sometimes the local council is Labour, spending the ratepayers' money wildly on play centres and sauna baths. Sometimes it is Conservative, returned on a programme of economy, and cutting down the books in the public library. It has a Labour member of Parliament as often as a Tory one. Thus it is flattered during the antics of a General Election as a microcosm of Britain,' Sir Lancelot explained. 'The streets are invaded by young men and women with television cameras, microphones and clip-boards, earnestly seeking which way the place will vote. They generally get it wrong. The inhabitants of Spratt's Bottom have an inconvenient relish for making all experts look fools, just like the rest of the country. This is where the workers with hand and brain mingle,' he announced, as they turned into the broad main street.

The pious Victorians had ruthlessly restored the Norman church. They had built a combined town hall, magistrates' court and police station, which together resembled a jail. On the seat of the Cherrymores squatted municipal offices. The smithy had vanished but the Elizabethan inn remained exactly the same, four centuries being no impediment to the smooth drawing of English beer.

The family butchers, fragrant grocers and obsequious drapers, had long been swept into the vast stores and harshly-lit supermarkets which changed shopping from a diversion to an expedition. One end of the High Street, overflowing with pedestrians laden with their shopping and their young, had dropped into disfavour. It presented only tumbledown little shops for cut-price drinks, spare motor-parts and Oxfam, the railway sidings, the smoke-less fuel depot and the corporation rubbish-tip. Here stood St Sepulchre's Hospital.

Sir Lancelot cursed.

'Why, there's a riot,' said Amelia with alarm.

'Bloody demo,' muttered Sir Lancelot furiously. 'The plague of our times. I mean,' he told her unctuously, 'the citizens are exercising their right to demonstrate peace-fully their grievances. It has become a national outdoor recreation as popular as football matches, with which its participants often confuse it.'

He slowed down. The cramped forecourt of the hospital was filled with bobbing heads, one or two in policemen's helmets. Above them waved a few ill-scrawled placards, on which Sir Lancelot could discern arguments like, WE DEMAND A CLEAN SWEEP, COCKROACHES OUT and WORKERS WANT A WASHDOWN.

'Bloody ACHE,' he growled.

'What ache?'

'The Amalgamated Confederation of Hospital Employees,' he said savagely. 'A union rag-bag. I mean,' he corrected himself, 'it represents the legitimate interests of all those worthy porters, tea-ladies, mortuary atten-dants and other functionaries whom we doctors could not work without. This morning, they are a little over-excited about conditions in the hospital. Admittedly, St Sepulchre's is not a clinical Bunter's, but it is perfectly adequate for its purpose. Unfortunately, the workers get extravagant ideas of what hospitals should be like. It comes from watching so much television.'

'Do *you* demonstrate?' Amelia asked. She stared with fascination as Sir Lancelot came to a halt.

'My social class writes pained letters to *The Times* instead.'

'Lancelot, you're going to draw blood from that lip of yours in a minute.'

'An occasion for tank-tactics, I think.' He blew his horn, let down his window and shouted, 'I have a pregnant lady. Gangway for the maternity department.'

'What did that young man call you?'

'A bleeding fascist, I think. That is the usual appellation of anyone who tries to impose the mildest discipline on anyone else. Fortunately, I was able to form a more accurate assessment of fascists than he, when for the best part of six years they were trying to kill me.'

The car edged through the jostling crowd into a short alley between the hospital buildings. At the end was the consultants' car park. Sir Lancelot drew up and opened Amelia's door. 'Here we are.'

'My God,' she said slowly. She stepped from the car submitting St Sepulchre's to its first good look. 'I don't believe it.'

'I'm sure you will appreciate,' Sir Lancelot told her smoothly, 'that even the hospitals of our country, rooted as we are in age-long tradition, often provide interesting historical monuments.'

'Oh sure. But this must have stood here when Stonehenge was a construction site.'

3

ST Sepulchre's had served the community of Spratt's Bottom in three capacities. When Oliver Twist was asking for more, it was the workhouse. With the Lunacy Act of 1890, which permitted all persons behaving oddly to be kept behind high walls, so as not to pain the susceptibilities of respectable citizens, it became the asylum. In World War I, it turned into a general hospital, filled with the debris of the trenches. In World War II, it half disappeared under sandbags, as a clearing station for air-raid casualties. The generous interchangeability of Victorian architecture allowed it to illustrate the useful flexibility of all British institutions, from the Monarchy downwards.

'A hundred and fifty years old.' Sir Lancelot tried to sound proud of it. He wondered if Amelia would notice the rusty stubs of sawn-off bars still to be glimpsed in the massive windows.' It could do with a lick of paint, certainly,' he admitted handsomely. 'But it matters less what a hospital looks like, Ms ... er, Amelia, than what it does. Remember that penicillin was discovered in a cramped little room behind Paddington railway station.'

He led her towards the tumbledown building, two ambulances standing open-doored outside the entrance marked CASUALTY. A brief and unenthusiastic shout came from the demonstrators, invisible in the forecourt.

'If anyone had called *me* a fascist, I should have got out of the car and hit him,' said Amelia.

'Perhaps I should have done exactly that, before I saw

sense in the advice of a fellow-doctor – "I can imagine no more comfortable frame of mind for the conduct of life than humorous resignation".'

'Which doctor?'

'Somerset Maugham.'

'I didn't know he was?'

'Assuredly. Until the end of his long life, he remained on the medical *Register*. He was presumably perfectly entitled to deliver a baby, had the occasion arisen and he happened to feel like it,' Sir Lancelot ushered her through the door. 'I fancy Dr Maugham would have been a sensible practitioner. He had arranged to be moved *in extremis* from the hospital at Nice to his bed in his villa at Cap Ferrat. It is bad enough being ill among strangers. A man is entitled to die where he has lived.'

'I see your point,' murmured Amelia, as he led her through the bustling casualty department into the main hospital lobby. She stood staring at the bright mustard walls, covered with posters warning the populace against the dangers of smoking, overeating and indiscriminate love-making. The red plastic floor was worn into brown puddles, the ceiling cracked and grimy and hung with arrowed notices. These indicated, in Sir Lancelot's imagery, various sections of the firing-line, to patients arriving as reinforcements for those retreating with their kit through the safety of the battered front-door.

'Sir Lancelot!' came a sharp voice. 'I must speak to you instantly.'

Sir Lancelot groaned again, but internally. Amid the swirling, misplaced, bemused and fearful humanity choking the small lobby stood like a salt-scoured lighthouse Mrs Florence Leatherby-Hunter. She was Nursing Officer in Charge at St Sepulchre's, but Sir Lancelot and everyone else afforded her the traditional and more fearsome title of 'Matron'.

Sir Lancelot forced another ingratiating smile. 'May I

introduce Ms Amelia Witherspoon? One of America's leading authors.'

The matron's glance flashed like the lighthouse beam. She was tall, slim, even in danger of being skinny, fair-haired, grey-eyed, divorced. She was no longer obliged to wear uniform, but her severe light-blue dress suggested one. On her left breast was pinned the shiny silver nurses' badge of St Swithin's. She apologized for her unfamiliarity with Amelia's name by saying, 'I am afraid that in my job I am far too busy to read books.'

'How great your sacrifice to humanity,' murmured Amelia smoothly.

The matron seemed not to hear. 'Sir Lancelot, what I have to say demands being said in confidence.' She drew him firmly into a corner. 'There is but one word to describe this place.'

'Spare my blushes—'

'Scutari. At least my namesake at the Crimea won public approbation with her accusations of crass stupidity and criminal neglect. Here, nobody takes the slightest notice. I do not know whether to feel appalled, amazed or merely amused at the way the Government expects me to run a hospital. I have insufficient nurses, and hardly any of those speak English. The porters seem to be per-manently either on strike or at tea-break. The building is falling to bits like Sodom and Gomorrah. The patients behave like touring pop-stars, expecting me instantly at their beck and call—'

'We all have our little local difficulties.'

'Don't be so infuriatingly unflappable. Good God, Lancelot! Even the captain of the *Titanic* could recognize an iceberg when he had one in front of his eyes.' Her look fixed him like an angler selecting a fat maggot. 'You're on the Area Health Authority. You have power. You're thick as thieves with both Jenny Porter and Ronnie Cherry-more, who sit on the local council as well. And you are constantly hobnobbing with Sir Charles from the Ministry in your club – where I think you are going far too often for the good of your liver. You'll forgive me saying so, I'm sure,' she ended more tenderly. 'Because you know I have your welfare close at heart, Lancelot.'

'It is either the club or Miss MacNish. I prefer to be poisoned by Scotch whisky than by Scotch cooking.'

'We must have a long talk about your domestic arrangements very soon. Who *is* that woman?' she broke off crossly. With a minute camera from her handbag, Amelia was photographing a pair of puzzled old men in striped towelling dressing-gowns, imploring them *not* to smile.

'Sir Charles sent her to me. She's come to write about the National Health Service.'

'*Here?*'

'I suppose on the principle that the most popular bit of Madame Tussaud's is the Chamber of Horrors.'

'I hope you take care what she writes. Remember that stupid fuss in the papers about the toe in the bread-and-butter pudding. Has Pip telephoned you?' Sir Lancelot nodded. Her expression softened again. 'How is the dear boy? I hope the tropics aren't sapping his vitality. He always was a sickly child.'

'The only ill-functioning part of him lies between the ears,' suggested Sir Lancelot.

'You've met his wife? Such a good match. She, too, is highly intelligent.'

'My acquaintance is restricted to an extremely greasy and dyspeptic dinner.'

'But she's cordon bleu. You must have drunk too much again. You really do need a woman to look after you, someone sensible and sympathetic, who understands you. Nurse—!' She glared at a small, pretty girl hurrying past. 'Have you not learned that a nurse *runs* only in case of fire or haemorrhage?'

'Holy Mother of God, yes, I have,' she said breathlessly. 'And the toaster's in flames in the ward kitchen. What shall I do?'

The matron's eyes narrowed. 'Fan them, Nurse, fan them.' She looked round, but Sir Lancelot had escaped.

'Where are we going?' asked Amelia. He took her elbow, and was hurrying her down a long, narrow, windowless corridor, choked with humans on their feet, on their backs, alive, asleep and dead.

'The operating theatres. You may find them interesting. They're constructed from the old workhouse mortuary. Ronnie!' He stopped short. 'What are you doing in that wheel-chair?'

Abandoned in the corridor was a tall, angular, sandy-haired young man, with large frank blue eyes. He wore jeans, an open flowered shirt, round his neck a string of multi-coloured beads, on one foot a sandal.

'I fell off my moped.' His voice was quiet, precise, firmly assured of its every word's accuracy, rightfulness and worth. 'I would have appeared to have fractured my ankle.'

'But my dear fellow,' exclaimed Sir Lancelot solicitously. 'Come along with me, and I'll have it X-rayed and plastered straight away.'

'You know I would find that reprehensible. I intend to take my place in the queue, exactly like everyone else. The porter was pushing me to X-ray, but I discovered he was off duty and insisted he left me here. Another will doubtless be along shortly.'

'But aren't you in pain?'

'I prefer pain to taking advantage of my fellow-humans.'

'Please yourself,' said Sir Lancelot briefly. 'But with the queue in X-ray, your fracture will probably have healed before you get a picture of it.'

'Mr Cherrymore?' A small, freckled, rounded girl in

uniform hurried up. 'I'm Nurse Tosker. I was sent from X-ray to collect you. Come along, now. We can't have you languishing without proper treatment. Besides, look how you're holding up the traffic.'

'Thank you, nurse. By the by,' the patient called to Sir Lancelot as she pushed him away. 'I'd prefer not to be called Ronnie any more. Only Ron. It's more democratic.'

'Who's that drop-out?' asked Amelia.

'A drop-out only from the peerage. He recently became Lord Cherrymore, but renounced it to become plain Mr Cherrymore. Like Lord Home, who became Sir Alec Douglas-Home to be prime minister, but turned into Lord Home again when he found he wasn't.'

'You British could do with a visit from Margaret Mead. Your tribal customs are more complicated than the Polynesians'.'

Sir Lancelot was hastening along the corridor. 'Ronnie – Ron, whatever he wants to call himself – is going into politics. He must be mad.'

'As an encrusted, blue-blooded Tory?'

'Good God, no. He's as left as a bar sinister. Yes?'

An angry-looking, middle-aged woman stood in his path. 'When's my husband coming in for his feet then? It's you doctors what's to blame. All right for some, if they've got the money,' she declared bitterly. 'Private patients don't wait to get their feet done. Oh, no! *And* they get their own room, *and* their own telly. My Harry, he's in agony with his feet—'

'I assure you, madam, that had we sufficient porters, nurses and facilities, I should eagerly slice my waiting-list to ribbons in a fortnight. And what's *your* grouse?' he demanded of a neatly-dressed young man hovering beside her.

'No grouse whatever, myself,' he said cheerfully. 'But one of our clients has. A writ, I'm afraid, Sir Lancelot. About that stomach you removed by mistake.'

26

'I have never so much as removed an adhesive plaster by mistake.' Sir Lancelot crammed the folded sheet of thick foolscap roughly into his pocket. 'Bloody money,' he complained, hurrying Amelia along. 'All people think about. Nothing'll come of this legal blackmail, but they all try it on. The slightest error in an overworked doctor's judgment, and they cash in like claiming on the football pools. A botched belly is good for a world cruise. Lose the wrong leg, and you can retire for life. No charity, no gratitude. God knows why I continue to practise at all,' he continued with rising exasperation. 'My father was presented with a clean starched towel and lavender soap at every bedside, and turkeys and Scotch every Christmas. The surgeons who taught me entered the ward with a trail of assistants and nurses, and would no more be waylaid by disgruntled patients in the corridor than Lorenzo the Magnificent stopped in the streets of Florence and asked the time. Now I creep into the insults of people with barely one O-level between them, and instead of patients being damn glad that I took the time and trouble of training myself to cure their ills – nine-thirty already,' he added, as the lights went out.

'The lights always go out at nine-thirty in the morning?'

'The power engineers are taking industrial action.'

'Seems more like inaction to me.'

'Exactly. When anyone in this country uses a word, it means just what they choose it to mean. The principle was discovered by another perceptive Englishman, the Reverend Lutwidge Dodgson.'

'Archbishop of Canterbury?'

'Much more important. He wrote *Alice in Wonderland*. The emergency supply will shortly be switched on.' They reached the end of the dim corridor. 'Here I must abandon you. We've reached the operating theatres.'

'But I'm coming in,' she insisted.

'I regret that unqualified persons are, in my opinion, as

unsuitable in an operating theatre as children at a dinner party. Besides, you might faint at the sight of blood.'

'No more chance than Count Dracula. I've haunted operating rooms round the whole world.'

'I forbid it.'

'Well, now. I'm beginning to think those porters and patients of yours have a point.'

'Oh, please yourself,' he said impatiently. 'I've work to do. Sister! Kit out this visitor. I'm scrubbing up.'

He changed into operating singlet and trousers, and put on rubber boots. He donned cap and mask. He went to the scrubbing-up basin. No water would come from the taps.

The fuse of Sir Lancelot's temper, which had been burning since he encountered the traffic warden, hit the explosive. He beat the long, shiny, arid handles with his fists. He called complicated anatomical curses on the Secretary of State for Health.

'Something the matter, Sir Lancelot?' The gowned theatre sister appeared at the door.

'I'm emigrating. To Arabia. I shall become an itinerant cutter with my instruments on a camel. At least, in the middle of the blasted desert,' he roared at her, *'I shouldn't have the laughable expectation of being provided with water'.*

'If you haven't scrubbed-up yet,' she consoled him, 'you can take a long-distance call from Mr Bisham.'

'I will not take any bloody calls from near or far—' Sir Lancelot abruptly grabbed the wall telephone. 'Bisham?'

'Hello, sir? I'm speaking from Llanfihangel-yng-ngwynfa. It's a place in Wales.'

'Obviously. It's two years since you worked in this dilapidated pesthouse, isn't it? How do you get the water running in the scrubbing-up room?'

'Kick the pipe behind the soiled-linen bin, sir.'

'Thank you.'

'And Sir Lancelot – you know I'm married?'

'Of course I do,' he snapped. 'I had a memorable dinner

28

with the pair of you, in that flat behind the Spratt's Bottom Post Office.'

There was a silence. 'Hello? Still there?'

'Yes, sir. You see, I'm still only a surgical registrar, and my finances demand that I spend my holiday in ten days' time doing some lucrative locum job—'

'Pin a postcard in—' Sir Lancelot stopped. He had a high opinion of Freddie Bisham. He was an able young surgeon, with the incomparable advantage of being trained by himself. 'I'll see what I can do,' he promised brusquely. 'Behind the soiled-linen bin? Good morning.'

Pulling on his rubber gloves, the scrubbed and gowned Sir Lancelot strode to the table under the yard-wide soup-plate of the operating lamp. A practised glance told him that his unconscious patient with a hernia was correctly prepared and towelled, that his assisting house-surgeon had a hangover, the theatre sister was suffering from premenstrual tension and the anaesthetist from homesickness. Gowned and masked, Amelia was gazing closely at the sterilized skin.

'We've catastrophic cross-infection in the hospital already, without your wiping your nose on the wound,' he told her in his usual operating-theatre manner, which resembled a peppery captain in a stormy morning on his quarterdeck.

Amelia's fine eyebrows disappeared under her cap. 'I take an intelligent interest in surgery.'

'So do I. I also take responsibility for anything that goes wrong. All right to cut, Ali?'

'Inguinal or femoral hernia?' asked Amelia quietly.

'Inguinal, obviously.'

'Direct or indirect?'

He answered with a cauterizing glare.

'I learned a lot of surgery from writing about it for the women's magazines.'

'Then I must apologize for learning mine from the Royal College of Surgeons.'

'You've missed clipping a bleeding point.'

'Will you not back-seat operate, woman?' he bellowed. 'Cut, man, cut,' he continued to his assistant. 'You're about as much use this morning as a jock-strap in a nunnery. *Swab, sister, swab!*'

'What happened to the attitude of humorous resignation?' asked Amelia.

'It is difficult to maintain in the cruciform position.'

There was a loud crack overhead, and it began to rain plaster.

'Bloody National Health Service,' roared Sir Lancelot. 'Bloody Bevan. Bloody Beveridge. At least, under the old system the bloody hospitals didn't collapse about your ears. Towel, sister! Whoever heard of an operation wound contaminated by the ceiling?'

Sister began to mutter miserably, 'I should never have taken up nursing. I did so love horses.' The assistant gazed upwards dumbly. The other gowned nurse bobbed round with a shiny bowl, trying to catch chunks of plaster. 'Oh, my goodness,' said the anaesthetist, 'Sir Lancelot has brought the house down.'

'Look out!' cried Sir Lancelot. With a sharp report, the massive operating light lurched towards the patient, dragging its electrical entrails from the roof.

Sir Lancelot slammed a swab on the oozing operation site. 'Field it,' he commanded the houseman, staring anxiously upwards.

'But I'm sterile, sir,' he objected in mindless confusion.

Amelia grabbed the heavy dish of the light just above the patient's exposed belly.

'Nurse,' shouted Sir Lancelot. 'Help the lady with the lamp.'

A lump of plaster caught the back of his head. The light went out.

'Ali! Emergency torch from the surgeons' room. Swing that lamp out of my way, woman,' he commanded Amelia. 'I'm going to finish this operation in double-quick time. Before the rest of the building buries us, making it the only hernia in surgical history with a seven hundred per cent mortality. Sister!' He glared. 'This is hardly the time for song.'

Her eyes screwed up with delight over her mask. '*Pennies from Heaven*, Sir Lancelot. Now the Ministry will be absolutely forced to give us a new operating theatre.'

4

'I do think everyone is making a mountain out of a molehill,' said Mr Clapper, the area health administrator, polishing his black-rimmed glasses with a large spotless handkerchief. 'Or perhaps I should say, a thunderbolt out of a passing shower?'

Sir Lancelot Spratt grunted.

'In one way the event was quite useful. A large and rusty water-tank was revealed, of which no one in the hospital had the slightest awareness. No wonder the canteen tea often tasted so horrible.'

Mr Clapper had been promoted from the administrator's office at St Swithin's. He was a small, fat man who gleamed from his smooth black hair to his polished black shoes. A relaxed smile stretched lips so pink and moist that they reminded Sir Lancelot of smoked salmon canapés. It was nine-thirty the following Thursday morning, exactly a week later. The crack which had sounded above Sir Lancelot's head had by then rung round the world. Television crews had sped to St Sepulchre's. Sir Lancelot's photograph shared the newspaper front pages with his patient's sitting up in bed. Amelia Witherspoon's hotel telephone had spread the name of Spratt's Bottom across the United States, which could shake its head over the dangers of socialized medicine, and the decline of a once-great nation so catastrophic that the dome of St Paul's was likely to go next.

Sir Lancelot accepted the power of the press as he accepted the power of microbes – equally capable of doing mankind great benefit or harm, but as a general rule to be avoided as carefully as possible. He thought that no self-respecting man should allow his name to appear in the papers, except upon death. But he could not avoid satisfaction at seeing the miserable shortcomings of the National Health Service dramatized into a national scandal. It might even galvanize the remote Civil Servants in charge of it, though they did not appear to read the newspapers even for the cricket.

'The turmoil is quite unnecessary,' continued Mr Clapper, replacing the glasses on his pink-rimmed eyes. 'The contingency was, of course, clearly foreseen by the Ministry. It is covered by circular SHM 58/68 ... no, that's *Abatement of Smoke from Hospital Premises*. Or perhaps *Flue Cleaning of Hospital Boilers*. Anyway, it is a straightforward matter of submitting the necessary repair slips in triplicate to the office of the building supervisor, who will allocate the appropriate employees of the hospital works department.'

'He has. But they've gone on strike. They discovered they were working in a disused mortuary, and wanted more pay to compensate for nervous stress.'

'Are you not concentrating on a ha'p'orth of tar, Sir Lancelot, and forgetting the magnificent ship?' Mr Clapper looked pained. 'The National Health Service really *is* magnificent. Administratively, I mean. I am naturally not concerned over the goings-on between doctor and patient. As I always tell my many assistants, it is for others to do the work, but it is for us to direct it into the proper channels.'

Sir Lancelot grunted again.

'I am not a religious man.' Mr Clapper gave a dreamy smile. 'But I like to think of our service since its reorganization – by a Conservative Government, at a stroke – as the New Testament NHS. The volumes which preceded it – the First Green Paper, the Second Green Paper, the Consultative Document, the very White Paper itself –

33

I compare to the Books of the Prophets. Power now flows from the Godhead of the Minister, through the DHSS into 14 RHAs and 90 AHAs, on to 205 DMTs, which bestow his blessing on the common people. Under the Old Testament NHS—'

'I hope these bloody committee members arrive soon,' said Sir Lancelot. 'It's essential I'm back in London by noon.'

He stood up and strode to the window. He wore his customary formal suit, emblazoned with a tie of flaming scarlet and yellow stripes. An emergency session of the Area Health Authority had been summoned. Though St Sepulchre's Hospital was a building wholly unfitted to treat the sick, it was an excellent one for holding meetings. Above the notice-tangled ceiling of the main lobby stretched a lofty panelled room with a vast stone fireplace, in which Sir Lancelot was alone with Mr Clapper. Down the middle was a table which looked solid enough to support a symphony orchestra. Round the walls hung portraits of black-coated Victorians with expressions of benevolence filtered through shrewdness.

This was the old council room. Here the workhouse board met to decide whether a scrap of mutton was allowable with the pease pudding, or to annihilate with its wrath errant and ungrateful paupers. Later, the guardians of the lunatics deliberated about strait-jackets and padded cells. Then the voluntary hospital governors speculated how to keep their doors open, with the donations of businessmen hopeful of knighthoods, housewives sticking passers-by with little flags on pins, and middle-class daughters tolerating an unpaid ten-hour nurse's day in the hope of catching a doctor-husband. Now the room echoed the discussions of the Area Health Authority.

'Ron Cherrymore's turned up, anyway,' remarked Sir

Lancelot, gazing down into the hospital forecourt. 'He seems to have found a friend.'

Chaining his moped to the lamp-post outside the main entrance, Ron became aware of rapid breathing in his ear. He straightened up to see the freckled nurse who had retrieved him from the main corridor.

'Don't you remember me?' she asked shyly. 'Nurse Tosker. Last week in casualty. I strapped your ankle. I do hope it's better?'

'Of *course* I remember you.' He shook her hand earnestly with both his, staring with frank eyes into her sandy-lashed ones. He still wore his jeans, flowered shirt and beads. 'Though it was only a strain, and not a fracture, might I express my admiration for the quiet, efficient way you did your duty? Obviously, you are devoted, and perhaps inspired, by our magnificent Health Service. Which as everyone knows, is the envy of all civilized nations.'

She gave a timid smile. 'It's not every day I have my hands on a lord.'

He dropped her fingers as though feeling something wriggling among them. 'I am *not* a lord,' he told her severely. 'I think everyone in Spratt's Bottom knows my views on the House of Lords. It would be better turned into a bingo hall for the people. The design would be convenient. The caller could operate comfortably from the Woolsack.'

'I mean you . . . you *feel* like a lord,' she said in blushing confusion.

'But surely all men feel equal?' he asked more kindly. 'On the outside, that is. No one could argue with that.'

'Oh, no. There's *something* . . . a touch of class. You smell different from the ordinary patients.'

'Smell?' He recalled that his late noble father had an aroma, but only after luncheon. He gazed at her, puzzled.

She was prettier than he had appreciated during his morning of intolerably uncomfortable tedium.

She smiled more boldly. 'So that's why I put you at the top of the queue.'

'I *queue-jumped*?' he asked in horror.

'I wasn't going to leave you sitting among the riff-raff, was I?'

'Nurse, I ... I am very cross.'

'I'm sure you're not. Not really. Do you know what I think, Mr Cherrymore—'

'Ron, please, No bourgeois formality.'

'Whatever you say, Ron – and I've read all those angry things you get into the local paper, about international capitalism and the local park being closed on Sundays, and all that – and I think you're far too kindhearted and nice to be really cross about anything.' She fluttered her eyelashes at him, giggled and hurried into the hospital.

'Good God,' he muttered. 'She's a complete virgin, politically.' A car horn sounded behind him.

'Good morning, Councillor Cherrymore.'

'Good morning, Councillor Porter.'

Jenny's carefully tended auburn hair appeared through the window of her MG. 'We'd better hurry. Sir Lancelot is in good practice for raising the roof.'

The pair came briskly into the council room. Sir Lancelot was at the head of the table. Jenny sat on his right, Ron on his left, both busily adjusting their blotters and documents, with the purposeful air displayed by the member of any committee from the churchwardens to the Cabinet. They were followed closely by the dean of St Swithin's, in a bad temper. It was typical of Sir Lancelot, he thought, to summon an unexpected meeting of the Spratt's Bottom Area Health Authority at a time wildly inconvenient for everybody, or anyway for the dean himself. He felt impelled to attend, being the university nominee. It pleased him to regard his valued mind as academic, fine-tuned, contemplative. Quite different from Lancelot, who was all cut and thrust, like an overweight member of the Three Musketeers.

'There would appear to be eleven apologies for absence,' said Mr Clapper, sitting opposite the dean on Ron's left. 'No, ten,' he corrected himself, as the door flew open.

'Sorry I'm late, mates.' Harold Sapworth, the ACHE shop steward, was young, ruddy-cheeked, with untidy hair, angular glasses and a thick dark moustache which seemed to have melted at both ends. He still wore his brown porter's coat. 'Little bit of industrial relations to sort out,' he told them cheerfully, taking a chair beside the dean. 'One of them dusky maidens among the nurses reckoned that one of the Micks on the kitchen trolleys had given her bum a pinch. The things that happen in hospitals.' He grinned. 'Wouldn't the patients be surprised?'

'There is perfectly adequate disciplinary machinery to settle intra-staff disputes of that nature, Mr Sapworth,' Mr Clapper told him coldly. 'It was circulated to all hospital authorities under cover of RHB (51) 80, HMC (51) 73 and BG (51) 80. Haven't you read them?'

'No, nor the dusky lady ain't, either. And any machinery you hand her, she'd know where to stick it, cogwheels first. Don't worry, a few words from yours truly sorted it out. I told her it was the normal greeting back in Kerry. They have to make sure people are real, they keep seeing things so much out there.'

'In my view, this is a clear-cut case to go in front of the Commission for Racial Equality,' said Ron severely, playing with his beads.

'Or before the Equal Opportunities Commission,' Jenny told him sharply.

37

'Oh Gawd, keep that lot out of it,' said Harold ardently. 'Industrial relations is like marriage. Bit of a dust-up with the old trouble-and-strife, you sort it out between yourselves. But once the wife's mother or the neighbours take a hand, once they keep telling her how she's hard done by, that's the finish. Ain't that so, Sir Lancelot?' He had known the surgeon some time, since pushing patients into his operating theatre at St Swithin's.

'Your attitude is, with respect, totally wrong, Harold.' Ron stared across the table in his frank, assertive way. 'This is a democracy. Everyone has their rights—'

'Which if everyone fully exercised, would bring this, and every other true democracy in the world, to disintegration,' Jenny interrupted.

Ron shifted his blue eyes to her. 'Your views are typical of your party's, which believes not in rights but in privileges.'

'While yours believes in fair shares for all – of the misery,' Jenny countered.

'I think we agreed that politics should be excluded from our meetings,' Sir Lancelot intruded. 'Otherwise, we shall find ourselves putting the world to rights while St Sepulchre's falls to bits.'

'Lovely morning,' observed Harold Sapworth, looking through the window. 'If you won the toss, Sir Lancelot, what would you do?'

'Bat. As chairman, I call to order this meeting about the structural state of St Sepulchre's—'

'Ah! I have the answer.' Mr Clapper snapped his fingers. They all looked at him expectantly. 'That circular covering the collapse of operating theatre ceilings was HM (65) 28, *Planned Preventive Maintenance*.'

'I expect you've got one in your office to cover the Last Trump,' said the dean testily. 'I don't suppose it'll be any more use.'

Mr Clapper pursed his thick lips, and started jotting on his agenda as though it were the dean's death warrant, composed with several procedural irregularities.

'From recent first-hand experience as a patient,' declared Ron, 'I can assure you that the hospital structure – though admittedly open to improvement, but even the Pavlov Institute in Leningrad is hardly perfect – is quite adequate for its purpose of giving the people the treatment they deserve.'

'St Sepulchre's isn't fit to house sick animals,' Jenny told him crisply. 'Personally, I should much prefer to be ill in the Battersea Dog's Home.'

'With private insurance schemes, your class is unlikely to find itself ill in either institution.'

'Lancelot, can't you control the discussion properly?' demanded the dean. 'I must be back in the West End for an important business discussion at lunch time.'

'Private practice should be subsidized, not proscribed,' Jenny countered. 'It's the only way to keep our home-trained doctors from flying off to California, and all the others flying here from Calcutta.'

'So you think that the state of medical care – whether you get treated now or never, in comfort or in squalor, by the doctor you chose or the one you get, whether you should live or die – depends only on how much you can pay?' Ron demanded contemptuously.

'Medicine is far too essential an activity to be complicated by idealism,' Sir Lancelot informed him. 'Order, please. I think I can release you sooner than you all anticipate.'

'Don't mind me, Sir Lancelot,' said Harold. 'I'm easy. I'd rather be sitting here than humping sacks of laundry.' He looked at his watch. 'When's coffee break, then?'

'Might I have a minute without interruption?' Sir Lancelot had an edge to his voice. 'Just before we assembled,

Mr Clapper here, with his customary powerful imagery, compared the National Health Service with both the Christian religion and some serenely sailing vessel. I am no theologian, and prefer to see it as a motley fleet commanded by admirals who have never been to sea in their lives. Some of the ships are in fighting trim. Most are seaworthy. Others like St Sepulchre's are drifting, rotting, rat-infested, pestiferous hulks, with the crew up to their waists in bilgewater and on the point of mutiny.'

'Hear, hear,' agreed Harold. 'How do you expect the lads to take a pride in their work, when they're still scrubbing dirt off the walls what's been there since the year we won the World Cup?'

'The answer is perfectly simple.' Ron swung his beads. 'The Government must increase taxes on the better-off to make such places medically seaworthy.'

'Damn,' said the dean. 'I've forgotten to cancel my lecture this afternoon on the liver.'

'This is all irrelevant,' said Sir Lancelot. 'Because the Government intend to sink us.' They started at him. 'I now speak in confidence. 'Last night in my club I met—well, someone high up in the Ministry. St Sepulchre's will close in six months. The official announcement will be made on Tuesday.'

'Thank God,' said the dean. 'The place has haunted my dreams for months. And the journey down is dreadfully tedious.'

'How sensible,' agreed Jenny. 'The Government will save half a million a year of taxpayers' money – from a health budget already overspent by three million.'

'What about the patients?' demanded Harold.

'The clinical work here will be transferred to St Swithin's,' Sir Lancelot replied. 'It has plenty of spare capacity. Like many hospitals in the centre of London, where people go only to work and dispose of their luncheon vouchers.'

'What about the relatives?' Harold persisted. 'It's a hell of a long bus-ride.'

Mr Clapper corrected him, 'The National Health Service does not exist purely for the convenience of the patients.'

'What about our jobs, then?'

'I admit,' Mr Clapper told him coldly, 'that it does sometimes seem to exist only for the convenience of the workers.'

'The decision is disgraceful,' said Ron.

'I am completely in agreement with Mr Cherrymore and Mr Sapworth,' revealed Sir Lancelot. The dean and Jenny looked shocked. It was as if Nicholas Nickleby had objected to the unexpected closure of Dotheboys Hall. 'My reasons are uncomplicated. Hospitals belong to their communities.'

'Spratt's Bottom a community?' The dean guffawed. 'People only use it to sleep and keep their cars in. You say as much yourself.'

'It would be less of one without St Sepulchre's. With everyone obliged to perform their lifetime's three fundamental activities of giving birth, being ill and dying, in a place they have never set eyes on before. The psychological scourge of our age is impersonality. The annihilation of the individual. In the days when my ancestors farmed down the road, everyone knew the village butcher, baker and constable. Now their bread and beer come from factories, and the most intimate transactions of their lives are conducted with total strangers.'

'Or machines,' the dean agreed. 'The number of wittily rude letters I must have wasted on computers.'

'We shall see, I think, once Spratt's Bottom has been roused by the threat to its hospital. A community can discover itself like a nation, when attacked.'

'There are always troublemakers who kick against any

major administrative decision,' Mr Clapper said wearily. 'Which are, of course, made for the public's own good. We ignore them.'

'You'll not ignore me, if you know what's good for you,' Sir Lancelot told him. 'I am starting a "Save St Sepulchre's" campaign forthwith.'

'Up the rebels,' said Harold. 'How many of the lads you want me to round up for the demo?'

'Really, Lancelot.' The dean gave a short laugh. 'You'll make yourself look ridiculous, walking up the High Street carrying a banner.'

'I feel so strongly, that I would readily do so while pedalling a one-wheel cycle. Though I fancy I have a high base-line for looking ridiculous. I shall anyway start with more subtle means.'

'What means?' asked Jenny.

'I'm sure, Miss Porter, that as a student of politics you will know the value of a public relations exercise? I sometimes think the two subjects are interchangeable.'

'I should prefer to rely on the good sense and just anger of the British people,' said Ron.

'People need to be told that they are angry and sensible,' Sir Lancelot elaborated. 'Otherwise they have other things to think about. It should not be too difficult, the whole country being aware of St Sepulchre's after the television news last Thursday. I propose a formal motion – any Ministry directive to shut the hospital be opposed by us, the Area Health Authority, by all means at our disposal. Those in favour?' Ron and Harold raised their hands. 'As Mr Clapper does not vote, and I have the casting one, the motion is carried. Meeting adjourned.'

'This is a farce,' complained the dean.

'It's democracy,' Sir Lancelot corrected him.

'What, with just five of us?'

'More than turns up for our union meetings,' Harold told him. 'That's how we get things done.'

The dean rose. 'I intend to waste no more time playing a part in it.'

'It's no good, Lancelot,' said Jenny, gathering her documents. 'Whitehall will win in the end. It always does.'

'Ah, time for a coffee,' said Harold, as an overalled lady pushed in a trolley. 'Got them chocolate biscuits I wanted, love?'

Ron caught up Jenny on the stairs. 'We'd better have a look at this ceiling of contention, hadn't we?' She agreed. As they walked from the lobby to the long windowless corridor, he said excitedly, 'I've got some tremendous news, Jenny.'

'You're presenting the prizes at a Fabian summer school?'

'I'm to be nominated as the next Labour parliamentary candidate for Spratt's Bottom,' he explained proudly. 'It's all fixed. The brother of that dreadful little man Sapworth – I mean, Brother Harold's brother – is on the selection committee. I've an excellent chance of getting in at the next election, the way things are going in the country.' He rubbed his hands. 'Then there'll be no holding me. I can see the glittering prizes already – parliamentary private secretary, junior minister, the Cabinet. Who knows? Prime Minister.'

'Congratulations.'

'Thank you. I've only one worry.'

'Yes?'

'My career is so promising that it would be quite greedy of me not to share it. Jenny . . . you and I are professionals, aren't we? And our professional politicians don't stay on shouting terms once they're outside the debating chamber. That's probably why democracy's lasted so long in this country. I'm offering you a great chance. Forget all this Tory claptrap, and come back to me.'

'That's a bit cool.'

'But we were happy, weren't we, as students together at the London School of Social Science?'

'Oh, yes,' she agreed. 'It was fun, living together in that room behind the British Museum on hamburgers and baked beans and Spanish burgundy. But don't read too much into it. Students are doing that all the time, everywhere.'

'But we *loved* each other,' he said solemnly, tugging his beads. 'In such a beautiful, innocent way. You were just the daughter of an ordinary little man who kept a corner newsagent's, who went to an ordinary comprehensive school before winning her scholarship—'

'That's why I became a Tory. Nobody in life helped me. I helped myself to life.'

'In those days you hadn't forgotten your drudgery behind the counter, and weren't quite so out of sympathy with the workers.'

'In those days you hadn't renounced your title, and weren't quite so out of sympathy with everybody.'

He looked at her haughtily. 'I hope you're not saying that I'm a hypocrite?'

'You know perfectly well, Ronnie – Ron – that every politician must occasionally be a cheerful hypocrite, just as every successful doctor must occasionally be a cheerful liar.' They reached the empty operating theatre, which had a large hole open to the sky. 'Well, Lancelot was always complaining about the ventilation,' she observed. 'By the way, I've some tremendous news for you. I'm shortly to be adopted as the next Conservative parliamentary candidate for Spratt's Bottom.'

'What!' He stared at her, knuckles white as he gripped his beads. 'You don't know what you're letting yourself in for.'

'Admittedly, I should be happier not standing against *you*, Ronnie. You have an intimidatingly strong local

44

following. But I suppose all's fair in love and the class war.'

'But women do disastrously in the Tory party,' he remonstrated angrily. 'Just look at Mrs —'

'God, what a shambles,' came Sir Lancelot's voice behind them. 'Sure you haven't made another cock-up and put on the demolition squad by mistake, Clapper?'

'I really must disabuse you of the belief that I am continually making mistakes,' said Mr Clapper in a hurt voice. 'Oh, dear. I had somehow forgotten this letter, which was handed in for you yesterday. It would seem to be marked "Very Urgent".'

He handed Sir Lancelot an envelope from his pocket.

'Bye, Ron,' Jenny said cheerfully. 'Nice to think we've got a date at the hustings.'

'I suppose that's democracy,' Ron said dully. 'Each party taking turns to play "them" and "us".'

'No, it doesn't,' she corrected him gently. 'Democracy means *us* taking turns to play *them*.'

Sir Lancelot was meanwhile reading,

> *Dr Edwin and Dr Marjorie*
> *Turnhorn,*
> *The Surgery,*
> *1 Apricot Avenue,*
> *Spratt's Bottom.*

My Dear Lancelot,

My wife and I have had a tremendous stroke of luck. One of our patients who was booked on a cruise has died, and his widow passed us the tickets. Unfortunately, we sail this very Saturday, and you know how impossible it is to find reliable locums at short notice. Are there a couple of young doctors you know, who might be prepared to live here for a month? No one from bog, bush or banana-patch, this practice being the most reputable and influential in the district.

> *As ever,*
> *Edwin.*

Sir Lancelot stood stroking his beard for some moments.

'Clapper, I take it I am entitled to free phone calls? Good.' He grabbed the wall telephone. 'Switchboard? Get me Nairobi.'

5

'AND how was Manchester?' Sir Lancelot asked Amelia Witherspoon.

'The hospitals were efficient. Otherwise, there was nothing wrong with the place which couldn't be cured by a good earthquake.' She climbed into his Rolls at Euston Station. It was shortly after twelve-thirty that same Thursday morning. He locked her overnight case in the boot and settled in the driver's seat.

'Talking of earthquakes, Lancelot, I was in an operating room in Bolivia when one started. It all came back to me last Thursday. You never know when any experience in life is going to be useful.'

'Had you not stopped that lamp injuring the patient, I should have ended up with so much egg on my face, that with the addition of a couple of anchovies I could have passed for a Scotch woodcock.'

'And how *is* the patient?'

'Eternally grateful. I have discovered that only the victims of our minor errors rush to law. Those we nearly kill leave hospital saying that the doctors and nurses were wonderful. His only complaint is absence of chips from the diet.'

'I owe you an apology. I was being uppity last week. You have a way, you know, of operating as though you were drilling the Grenadier Guards.' She smiled. 'I thought you were treating me as an inferior being. I have since found that all Englishmen treat women thus.'

'It is I who owe you one, Amelia,' he said handsomely. 'I had rather assumed that your interest in surgery was

47

that of a *tricoteuse* under the guillotine. If I *do* issue somewhat forceful orders, please believe me that it is exclusively for the good of the most important person in the room. The patient.'

She took a packet of cigarettes from her handbag, opened them but hastily put them away again. 'Are we going back to that ancient monument you call a hospital?' They had turned into Regents Park.

'Oh, I shan't be operating at St Sepulchre's for at least a month, until the roof's fixed.' Noticing her surprise, he added, 'We in Britain like to think carefully before taking action. Watt didn't simply fit his steaming kettle with wheels, did he? And after Fleming discovered penicillin in that poky little laboratory, it took another twelve years for anyone actually to make it.'

'Where *are* we going, then?'

'Lord's.'

'She raised her eyebrows. 'The House of Lords?'

'No. Somewhere providing equally stately spasmodic entertainment.'

It was the first day of the Test match. The weather was perfect. The ground was full. Sir Lancelot indicated he was off duty by wearing above his formal suit a boater with a scarlet-and-yellow band. He conducted Amelia from the Grace Gates, behind the pavilion towards the Father Time stand.

'I guess I can check into Bunter's later,' said Amelia, staring round bemusedly. 'It looks sort of ecclesiastical.'

'It has indeed been called "the cathedral of cricket",' he agreed. 'It is Thomas Lord's cricket ground, which has been here since the Battle of Waterloo. It has also been described by the distinguished architectural expert Sir Nikolaus Pevsner as "A jumble without aesthetic aspirations, quite unthinkable in a country like Sweden or Holland". Which is itself rich flattery to English ears. You might notice that I am wearing the tie.'

'I thought it was something surgical – blood and golden sovereigns. Who do I root for?'

'England are playing Australia. But one does not root.'

'Museum!' she exclaimed, pointing to the sign over an open doorway. 'I can't see baseball fans leaving their seats to peer through glass cases.'

'Perhaps that is indicative of the difference between the two games? It contains W G Grace's boots and suchlike. He was the Babe Ruth of cricket, and I am proud to say a fellow medical man.'

Amelia was amazed at the relaxed boyishness of Sir Lancelot's mood. She wondered if he was on drugs. 'Can't we go in this place?'

'Alas, only one woman is ever allowed in the pavilion. And Her Majesty will not be coming before tea-time on Saturday.'

'Saturday? How long does it all last, for God's sake?'

'Five days.'

'But I've a busy schedule—!' began Amelia in panic.

'One watches only a fragment, the result being of indifference compared with the game itself. You may not be aware that the Oxford dictionary defines cricket as "Fair play between honourable opponents". And that the expression "not cricket" to describe a man's underhand behaviour is so libellous as to attract enormous damages, particularly as all our judges are devotees of the game. Meanwhile, I have brought a bite of lunch from Fortnum's,' he added, indicating the large wicker basket at his side.

'Why, it's Sir Lancelot,' a gnarled spectator greeted him. 'We're all grateful to you today, sir. It's your knife that got Jowler back in action.'

'Thank you, sir.'

They sat in the sun on the grass, behind the mid-wicket boundary.

'It looks pretty,' she admitted. 'A ballet of white on

green. Why are they wandering about in all directions?'

'It's over.'

'Already? Then what do they do for the other four days? Why's that man performing a strip act for the other man dressed like a bar-tender?'

'Jowler is removing his sweater preparatory to bowling, and handing it to the umpire.'

'But he's going the wrong way.'

'Patience.'

Jowler stopped almost at the pavilion steps. He turned with a toss of his jet-black forelock, lowered his head like a short-tempered bull pursued by a swarm of bees, and bowled at the Australian.

'Well played, sir,' murmured Sir Lancelot.

'But nothing happened,' exclaimed Amelia.

'Precisely. The batsman displayed high skill in avoiding touching it.'

'He missed? That's good?'

He consoled her, 'It takes several generations of English ancestry to understand all this.'

'Would Scots do? I have some.'

'No. Only the English play cricket. The Scots toss cabers, the Welsh sing hymns and the Irish find the leprechauns get into the pitch.'

Jowler charged. The crouching fieldsmen leapt in the air, yelling.

'My God,' gasped Amelia. 'They're trying to kill the poor man.'

The umpire's finger rose, with it Sir Lancelot and the rest of Lord's. The batsman trailed disconsolately towards the pavilion. Jowler took his sweater with the air of a headsman wiping his hands. 'L b w,' said Sir Lancelot warmly. 'At this rate, we'll win the Ashes.'

'The what?'

'We play for what I suppose you'd call the garbage. Is it all too boring?'

Amelia drew her knees up on the grass. 'I'm fascinated. Where can a woman these days find an entirely new experience?'

They stayed until the close of play.

'I think I'm getting it,' Amelia decided. 'One side is out there, and one side is in, until they're out.' Sir Lancelot nodded. 'Then *they* go out, and the other side go out to go in, until they're down to one who's not out, when they're all out.'

'I wish my students at St Swithin's were as quick-witted.'

'And now, everyone who's out comes in,' she continued, observing the long-shadowed players ambling towards the pavilion. 'Including the two who are not out, and join the ones who are in, some of whom are out, and they all go out for a beer. OK?'

'Which prompts me to suggest you join me for a drink at my club.'

'A male chauvinist sty. No thank you.'

'We are perfectly heterosexual after six o'clock in the evenings,' he assured her. 'As you are with a member, you will not even be obliged to use the side entrance.'

Amelia had expected Sir Lancelot's London club to resemble in massive, dusty, dark spaciousness the New York Public Library on Fifth Avenue. She discovered a Georgian building tucked from sight in the lanes which cluster intimately round St James's Palace. Its rooms were delicately proportioned, hung with bright pictures and pretty curtains. The members seemed all intimate friends of Sir Lancelot. The drink became dinner.

Amelia sat at the candle-lit table, as Sir Lancelot handed back the wine-list to the green-liveried steward. 'How's the fistula?'

'No trouble at all, Sir Lancelot, thank you,' the man told him happily. 'You did a really good job on me, I must say.'

'Do you mind if I smoke?' enquired Amelia.

'It is strictly against club rules in the dining-room.'

She put her cigarettes away.

'May I pay you a compliment?' he asked.

'Flattery will get you nowhere, Lancelot.'

'On the contrary, I have invariably found that it will always get you somewhere. You are the only woman – since my poor wife died – whose company, after eight unbroken hours, I did not find tedious. The others varied only in degree, between the supportable to the embarrassing and then the intolerable.'

'Now aren't you charming?' Amelia fixed him with her blue eyes. 'May I pay one to you? Although, like all Englishmen, you speak as though in need of major otorhinolaryngeal surgery, you dress as though in mourning for your favourite horse, and you behave as though you were continually contemplating your severe constipation – you have something rare in this world. Style.'

Sir Lancelot seemed pleasantly surprised. 'I did not accord to your expectations?'

'No. I expected you to be cold, sneery, arrogant, satisfied with nothing but your own importance, with no conversation, full of surgical jargon and on a strict diet.'

'The last fault would be the worst. The chef here is excellent.'

With the Stilton, Sir Lancelot said, 'I must recommend the port. It was laid down to celebrate the Coronation of the Queen, or the Silver Jubilee of George the Fifth, I forget which.'

'This place is a bastion of privilege, isn't it?' She looked round with narrowed lids. 'Moated and turreted, with boiling oil over the drawbridge for unwelcome strangers.'

'Yes.'

'Doesn't it make you feel ashamed?'

'No.'

'Why? It does me, as an American.'

'Because the country bristles with such bastions, if admittedly on a more modest scale. Only regular custom is necessary, for the priceless privilege of expressing unfettered opinions in congenial company. Fortunately, I can enjoy myself at all social levels, being indifferent to the trappings. Had you not been with me today, I should have lunched off cheese sandwiches from a paper bag and bottled beer, like everyone else. Though admittedly, the cold duck and claret was most acceptable.'

'Where are these bastions?' she asked suspiciously.

'Would you care to inspect one? It has views of the lights across the Thames, so you will be privileged to see exactly what inspired your fellow-countryman James Whistler.'

As Sir Lancelot drove through the dusk-softened streets of west London, the amusing and interesting possibility first came to Amelia that her stately companion was intending to make her.

The tiny pub was almost unfindable down a riverside alley. It had oak beams, a sagging floor and a dozen customers sipping pints with the grave British air of doing so for medicinal reasons. Sir Lancelot had removed the landlord's appendix.

'This is quite wonderful,' Amelia volunteered readily. They leant against a brick parapet on the terrace, watching the river darken, while the evening air wrapped them like an old shawl. 'We've nothing like it back in the States.'

'We have no Las Vegas,' said Sir Lancelot gallantly.

'Want to exchange?'

A gratifying discovery came to him. His extraverted companion was growing relaxed. It was the first time, since he had met her the previous week. Sir Lancelot's knowledge and experience of women was infinite. A hundred taxed his brains every day. A hundred more backed up his work every minute – and they were often the more difficult. He had classed Ms Witherspoon as an insecure intellectual, one of those drawn so often to his

53

consulting couch with phantom pains and shifting symptoms. They responded to comforting like cats, but they never purred before they had scratched. He felt pleased that he was doing her so much good.

'What's the barman shouting for?' she asked.

'Time.'

'Can't he read the clock?'

'All pubs shut by law at eleven, and during the afternoon. This is to prevent drunkenness among the munition workers of World War I.'

'But I'm just getting the taste for warm beer.'

'The law does not apply so rigorously to night clubs,' he suggested. 'They were presumably not patronized as freely by World War I munition workers.'

The door was unmarked, in a narrow, litter-strewn, murderous-looking street in Soho. Inside, thickly carpeted, gold-banistered stairs led down like the entrance to Aladdin's cave.

'Why, it's Sir Lancelot,' delightedly exclaimed the coat-check girl in fishnet tights.

'How's the kidney?' he asked kindly.

'Fine,' she smiled. 'Thanks to you.'

The head-waiter in tails hurried across the lobby. 'Sir Lancelot! What a pleasure. Luckily, I have one excellent table left.'

'Evening, Guiseppe. Varicose veins all right now?'

Sir Lancelot and Amelia sat beside the dance floor.

'Hello, my dear.' Sir Lancelot smiled at the topless waitress approaching with a bottle. 'Nice to see that mammary fibroma I removed has healed without complications. But I didn't order champagne.'

'Compliments of *il padrone*, sir. He hasn't forgotten your treatment of his little accident.'

'The poor fellow ran on to the end of a drawn knife,' Sir Lancelot explained to Amelia.

'Have you operated on absolutely everybody in town?'

54

'My profession has the advantage of meeting interesting people from different walks of life.'

The waitress left the bottle in an ice-bucket, and kissed him.

'God, I've discovered something,' exclaimed Amelia. 'Surgery is sexy.'

Sir Lancelot considered this, inspecting the bubbles in his glass. 'I think you are right,' he decided gravely. 'Because we are men of action. Ruthless, commanding, indomitable. As masterful as any woman could sigh for.'

'Oh, Lancelot!' she lamented. 'Hasn't the light of women's lib yet penetrated the mullioned windows of your soul?'

'A passing fad. Women have changed little biologically since they enjoyed being hit on the head by the caveman's club. Would you care to dance?'

'Let's try.'

'How I admire your American zest. The last Englishwoman to whom I addressed the suggestion here said, "Must we".'

'How uncivil.'

'A princess must be allowed a little imperiousness,' he said modestly.

At two in the morning, Sir Lancelot drove Amelia away from Soho in his Rolls. She was happy. The build-up was ponderous – fourteen hours, starting at Euston Station – but possibly it was the British way of going about things, like repairing operating-room ceilings. He was kindly. He was a knight. He wasn't all that bad-looking. He seemed vigorous enough. He couldn't be more fumble-fingered than that general from the Pentagon. Then she saw they had drawn up at Bunter's.

'Here we are,' announced Sir Lancelot. 'I'm afraid that I have submitted you to a long day. But in a few minutes now, you'll be tucked up in bed. I'll get your case.'

He stepped from the car. A sign met his eyes. HOTEL CLOSED. He became aware of a huddle of men on the pavement, leaning so sleepily against the wall that their placards OFFICIAL STRIKE and COMMIS DEMAND JUSTICE stood askew.

'Why, it's Sir Lancelot,' came a familiar voice.

'Sapworth! What are you doing here, man? You're a health worker, not a flunkey.'

'It's all right, squire. I'm taking over from my brother on the picket line. It's his birthday. Few friends in, and that.'

Sir Lancelot drew himself up. 'And what if ACHE gets to hear? Poaching is an extremely serious union crime.'

'Well, I'm not going to tell them. And neither are you.'

'How do you know?'

'Because I can trust you anywhere, Sir Lancelot.'

'That's all very well, but I have a lady in the car who's booked a room for the night,' he complained shortly.

Harold Sapworth sighed. 'We of the union regrets that at this moment of time the situation of industrial action causes the public inconvenience, but we have a just case which we are prepared to put on the negotiating table once anyone shows any commonsense—'

'Oh, do shut up, Sapworth,' Sir Lancelot said irritably. 'You're not on television. Where's the lady going to sleep?'

'Not here, squire. The lads are out, one hundred per cent solid.'

'What's the bloody dispute about, anyway?'

'Search me. I think one of them got sacked for sticking a fork into the head waiter. Mind, they got cushy jobs in there, I reckon. People stay in hotels in a mood to enjoy themselves. Which you can't say exactly of St Sepulchre's.'

'Very well, very well,' he muttered. 'Have to try some-

56

where else, I suppose. Not that there's much hope, at this time of night and this time of the year.'

'There's an all-night ladies' at Piccadilly,' Harold said helpfully. 'But I don't suppose it's too comfortable, sitting up till breakfast time.'

'I shall have to take responsibility for my companion. You realize you are putting me to considerable personal inconvenience?'

'Sorry, Sir Lancelot. But it's democracy, ain't it?' He glanced over his shoulder, and passed across a slip of paper. 'Something good for Ascot. My brother's in the turf business.'

Sir Lancelot slammed the driver's door behind him. 'You saw the situation?' he said sternly. Amelia nodded. 'We can try Claridge's, the Connaught, the Ritz, if you wish. Otherwise, I can offer you a bed for the night.'

Amelia's eyes narrowed slightly. 'How kind.'

'My housekeeper is, of course, in residence.'

'Oh, of course.' She thought romantically of Lancelot and Guinevere. The Rolls became a white palfrey.

Inside Sir Lancelot's front door at Lazar Row, she exclaimed, 'What a charming little house! You could imagine Elizabeth Barrett Browning coming down-stairs—'

He laid a finger urgently on his lips. 'My housekeeper. A very light sleeper.'

They went upstairs.

'What a bed!' she whispered intimately in his ear.

'The sheets will be fresh today,' he breathed back. He gently set down her case on the floor. 'I hope you'll be comfortable. The hospital refuse collection is often noisy at six-thirty. The bathroom leads off. Good night.'

Amelia sat on the bed. She lit a cigarette. She frowned. Why had he left her so abruptly? She decided it was pure habit. Take off your clothes, the doctor will be with you in a minute.

She undressed. She smoked another cigarette. The bed-side clock passed three. She opened the door. A light shone downstairs. In her nightie, she tiptoed to the hall. Sir Lancelot was in the front room, on a leather sofa under a tartan blanket, his mouth open, snoring. She looked at him sadly. She sighed. She said slowly, 'No wonder they lost India.'

6

Sir Lancelot dreamt he was being chased by a man-eating hen. He woke to a loud squawk, which he discovered to come from Miss MacNish. She was in her green overall, glaring at him from the doorway. 'Could ye noo get up the stairs when ye got home at last?'

Sir Lancelot wondered what he was doing in his sitting-room. 'What time is it?'

'Seven o'clock, on Friday morning.' He sat up, rubbing his eyes. 'Stark naked, too,' Miss MacNish added with disgust.

'I gave up my bed to an American, who had no hotel room. As a Scot, you will appreciate the duties of hospitality.'

She continued eyeing him severely. She disliked finding anything out of place in the house, particularly Sir Lancelot. 'Shall I take him a cup of morning tea?'

'Good God, no! Not on any account.'

'Why not?' she demanded accusingly.

'Because Americans don't drink tea.'

She looked suspicious. 'What sort of American might he be?'

'A literary person. Like Ernest Hemingway.'

'I see. Do you suppose he likes porridge?'

'Who in the world could possibly dislike the stuff?'

'How long's he staying?'

'So little time, you will hardly notice the presence of another human in the house at all.'

She left him. Sir Lancelot rose in his Y-fronts, wrapped the rug round him, and made for the downstairs bathroom. Splashing cold water on his face, he calculated the chance of Amelia's escaping without detection. She had been late to bed, and would probably sleep until Miss MacNish left for her morning shopping. The housekeeper was an early bird for cut-price worms.

He dressed, and went into the back dining-room. Miss MacNish was leaning against a chair. She seemed to imagine he yearned for company at breakfast, he reflected, when it was a meal which should enjoy the privacy of all other early-morning functions.

'Aye, I once had an uncle and aunt who emigrated from Bonnie Glasgow to America.' She sighed. 'They went to live among Red Indians and savages. Some had never even heard of Scotland.'

Sir Lancelot spooned up his porridge in silence.

'Those puir people that live in America! Nothing but hamburgers and shooting one another. Still, some Americans are quite agreeable,' she conceded. 'I hope your friend is.'

'My friend is perfectly charming.'

'Mind, they're sex crazy. My mother would never go out in the black-out.'

'Miss MacNish, I wonder if you'd slip out as soon as the shops open and buy me a ... a ... an umbrella.'

'But it's a braw morning,' she objected.

'In our climate, you never know what to expect.'

'Hi,' cried Amelia, throwing the door open. 'That bed of yours, Lancelot! So *springy*. So much room to move. It would have suited Madame Pompadour in her prime. Invite me for another night whenever you feel like it.' She kissed him. She had slept well. She felt fine. They had finished the night before with crossed wires, but they had the day ahead to untangle them. 'You look fresh, Lancelot, for a man who sleeps with his mouth open, making a noise like a tuba serenade,' she continued ebulliently. 'What's that you're eating?'

'Porridge,' said Sir Lancelot, in the tone of Scrooge addressing Marley's ghost.

'So *that's* what porridge looks like? Yuk. You must be the famous housekeeper?' She smiled at Miss MacNish. 'Lancelot's been telling me how you're a real bit of auld Scotland, like bagpipes, haggis and the Loch Ness Monster. Hoots and och aye!' Amelia clapped her playfully on the back. 'Will ye no pick up your kilts and do a Highland reel for us, lassie?'

Miss MacNish quivered like Arthur's Seat in a heathaze. 'If you'll excuse me, Sir Lancelot, I shall leave you alone with your—your person.'

'Off for a wee dram?' suggested Amelia smilingly. 'Have one for me, too. It's the best drink of the day.'

Miss MacNish's eyes flashed. 'Strong drink is the abomination of the Devil.'

Amelia laughed. 'That Scottish bluenose bit is perfect. Do us another act.'

The housekeeper looked heavenwards and strode through the door, muttering something of which Sir Lancelot could distinguish only the words, 'Burke and Hare.'

'She's quaint, isn't she?' Amelia sat at the circular table. 'I'll just have coffee. May I smoke?'

'No, you may not,' roared Sir Lancelot.

She put away her cigarettes, looking alarmed. 'Something wrong?'

'Miss MacNish did not approve of your occupying my bed last night.'

'Jealous? I'd hate to upset a beautiful relationship.'

'Like many Scots, she can be somewhat narrow-minded,' he said more calmly. 'She regards all that is enjoyable as sinful. She is also nervous of anything impeding her passage to Heaven. A place for which she has an inordinate desire, considering that she imagines it to resemble Scotland on a Sunday.'

61

Amelia looked shocked. 'You don't say she was serious? I thought she was a little bundle of fun.'

'Fun!' muttered Sir Lancelot. 'But she is an incomparable housekeeper. And they are considerably more difficult to come by in London than mistresses.'

The door opened. Sir Lancelot's heart fell. She was carrying her budgerigar.

'Miss MacNish,' said Amelia humbly. 'Will you forgive me, if I've wounded your feelings? We Americans, you know, are very brash—'

'Sir Lancelot, I am tendering my resignation. I will not work in a hoorhoose.'

He frowned. 'A what?'

'Please have my things sent to my sister's in Putney. I kept them packed for such an eventuality.'

'Just a minute—' Amelia spoke like a rasp. Her glance struck like a blowlamp. 'When a lady spends a night under a gentleman's roof, she does not expect to be labelled as a harlot—' Her eyes narrowed to slits. 'By the servants.'

'*Servants?*' cried Miss MacNish. 'But I am Sir Lancelot's housekeeper.'

'He hires you, doesn't he? Oh, hell, yes, all men are equal, I'm a good democrat. But they're not entitled to be equally rude,' she said furiously. 'Anyway, not to me. OK? You keep your impure thoughts to yourself.'

'*Impure?*' exclaimed Miss MacNish. Then Sir Lancelot's curious gaze saw her crumple in the heat of Amelia's attack. 'Perhaps I was a wee bit hasty,' she muttered. 'I didn't mean any disrespect to a guest of Sir Lancelot's.'

'You didn't?' said Amelia. 'Well, you achieved it.'

'I was brought up very strictly in Edinburgh,' she continued submissively. 'Until I was a grown woman, I thought sex was a time of day.' The other two stared at her in silence. 'I hadna much chance to find otherwise, since I've only lived with Rob Roy.'

Sir Lancelot frowned. 'Who?'

She held up the bird, which said, 'Owjado?' 'Sir Lancelot, I will give you another chance.'

'You will, will you?'

She said graciously, 'I withdraw my resignation.'

'Good. Then I can fire you.'

Miss MacNish looked aghast. 'Do I understand that you are voluntarily dispensing with my services?'

'You do.'

'But . . . but that's outrageous,' she said in amazement.

'I believe the Government provides some sort of tribunal, which you can appeal to if you consider me unjust.'

'I'll do no such thing.' She drew herself up. The budgerigar flapped its wings and started chirping. 'I shall make it my business not to set eyes on you again in this world, Sir Lancelot. In the next, such precautions will not be necessary.'

The dining-room door slammed. They sat without speaking. Sir Lancelot blew out his cheeks. 'Amelia, thank you. I've been steeling myself to do that for months.'

'Then why didn't you?' she asked, still nettled.

'It seemed as difficult as Macbeth evicting his Lady from Glamis.'

'But look at the trouble it would have saved him later.'

'Lancelot, your front door's open.' The dean's cheerful voice came from the hall. Sir Lancelot groaned. It was too late to head him off. 'What's the drama, so early in the day? I've just seen your housekeeper leave, *with* her budgie—'

The dean stopped in the dining-room doorway, eyebrows leaping like caterpillars dropped on a hotplate.

'Ms Witherspoon,' Sir Lancelot introduced Amelia, glaring at him fiercely. 'The lady I mentioned, from America.'

'Really, Lancelot,' exclaimed the dean in confusion. 'She doesn't look at all like a bitch with a bone.'

'Oh, thank you,' said Amelia. 'Everyone's so complimentary this morning.'

'I mean, the only literary ladies I've met seemed rather definitely hardcover editions.' The dean recovered himself, sitting down. 'Mind if I join you?' He rubbed his hands and reached for the coffee-pot. 'A breakfast-time appointment, eh? You Americans are so zealous. Personally, I do not regard breakfast as a social meal.'

'Oh, no, neither do I. But Sir Lancelot and I spent the night here.'

'Really, Lancelot, I hope the students' magazine doesn't get hold of this,' the dean muttered. 'Anyway, I can't stay long. I'm glad I caught you this morning, because I've discovered something amazing about Hamilton Tosker. What a captain of industry! What a benefactor of humanity!'

'Personally, I think he's still got broad arrows on his underwear, but I'm no judge of business ethics.'

'The package-deal hospital idea is going splendidly.' The dean ignored Sir Lancelot's remark. 'We're discussing it at another working lunch today. That reminds me, I must cancel my lecture to the students on the thyroid. It's all so easy when Tosker has the right contacts in the right places. Even quite important politicians seem to fall over themselves, just to please him. As for the doctors, they're queueing up. I've already recruited one of the younger St Swithin's surgeons – no names—'

'Yes, he's a greedy devil,' guessed Sir Lancelot.

'So there'll soon be a vacancy on the consultant staff.' The dean tipped up the coffee-pot, finding it dry. 'Do you know where the Toskers originally come from? Spratt's Bottom!'

'That health resort,' murmured Amelia.

'I do sometimes think the Luftwaffe would have done this country a great service by hitting St Sepulchre's in 1940,' reflected the dean. 'Or better still, the Zeppelins in

1915. Anyway, Hamilton Tosker wishes to visit Spratt's Bottom and see if he can trace any relatives. As he puts it, he will go there like a rouseabout fossicking among the jumbucks, because a roo can kick a nugget into a no-hoper's dillybag. I believe he means that he might discover some delightful kinsman. The Australian language has the lurid if obscure beauties of the later pictures by Turner. Why is there no more coffee?' he demanded peevishly.

'Because I have given Miss MacNish the push.'

The dean looked amazed. 'But who's going to cook for you?'

'I don't care if nobody does. Principles are more important than hot dinners.'

'I can cook,' said Amelia suddenly. 'Not much, but omelettes and toasted cheese. And I'm absolutely brilliant at defrosting and opening cans. How about me making your dinner tonight, Lancelot?'

'My dear Amelia, what an agreeable suggestion. Look here – why not stay on a while? Until that nonsense at Bunter's is finished? You can move into Miss MacNish's apartments. They are totally self-contained, with a stout lock on the door, to which she herself added a pair of ten-inch steel bolts, a chain and a burglar alarm.'

'That's a thought,' Amelia said speculatively. 'A hotel room in a foreign city is anyway only luxurious solitary confinement.'

'What *is* the matter, dean?' Sir Lancelot demanded.

'Rag week is coming up, and you know how the students put on a satirical revue about the consultants—'

'Lionel, the students, you and Miss MacNish all have incurably dirty minds.'

'Yes, and I didn't much like the look her budgerigar gave me, either,' said Amelia.

7

EARLY the following Monday, a thick-set, good-looking young man with a neat haircut and a Chester Barrie suit, carrying a black, square executive case, was standing at the corner of Apricot Avenue in Spratt's Bottom. The avenue was long and straight, shaded from the morning sun by precisely spaced, identical rowan trees, and lined by neatly-cut privet, box and laurel. He stared bemusedly at the house names, all of which seemed to be *The Squirrels*, *Mentone* or *Pilgrims' Rest*.

The roadway was busy with Minis, Imps, Dafs and Golfs, driven by women so dishevelled they appeared just dragged out of bed, rightly. Beside them sat men neat in City clothes. The pavements streamed with more dark-suited men taking the same direction, with briefcases and the folded *Daily Telegraph*. Motorized or on foot, the harassed but unconquerable army of the middle-class was about to entrain towards its daily battle for self-preservation.

As the stranger started strolling up the avenue, he noticed with curiosity another coming bemusedly towards him. He wore a broad-brimmed khaki hat decorated with a strip of zebra-hide, his tall, gangling frame in a safari suit of the same colour, a scarlet scarf looped loosely round his neck, over his shoulder a half-empty rucksack. About to seek directions, the man in the blue suit exclaimed, 'Pip Chipps!'

'Freddie Bisham!'

'What *are* you doing, wandering round this appalling suburb at breakfast time?'

'*Is* it breakfast time? I've just got off the plane from

Nairobi. I'm doing a locum for one of the Dr Turnhorns.'

'But *I'm* doing a locum for another of the Dr Turn-horn's.'

'No! How did you get the job?'

'Through Sir Lancelot.'

'So did I. Well, well, well!' They slapped each other violently. 'Why it must be four whole years!' said Pip. 'That farewell party at St Swithin's—'

'Bedpans of champagne,' smiled Freddie fondly. 'But why lose yourself in Kenya?' he asked, after several minutes of reminiscence on the pavement.

'Nutrition. All very scientific. I'm a better doctor if I don't need to talk to patients. Perhaps I should have been an anaesthetist?'

'Why not a pathologist?' laughed Freddie. 'Then your patients would have been even less trouble.' He spotted a brass plate. 'We're here.'

A well-raked gravel drive led between gaudy flower-beds to a large mock-Tudor house. It had twisted brick chimneys and leaded windows of pink- and green-tinted glass. Freddie's ring at the church-like oak door produced chimes resembling the preliminaries to Big Ben striking the hour.

The door was opened instantly by a short girl in a white overall, a starched white cap on her dark curls, white stockings and white shoes. One side of her bursting bosom bore thermometer, throat spatula, pen-torch, coloured felt-pens and watch on a cord. The other, a large red cross. She was so young that she appeared an overdeveloped child dressed up to play doctors and nurses.

'I'm Cindy.' She smiled broadly as they introduced themselves. 'I come in daily. It's a nice house in a classy district,' she assured them, 'if some of the patients do get up your snout.'

The well-polished parquet of the hall was covered with metal-and-canvas chairs littered with worn magazines.

There was a desk with two telephones, and they noticed a pair of white doors leading to the surgeries.

'Here's the lounge.' Cindy led them into a large room with an orange tufted nylon carpet spread with vivid-patterned rugs. A plum-coloured, gold-braided three-piece suite of cut moquette, with a pair of silver-corded pink pouffes, clustered round a wide brick hearth containing electric logs, embellished with shiny horse-brasses, fire-irons and toasting-fork. The wallpaper was bright blue with fleecy clouds, which set off a flight of china ducks. 'The kitchen's through there.' She indicated a Moorish arch with a curtain of multicoloured bright beads. 'Also the stairs to the bedrooms – dreamy duvets. That door opposite leads to the surgeries. The windows slide back on to the patio, where you can have your barbecues.' Outside stood a sundial, birdbath and a pair of gnomes fishing in a lily-pond.

'Where did you train?' Freddie asked her.

'What for?'

'I mean, what hospital did you go to?'

'Oh, Guy's.' The two doctors looked impressed. 'I had my tonsils out.' Big Ben chimed. 'Oh, them patients! Monday mornings, it's like the first day of the sales. Nothing brings on a housewife's headache like facing five days locked up alone with her kids.'

'Sexy Snow White has a point,' murmured Freddie, as Cindy hurried to the hall.

'Do you suppose there's any wildlife in here?' asked Pip, head in the shiny house-plants which filled one corner to the ceiling.

'Hey, look at this,' cried Freddie, throwing open a repro-Jacobean cabinet. 'Gin, whisky, vodka, port, egg flip ... even stuffed olives and little onions. This could be just like the old days,' he said warmly. 'When you and I shared that dreadful flat as students.'

'Living on baked beans, tinned pilchards and marmalade sandwiches,' smiled Pip. He picked up a pudgy choirboy with flowing surplice whose hymnal made a convenient ashtray. 'But didn't you use to work down here, Freddie?' he remembered. 'After that farewell party at St Swithin's, you went to be surgical registrar at St Sepulchre's.'

'For a while.' Freddie relaxed on the button-back plastic recliner, facing the colour TV with busts of Mozart and Schubert on top. 'We won't have to live on baked beans and marmalade. I've got a wife.'

'No!'

'Marriage, like death, comes to us all.'

'I know. It's come to me, too.'

'No? Well, well! I married a physiotherapist,' Freddie volunteered.

Pip scratched his sharp, sunburned chin. 'Interesting.'

'Why?'

'Because ... she'd know all about deep, relaxing massage,' Pip said vaguely. 'Must be nice after a long day.'

'Dawn doesn't actually work in Soho – what made you jump?'

'Dawn. Uncommon name.'

'*Is* it?' Freddie was a practical, forthright surgeon, who found the ideas of his academic friend Pip as difficult to grasp as butterflies.

'Mine's called Evangelina, but everyone calls her Eva.'

Freddie jerked up. 'You met her in Kenya?' Pip nodded. 'Good!'

'She'd just come out from England.'

'Ah!'

'She had a job with the Health Department in Nairobi, as a statistician.'

Freddie leapt from his recliner and began pacing the tufted nylon. 'Statistician? Needs a lot of brains.'

'Eva *has* a lot of brains.'

69

'I know.'

'But you've never met her ...'

'I mean, if she's a statistician, she *must* have a lot of brains.'

Pip scratched his chin again. 'How long have you been married?'

'About a couple of years.'

'Me too. Where's yours now?'

'Coming down in the Jag with the luggage. I had to get here for morning surgery. Where's yours?'

'Coming down in her parents' Rover. I had to go straight from the airport.'

Freddie stared at him solemnly. 'This month could be a great giggle.'

'Why not? We've a perfectly comfortable house, bags of drink, and I shouldn't think too much work. Half the population of a place like this will be sizzling like Frankfurters on insanitary Mediterranean beaches.'

'I'm sure the two girls will get on famously.'

'They should do. They've got the most fascinating topic of conversation in the world—'

'Us!' they said together, suddenly laughing and slapping each other again.

'Now, Doctors.' Cindy came into the lounge briskly from the surgery door, bearing a pair of white coats. 'There's two cases stretched out ready. A rheumatoid arthritis of the elbow-joint benefiting from intra-articular injections of 50 milligrams of cortisone, and an acne vulgaris doing nicely on ultraviolet light.'

'You speak the language,' Freddie complimented her, taking a stethoscope from his case on the plastic-marble coffee-table.

'I just keep my eyes and ears open. It's a matter of using your loaf and picking things up as you go along, isn't it?'

'The principle on which we learn medicine,' Pip told her.

'You'll never find out about real people just by reading books. Oh, them patients,' Cindy complained, as the chimes rang out. 'Must be a new one. All the chronics know I leave the door unlatched.'

Cindy found on the doorstep a tall, slim, suntanned woman in a smart lightweight rust-coloured suit. 'Dr Chipps?' asked the visitor.

'You'll have to queue up like everyone else,' Cindy said severely.

She smiled. 'I'm Mrs Chipps.'

'Oh, do come in, make yourself at home.' Cindy led her into the lounge, which was empty. 'The doctor is with a patient at the moment.'

Eva looked round with the expression of a woman unable to find a taxi at Harrods and obliged to join a bus queue. 'Poultry are *not* a decoration,' she murmured. 'I suppose we must be glad of a roof over our heads,' she announced to Cindy. 'When we've just set foot in the country.'

'Of course, there's the other locum doctor living here.'

'*Other* doctor? Sir Lancelot said nothing over the telephone. I happen to be very sensitive over sharing bathrooms. I suppose he's married?'

'Well, he hasn't got one with him. He seems a nice sort of feller. Quiet. *Very* good looking.'

'Aged?'

'Oh, he's well into his twenties.'

'Mm, really,' said Eva, looking more interested.

'Do you know something, Mrs Chipps?' Cindy confided, eyes sparkling. 'As soon as I saw him, I thought, that's the sort of man I take to. Polished. Worldly. The kind a girl could put her trust in. As reliable as the Rock of Gibraltar.'

'Perhaps we can all three manage to rub along together,' decided Eva, inspecting her reflection in the patio doors.

'Here's his brief-case.' Cindy read the label. 'Mr Frederick Bisham, FRCS.'

'I must go back to London at once,' said Eva.

'But you've only just arrived,' exclaimed Cindy.

'That doesn't matter.' Eva was striding towards the door. 'The locum's off. We shall tour the Lake District instead.'

'But you can't let down the Dr Turnhorns,' Cindy complained shrilly. 'Think of all them sick people, suffering in the waiting-room.'

'I don't give a damn if Spratt's Bottom's in the grip of bubonic plague.'

Pip hurried into the lounge through the surgery door, stethoscope dangling. 'Hello, darling. Drove the car all right? Nurse, I want a 5 millilitre syringe and an ampoule of cortisone – you were perfectly right about that elbow.'

'We can't stay here another moment,' cried Eva, as Cindy scurried away.

'I agree the decor's horrible. But we're being paid to look at it.'

'It's not that. I don't feel well. I probably picked up something before we left. Lassa fever.'

'You get that in the Sudan, not Kenya,' said Pip thoughtfully. He added tenderly, 'Poor dear ... but we can't possibly back out. I told you the sort of ogre Sir Lancelot is. If I upset him in the slightest, all my careful plans for the future would disappear up the sigmoidoscope. And what about my Auntie Florrie? She'll be along any moment to run her nutmeg-grater glance over you.' Eva sat abruptly on the recliner, hands twisted. 'What *is* the matter, darling?' he asked gently.

'Pip – have you ever had the strange feeling of being in a place before?'

He nodded, holding the brass pole of the electric oil-lamp, its shade made from a flat Malaysian straw hat. 'It's what we doctors call the "déjà vu" phenomenon. You get it from a neurological disturbance.'

'I've got it because I *have* been here before.'

'Go on? In Spratt's Bottom?'

'In the horrible hospital. I was ill.'

'What was wrong with you?' he asked in surprise.

'I don't know. I mean, I . . . I had loss of memory.'

'But you never once mentioned it,' he complained.

'Of course not. If you suffer loss of memory, believe me, you want to forget it.'

Pip wrapped his white-coated arms round her tenderly. 'You poor, poor, angel.'

'I steeled myself to face Spratt's Bottom again for your sake. Now I'm here, I find I can't.'

'Of course, you had a terribly traumatic experience in the place.' He scratched his strawlike hair. 'But my love, if we leave even before we unpack, Sir Lancelot will blow the ends off his carotid arteries.'

Cindy's head appeared round the surgery door. 'Syringe ready, doctor.'

'I mustn't abandon my patient. We'll talk about it later, eh?'

Eva walked distractedly about the room. She picked up a tinted-glass Spanish wine-flask like a hospital bottle, and opened the head of a large straw Spanish donkey used as a wastepaper basket. She slowly rubbed her hands together, frowning deeply. She jumped. Big Ben had chimed.

'Excuse me—' From the door to the hall there appeared diffidently a short, plump, dark, pink-cheeked, cheerful-looking young woman in tight jeans and yellow T-shirt. Hands and eyelashes fluttering, she asked with a smile, 'Are you the nurse?'

'No, I'm the doctor's wife,' Eva told her crisply. 'You'll have to wait outside, like everyone else.'

She gave a suppressed laugh, fingertips to lips. 'But I'm the doctor's wife, too. Mrs Bisham. You all right, dear?' she asked with sudden concern.

'But Freddie – Mr Bisham – is not married.'

'Well, he's been behaving like it to me this last couple of years. What a pretty lounge.' She gazed round. 'What lovely ducks.' She fondled her necklace of shiny, odd shapes of metal, which Eva thought outstandingly ugly. 'We're going to be ever so happy here, I know.'

'We happen to be living here too,' Eva informed her coldly. 'My husband's the other locum. We've just flown in.'

'Now, isn't that nice? We'll be company for each other, when our menfolk are busy. I'm Dawn.'

She offered a hand. Eva found it unpleasantly damp.

'I'm Eva Chipps.'

'How funny.'

'It isn't a particularly comic name.'

'My husband had a great friend called Chipps. When he trained at St Swithin's. I trained there too, as a physio. But we didn't meet until dear Freddie and I were both working at Spratt's Bottom.' She sighed romantically. 'St Sepulchre's Hospital! Our trysting-place. Where are you going?'

'To the loo. I feel sick. Jet lag.'

Dawn crossed to the reproduction of Monet's *Corn Poppies* over the brick fireplace. 'I do so love art,' she said to herself.

Freddie hurried through the surgery door. 'You got here quickly darling. I'm up to my neck in it already, as you can see. Where's that bloody ophthalmoscope?' He started rummaging in his bag. 'Guess who Sir Lancelot found for the other locum? My dear old pal Pip Chipps. You remember – I told you terrible tales about the flat we used to share before I qualified. It's odd, you know, that you never ran into him at St Swithin's.'

Dawn stretched lazily. 'Big place, St Swithin's. But I've just met his wife.'

'Ah, yes, his wife.' Freddie straightened up, ophthalmoscope in hand. 'And how would you describe her?'

'Glistening, with sharp edges and cold inside. She reminded me of our fridge.'

He took from the bag a small square bottle containing an appendix preserved in white spirit, kissed it, and placed it delicately on the plastic coffee-table beside the Spanish wine-flask. 'I must put out my lucky charm, which goes with me everywhere.'

'Freddie—' Pip appeared distractedly at the surgery door. 'I can never remember dosages. How much ergotamine tartrate do I give my wife? She's got severe migraine.'

'Point-two-five to point-five milligrams.' He extended an arm proudly. 'Pip, meet the wife.'

'We've met,' said Pip absently. 'Hello, Dawn.'

'Hello, Pip. You *are* looking brown. Been in the sun?'

Freddie thrust his fingers through his thick hair. 'Hey! How? When?'

'Pip, what *are* you doing all this time?' Eva appeared from the hall, holding her head. 'I'm absolutely splitting.'

'Freddie, meet the wife,' said Pip.

'We've met,' said Freddie.

Dawn giggled. 'Isn't it a small world?'

'You *know* Dawn,' said Freddie, frowning slightly. 'How?'

'It was at St Swithin's. After you'd left,' Pip told him. 'After the party with the bedpan loving-cup. I had trouble with the back, so I went along to the department of physical medicine. And there was Mrs Bisham. Of the future, of course.'

'And then what happened?'

'How kind of you to ask. It got better quite quickly.'

'Dr Bisham—' Cindy's head appeared round the

75

surgery door. 'Mrs Egham's been all exposed for ten minutes, and say's she's not going to be the first patient who develops pneumonia as a complication of nettle-rash.'

'Give her *Punch* to read. I don't care a damn if your whole backbone fell through your pelvis and made a nasty mess on the floor. But I'm just slightly interested in knowing exactly how *well* you knew Dawn?'

Dawn started to giggle again.

'Aren't you being a bit truculent?' asked Pip. 'And a bit paranoid?'

'Surgeons are entitled to be truculent. It's part of the act. As I've known you for years to be a creeping Casanova, I'm entitled to be a little paranoid.'

Dawn was squirming with giggles, holding the oil-lamp for support. Eva stood clasping her temples with her mouth open.

'Come to that,' Pip counter-attacked, 'how did you come to know Eva?'

'Simple,' replied Freddie, with a surgeon's brisk confidence. 'Eva fell ill while visiting Spratt's Bottom. I treated her at St Sepulchre's. Nothing to it, you see.'

Pip looked puzzled. 'What was a surgeon doing, treating her for loss of memory?'

'Stop—!' Eva threw her arms apart. She looked like Joan of Arc hearing the scratch of English tinder-boxes. 'Pip, darling. A terrible moment has arrived in my life. In your life. In all our lives. I have a confession to make.'

'Dr Chipps—' Cindy's head reappeared. 'There's a man certain he's swallowed a bee, and he's frightened it's going to sting him inside somewhere sensitive. Oh, blimey,' she muttered, as Pip waved her impatiently away. 'Better treat them myself, I suppose.'

'Pip, darling,' said Eva dramatically as the door shut. 'Freddie and I lived together: Here, at Spratt's Bottom. We had a little flat behind the post office.'

76

'It got dreadfully noisy when they sorted the letters early in the morning,' Freddie reflected.

'It was just for a month or two. I must admit that it was a very, very beautiful experience at the time. You were in Kenya, Pip. Freddie kept talking about you. When we split up – in a perfectly adult way, we were intellectually incompatible, quite intolerably – I went out there too, just to be far away from my memories.'

'Freddie's perfectly tolerable to live with,' Pip said meditatively. 'I lived with him for a year myself.'

'Oh, Dawn—!' Eva tragically took two damp hands in her own. 'Never did I imagine that Freddie and I would ever meet again. How can I ask you to forgive me?'

'Oh, don't mention it. Your husband and I lived together, too. In a little flat behind the St Swithin's hospital laundry. It was terribly noisy all night long.'

'Dr Chipps!' Cindy was in the surgery doorway, hands on hips. 'If you don't come at once, I'm walking out. Them bees are swarming.'

'Back in a jiffy,' Pip mumbled, hurrying after her.

The three stood looking at each other in silence. 'Well,' said Freddie cheerfully. 'That should give us all something to talk about during the next month, shouldn't it?'

'Eva dear, don't look so upset,' Dawn told her kindly. 'Everybody lives with everybody these days. Look what it saves on gas alone.'

'Of course, you're perfectly right, Dawn dear,' she decided. 'The incidents have utterly no significance, none whatever. I sometimes think that I am too serious-minded. It comes from my mother being a professor of moral philosophy.' She purposefully straightened her shoulders and clasped her hands. 'How did you two happen to meet?' she asked, trying to sound conversational.

'I wrenched my leg playing cricket,' said Freddie.

'So I massaged him in the physio department at St Sepulchre's,' Dawn continued. 'On Monday, I started on the calf. By Tuesday, I'd reached the patella. By Wednesday, I was on the thigh. On Thursday, I reached the hip, and on Friday he asked me to marry him. What did he do to you?'

'He took my appendix out—' Eva stopped.

She pointed towards the coffee-table. 'The bottle. That's it. I'd recognize it anywhere.'

'Freddie!' exclaimed Dawn crossly. 'All this time, I've been looking at another woman's appendix on the mantelpiece.'

'Honest, darling,' he explained. 'I didn't put it in a bottle because it was Eva's appendix. But because that appendix was the very first I ever took out in my life.'

'Why, you rotten little surgical swine,' Eva exploded. 'You told me then you'd taken out hundreds and hundreds.'

'Well, I had to give one of us confidence for the operation.'

'Freddie,' said Dawn firmly. 'You're going to take that appendix and give it a decent burial in the garden.'

'Certainly not. It's my talisman. It's brought me luck. Why, it brought me you.'

'It happens to be *my* appendix,' said Eva briskly. 'I think I'd like it back.'

'You can't. Whoever heard of an appendix transplant?' asked Freddie. 'I refuse to argue with you any longer. I have patients to see.' He slipped the bottle into the pocket of his white coat and stalked from the room.

'Freddie really *is* a wonderful surgeon,' Dawn said lovingly. 'So delicate, such sensitive hands.'

'You think so, do you?'

'Oh, yes. He's got ambitions for heart operations.'

'He has, has he?'

'You ought to see some of his work.'

'I do,' said Eva briskly. 'Frequently.'

She pulled up her skirt, tugged down the top of her

tights and lilac pants, and exposed a long, broad, sunken brown line.

'You see? He scarred me for life.'

'Yes, it does rather look as though he did it with a bulldozer,' Dawn told her contemplatively. 'But you must make allowances. Remember, it was his very first try.'

'Oh, I feel awful,' Eva burst out, collapsing on the cut moquette.

Cindy appeared from the hall. 'Mrs Chipps ... Mrs Bisham ... I've just had two phone calls. One from a Sir Lancelot Spratt. He's coming tonight for dinner. The other from the matron of St Sepulchre's. She's coming tonight for dinner, too. Will you be wanting anything extra from the milkman? He's waiting outside with eczema.'

8

SIR Lancelot drove to Spratt's Bottom that Monday evening in a disturbed mood. He had spent the afternoon in the Park Lane offices of a firm of public relations experts, their name grudgingly sought from the dean. Apparently Mr Hamilton Tosker would have trusted them to make Joseph Stalin look like Father Christmas. Sir Lancelot had anticipated some velvet-suited neurotic smelling of alcohol and perfume, but he found a brisk young man with hair the colour of lacquered chestnuts, whose only deviation from everyday mankind was being surrounded by unbelievably beautiful women.

'Do you think you can pull it off?' Sir Lancelot asked, putting his plan.

'Public relations can accomplish almost anything.' The expert sat at a desk bare except for a silver bowl of roses and the signed photograph of a former Prime Minister.

'Perhaps I'm being overcautious,' said Sir Lancelot doubtfully. 'If a lot of people want something, they soon make themselves felt. Look at the French Revolution.'

The expert smiled. 'The most successful public relations exercise in history. Anyone could have walked into the decrepit old Bastille. *Storming* it was so much more impressive. We'll have this hospital given the kiss of life, don't worry. What's it called?'

'St Sepulchre's.'

'Mmm, hardly the most saleable of names. We'll organize local pressure groups, councillors, the MP, and so on. You must take the editor of the local paper out to lunch. *They* are closing *your* hospital, you know. We'll get a letter in *The Times* from one of those teams of signatories who're always ready to be identified with worthy causes. I'll have a question asked in the House—'

'Surely you cannot rig so important a constitutional procedure?' Sir Lancelot looked shocked.

'Oh, it's a whole industry,' the public relations man told him lightly. 'And we must infiltrate the Ministry. There's usually some rivalry or other to be exploited. We'll have a few well-organized spontaneous demonstrations. Car-stickers and leaflets. Perhaps a stunt – you and a nurse dropped on the hospital by helicopter?'

'No,' said Sir Lancelot firmly. He caught the whiff of burning boats. He was fierce about saving St Sepulchre's, but he trembled at making an even worse public spectacle of himself than walking behind the bowler's arm at Lord's.

And Amelia had left Lazar Row. The prong-prodding commis had been reinstated at Bunter's. He felt disturbed that she had gone, and more disturbed that he did not know precisely why.

'That apartment up there is luxurious,' she had com-plimented him. 'You really spoiled Miss MacLockjaw, or whatever her name was. By the way, there's about a ton of birdseed tucked in the closets and places.'

At least it stopped the dean persistently greeting him with a leer which suggested that he made Don Juan look like John Knox.

'The Turnhorns have a most rewarding cellar,' Freddie was meanwhile saying in Apricot Avenue, sniffing a cork. 'This claret is really quite authoritative.'

'You always were so knowledgeable about wines,' murmured Eva, laying the table. The two couples had recovered their lively spirits. The party would be a cel-ebration of their reunion. They had decided to dine on the patio, by the light of gas candles. The poplars at the end of the garden were striping the lawn, the herbaceous borders gleamed in the descending sun which tinged the lily-pond with gold.

'It's like wearing the right clothes or driving the right car,' Freddie told her. 'It all helps furthering a surgical career. What happens in the operating theatre isn't everything, not by a long chalk.'

'Pip can't tell Beaujolais from cherry brandy.'

'Well, Dawn can't cook anything except moussaka. Which resembles Irish stew made with engine oil.' He noticed the necklace of little gilt Eiffel towers round her bronzed neck, above her low-cut dress of dark green Thai silk. 'Didn't I give you that?'

'*Did* you? Yes, so you did. On our trip to the rugby international in Paris.'

'Do you often wear it?'

'Almost always. I'm very fond of it.'

There was a short silence. A cuckoo gave voice.

'I suppose what happened between us can never fade away,' he said. 'It's like antibodies in the blood after an attack of measles.'

She asked quietly, 'Why did you leave me, Freddie?'

He poured a drop of claret into a glass and sniffed again. 'Living with you was like driving some super, sleek sports car. All day long. A great experience, but it takes it out of you. I'm the sort of bloke who's happier chugging along in some slow old banger.'

'And I suppose *I* found you not demanding enough intellectually. Oh, I know that you're a terribly clever surgeon, Freddie. But that's something you do with your hands, isn't it? Like repairing the lawn-mower.'

He sipped the wine, smacking his lips. 'At least, we're being frank.'

She adjusted the fish-forks. 'Mutual frankness is a privilege which few pairs of human beings can enjoy.'

'Now we're stuck here for a month like four survivors on a life-raft. But we'll live,' he said cheerfully.

'Yes, I'm sure we'll get along splendidly.'

'Where's Pip?'

'Wandering about somewhere. He does wander, quite a lot.'

Her husband was beyond the Moorish arch, in the fully-fitted kitchen with electric spit, grained formica veneer, matching fridge panel and breakfast bar. Eva had left Dawn in charge of the gravy.

'I'm always telling Eva, it doesn't matter in the least *what* a man eats.' Pip was absentmindedly swallowing peanuts from a heaped glass bowl. 'So long as he receives an adequate daily intake of protein, fats, carbohydrate, vitamins and minerals. Which a lot of men don't, and not only in Kenya. Do you realize, Dawn, that one-third of the whole world doesn't get enough to eat? A third of our fellow-humans, always hungry! While here in Spratt's Bottom, they guzzle away until they inflict themselves with obesity, heart disease, strokes, ulcers, arthritis. They get neurotic, because they're not making enough money. But they have solid houses, pure water, excellent drains and a surfeit of doctors to attend their most trivial ailments. For a lot of people on this planet, nobody cares much, or even notices much, if they're alive or dead. I can't decide if the situation's more amazing than appalling. I don't know whether to laugh my head off, or put it under a bus.'

'Fancy you, going to work among the blacks.' Dawn peered intently into the saucepan.

'That's what made me a doctor.' His eyes were bright as he chewed the nuts. 'When I could treat my patients by the million instead of face-to-face, when I had a challenge which doesn't appeal to the commonplace mind, and when success is marked by something more inspiring than money. You remember how I was always in trouble at St Swithin's? Only because I was too shy to assume the role of God at the bedside, like Sir Lancelot.' He noticed above the neck of her black dress with the crimson sunflowers a chain bearing a silver St Swithin's crest. 'I gave you that, didn't I?'

'Perhaps you did. Yes, it was the day you passed your finals. It made you suddenly fond of the place.'

'Do you wear it much?'

'Oh, ever such a lot.'

He started to eat another handful of nuts. 'Dawn, I really do know you terribly well, don't I?'

She stirred the gravy with a wooden spoon.

'Sometimes I feel that I know you better than I know Eva,' he continued.

'Oh, damn! I think I've burnt it.'

'Pip—' Eva rattled through the bead curtain. 'Freddie wants you to help him decant the port.' She took the spoon firmly from Dawn. 'How do you find him?' she smiled at her, as Pip disappeared.

'Just the same.'

Eva looked amazed. 'I thought I'd cured the terrible lack of confidence which so held him back at St Swithin's.' She seemed to be mentioning a vital but painful operation.

'And how do you find Freddie?'

Eva had her nose over a spoonful of sauce. 'More charming, I think.'

'Oh, thank you,' said Dawn doubtfully.

Eva tied on a frilled check apron, and briskly started chopping mint. 'Odd, how we married two such entirely different doctors.'

Dawn helped herself to the cheese footballs. 'Don't they *all* have this tremendous, mysterious attraction? I suppose they see so many women without their clothes on, we all feel we have to try harder.'

'What precisely attracted you to Freddie?'

Dawn sighed. 'He was a surgical registrar. Nothing in a hospital is more sexy than a surgical registrar.'

'Of course, hospitals are places run entirely by women

84

who want to get husbands, or want to get away from them. Pass me the tarragon vinegar.'

'Why were you attracted to Pip?'

'Because he is very much more intelligent than he likes to let people believe.'

'Funny, I shouldn't have thought so.'

'Tell me about your honeymoon?'

'We went to Cornwall and had flu.'

'We went on safari and were eaten by mosquitoes.'

'Better than by lions, I suppose.'

Pip's head appeared through the bead curtain. 'His car's here,' he announced breathlessly. 'All on parade. Don't worry, Dawn. He may be a pain in the guts, but it's all wind.'

Freddie was rummaging distractedly through the Jacobean cabinet. 'I hope we've a bottle of single malt, to warm up our surgical Genghis Khan. He always arrives in a state of social frostbite.'

Big Ben chimed.

'My favourite whisky, Bisham. Very thoughtful to get some in,' said Sir Lancelot affably, a few moments later. The four stood in a line, smiling with hands clasped before them, as demure as schoolchildren on prize-day. 'I know already that I am assured of a good meal. Not the customary suburban dinner-party, consisting of avocados, frozen duck, soggy soufflé and character assassination.'

'I'm giving you my gigot,' said Eva proudly.

'Capital. You're damn lucky, Bisham, having a wife who's such a good cook.'

Freddie smiled at Dawn. 'I don't think that my wife would claim to express her best talents in the kitchen.'

Sir Lancelot seemed surprised. 'One experience certainly satisfied me. But I suppose you registrars live it up these days. Both you young fellows enjoy one thing in common – wives far too good for you.' The couples exchanged glances of befitting winsomeness. He took another gulp of whisky, and continued with gratifying glowing geniality, 'It must be four years now since you entertained me in your own homes.' Their glances changed to blank stares. 'What is the matter?' he asked sharply.

'Nothing, sir,' said Freddie hastily. 'One of those sudden silences that can affect any gathering. An angel passing overhead, I believe.'

'Why not make yourself comfortable, Sir Lancelot?' said Eva quickly, vigorously pummelling the yellow satin cushions on the purple sofa.

'Do put your feet up, Sir Lancelot,' invited Dawn, sweeping a pink pouffe under his heels.

Sir Lancelot looked more surprised, but continued the conversation. 'How do you find being a housewife in Nairobi?'

'Basically, no different from Spratt's Bottom,' Eva told him.

'But you've never been to Nairobi,' Sir Lancelot objected.

'Oh! No, of course not. But . . . but I've been to Spratt's Bottom.'

Sir Lancelot frowned. 'Bisham, is this whisky extra proof?'

'Another glass, sir?' pressed Freddie.

'Well, it might not be a bad idea.' Sir Lancelot leant back. 'I think I may congratulate myself on discerning, four years ago, that Eva would be invaluable in keeping her husband's career firmly on the rails. Which may lead to the palatial terminus of a consultant post.'

'But I don't want to be a consultant, sir,' said Pip.

'I didn't say anything about you, Chipps,' Sir Lancelot told him shortly. 'Doubtless, your capacities are better extended among the snakes and monkeys. But you, Bisham, I know entertained hopes of the staff at St Sepulchre's.'

Freddie looked anxiously at Dawn and Eva. 'Modesty would not be honesty, sir.'

'In which case, you may be disappointed. The place is threatened with closure.' Freddie's face fell. 'That's why I put you and Chipps in this job. As advance troops in my campaign to keep St Sepulchre's open. My success or failure may anyway prove irrelevant to you,' he continued grudgingly, 'because an unexpected vacancy will shortly arise at St Swithin's. One of the surgeons has been sold to the Arabs by the dean, who would seem to ape the qualities of manager to the Arsenal Football Club. Play your cards right, Bisham, and I can guarantee that you and Eva will join the pleasant circle of St Swithin's consultants.'

'Sir Lancelot—' Eva's eyes flashed. 'There is something I must tell you instantly.'

'You're pregnant? Congratulations.'

'No, no, no!' she said impatiently. 'But you've got it all—'

Freddie clapped a hand over her mouth.

'What the devil?' demanded Sir Lancelot.

'She has a terribly nasty throat, sir. Streptococcus. Resistant to antibiotics. Wouldn't like you to catch it.'

Dawn started to giggle.

'What *is* going on?' asked Sir Lancelot. A tuneful hiccough came from his top jacket pocket. 'Damn. My bleep.'

'The phone's in the hall, sir.' Freddie threw open the door. He shut it behind the surgeon quickly. 'Listen,' he said urgently, 'we've got to keep the old boy in the dark.'

'I refuse,' said Eva. 'Utterly. It's humiliating.'

'It's only for tonight,' Freddie implored. 'He's far too busy to stick his talons in our nest again. I'm playing for high stakes,' he added. 'St Swithin's itself.'

'Go on, Eva. Be a sport,' Dawn urged.

'That's all very well for you, Dawn,' Eva responded. 'But what does my Pip get out of it?'

'Money, a job, a lab for his nutrition work. That's what you want to screw out of Sir Lancelot, isn't it?' Freddie asked. Pip nodded. 'You certainly won't, if he finds we're not coupled the way he thinks.'

'But even a straitlaced old fogey like Sir Lancelot can't object to our living in what he would call sin,' Pip protested.

'He would almost certainly object violently to the discovery that he's made a lunatic mistake. When he puts us in this job thinking we were the other way round. It would be like diagnosing jaundice in a Chinaman.'

Pip nodded. 'He hates being made to look a fool. When his operating trousers split in the middle of a gastrectomy, you'd have imagined the same thing had happened to Hitler addressing the Reichstag.'

'Oh, very well, very well,' Eva agreed reluctantly, taking Pip's hand. 'If it's for the good of us all. Though God knows how we're going to get through dinner.'

'What's that necklace?' Pip noticed the Eiffel towers. 'I haven't seen you wearing it before.'

'Haven't you, dear?' said Eva. 'I've had it quite a time.'

Sir Lancelot returned. 'The dean, if you please. From the Dorchester Hotel, where he is guzzling with his new little friend Hamilton Tosker. You know, the Australian millionaire and racehorse-owner who won the Melbourne Cup three times running, and therefore exists there in a state of canonization. The dean wants me to lay on a slap-up lunch at the pub when he visits Spratt's Bottom next week. Damn cheek. Still, Tosker might have some suggestions on getting my operating-theatre roof repaired before the snow starts coming through. Which brings me to the point. I want you, Bisham, and you, Chipps, to furnish all your patients with the leaflets I am shortly sending, and the car-stickers bearing our slogan, "Save St Sepulchre's – St Sepulchre's Saves Spratt's Bottom". You might mention something to this effect while performing your examinations.'

The pair nodded. All four stood round the sofa respectfully, Pip holding Dawn's hand, Freddie Eva's. 'The doctor's word is terribly potent,' Sir Lancelot continued. 'The patients go home and squeeze each phrase, until it is dry of all drops of hope, warning, exhortation and – if they are singularly fortunate – information. I think we all learn as first year medical students, never to let fall within the patient's hearing any remark in the slightest unconsidered.'

'Freddie has the most lovely bedside manner,' said Dawn fondly.

Sir Lancelot blinked.

'Freddie, you're wonderful with patients,' said Eva quickly, kissing him.

'Oh, yes!' exclaimed Dawn. 'And so are you, Pip.' She took his head between her hands and kissed him for so long that Sir Lancelot began to stir uncomfortably.

'Nice to see so much affection between young couples,' he said gruffly. 'Particularly after four years of marriage. Glad to see you're sporting the St Swithin's crest, my dear.'

'I've never seen her wearing it before,' volunteered Freddie. 'I mean, Pip's never seen her wearing it before. Another dose of the malt, sir?'

The doorbell chimed.

'My God!' cried Pip. 'I'd forgotten Auntie Florrie.'

As if sleepwalking, he went into the hall.

9

'DEAR Pip, how wonderful to see you again.'

The matron strode into the lounge in her turquoise dinner-dress. 'And how splendidly fit you look. I was quite concerned that you might have become infected with hookworm or bilharzia or those other disgusting tropical things. But why must you appear at this hour on an English June evening as though going out to shoot elephants at any moment?'

She indicated his safari suit. Pip stood staring with his mouth open.

'Pip! Is this all you can do for your auntie? I am hardly enamoured with a view of your tonsillar fossae.'

'Oh, sorry.' He kissed her. 'This is an emotional moment.'

She patted his cheek. 'That's better. So nice to know that you still love your auntie. Good evening, Lancelot.' The surgeon had politely risen. 'Sorry I'm late, but the kitchens have flooded at St Sepulchre's. The patients are obliged to sup off cocoa and sandwiches, but fortunately they are little worse off than usual, because the cooks have been on strike for a week. Eva . . .' The matron fondly took each of her hands. 'How wonderful you look. Positively dazzling. When I used to travel in the tropics with my own husband, I noticed how so many Englishwomen's complexions simply went to pieces in the strong sunlight. They looked like cracked, dried-up river beds. You seem to have avoided that.'

'It's been a good summer so far,' Sir Lancelot observed, frowning. 'But not that good.'

'You must be Freddie Bisham?' The matron politely

extended her hand. 'You left St Sepulchre's before I arrived. Though of course, I hear so much about you. Quite one of the most brilliant registrars in surgery. And one of the most popular among patients and staff.' She smiled coyly. 'Particularly among my nurses, I understand. Though you weren't a nurse, Dawn, but a physio?' She patted her cheek, too. 'Are you still keeping it up? Good! I believe most firmly that marriage is a woman's pastime, not her career.'

'Your usual dry sherry, Auntie?' Pip interrupted.

'Thank you.'

'Do I gather that you've already met Mrs Bisham?' asked Sir Lancelot.

The matron shook her head. 'No. Only this evening.'

He pulled his beard. 'Is there some rat which everyone is trying to keep from the perception of my olfactory nerve?'

'Why don't you and the matron take a turn in the garden, sir?' suggested Freddie. 'It's such a lovely evening.'

'Yes let's, this minute,' agreed the matron, taking her glass. 'There's something I particularly want to discuss with you, Lancelot, before we all get down to the jollity.'

She drew him on to the sunlit lawn, bedewed by sparkling drops from the whirling sprinkler.

'How gratifying to find Pip so suitably matched,' she said. Sir Lancelot grunted. 'Young Bisham and his wife seem to make quite a pretty pair, too.' Sir Lancelot grunted again. 'Isn't it sad about St Sepulchre's? I heard the news.'

'I am going to fight to keep it open,' he said forcefully. 'Until the Government is forced to hose money into the place, to quench the flames of public anger.'

'I can't see how St Sepulchre's could possibly be improved,' she said doubtfully. 'Even if they struck oil in the basement, it would only add to the mess.'

'Sheer defeatism.'

'The dean told me this morning that your housekeeper had left you.'

Sir Lancelot grunted once more.

'It is absolutely grotesque, a man in your position not having a woman to look after him.'

'I shall advertise for another in the *Lady*.'

'Oh, Lancelot . . .' They were concealed from the patio behind a well-clipped laurel at the foot of the lawn, in an arbour containing a rustic seat. To his intense embarrassment, Sir Lancelot noticed two tears on the matron's fair lashes. 'Sometimes I worry about you even more than I worry about Pip.'

'That is very civil of you.'

She laid a long-fingered hand on his lapel. She told him softly, 'You don't want a housekeeper, Lancelot. You want an intelligent and sympathetic woman, one who knows you of old, one who can allow for all your little habits and mannerisms, which to a stranger might seem alarming, if not revolting. You want a woman who will devote her whole life to you.'

'That's what Miss MacNish kept saying. But I fancy she was more interested in her budgie.'

The matron's hand crept softly to his bristly neck. 'Don't you want me to make you happy?'

He patted her forearm. 'Florence, I am much touched. What man could fail to be? I am sure that you would make me very happy indeed. But like all surgeons, I am a realist. And I see that I should fail to make you happy in return. Far from our trotting in harness, you would be as miserable as Mr Lester Piggott on a mule.'

'Dear Lancelot,' she sighed. 'All of us in the hospital fear your tongue. But the object of your harshest criticism is you yourself.'

'That is surely the case with any self-respecting man who has charge of others, and the lives of others?'

'You quite like me, don't you?'

He did, he felt, from time to time. 'Yes, Florrie, I do.' He kissed her. 'Now come and sit down on this bench, and I shall tell you of my plans to save St Sepulchre's.'

Eva was kneeling before the sizzling roast in the oven, when she found Freddie leaning over her.

'Eva—'

'Freddie—'

They clasped each other.

'From that moment you kissed me, Eva—'

'Yes, yes! I wanted you more than ever.'

'Like behind the post office—'

'Freddie, darling,' she said breathlessly. 'For years, I've hardly been able to post a letter without a tremendously thrilling feeling.'

'But what can we do?' he asked hopelessly.

'I just don't know.'

'Can we get rid of Pip?'

'How? He notices much more than anyone thinks, you know.'

'Golf.' Freddie snapped his fingers. 'He's still keen?' She nodded vigorously. 'I'll fix him a round with the pro. He was one of my patients.' He held her tighter. 'He can suffer frustrations in the bunkers, while we're getting rid of ours on the bedsprings.'

'But what about Dawn?'

'Ah.'

'Is she easygoing?'

'No, she sticks like Elastoplast.' He snapped his fingers again. 'Shopping. I'll give her a fistful of money and send her to London. A lot of suburban husbands do that. It's why Harrods is always so crowded. What's the matter?'

'My appendix scar. It itches when I get sexy.'

Dawn was setting on the patio table six plates of plump, peeled prawns, spoking a hub of pink cream. '*Bouquet garni* with aurora sauce, for starters.'

93

Pip absently picked a prawn and munched it. 'Dinner's going to be like playing two games of bridge at once,' he said gloomily.

'Typical Freddie,' she said resignedly. 'Always chancing his arm. It's not the first mess he's got into. Quite a number of people in Spratt's Bottom have bits missing that might still be usefully attached.'

Pip ate another prawn. 'Now *I* always like to think things out carefully. I should never have spun this cat's cradle, which I fear will soon be a tangled heap at Sir Lancelot's feet.'

Dawn helped herself to a prawn, dipping it in the sauce. 'Would it matter?' she asked quietly.

'Oh, Dawn! From that second I felt your lips—'

'Oh, Pip!' She gulped down her prawn and kissed him.

'For years, I've hardly been able to pass a laundry without thinking, "Came the Dawn".'

Her nails dug through his safari suit. 'From the moment I saw you, I knew this had to be.'

'But there's Freddie.'

'Can't we get him out of the way?'

'Is he still a cricket fan?' She nodded. 'Personally, I'd rather spend a day in the cemetery watching the funerals. But I know someone at Lord's, I can get him a ticket for the Test match tomorrow. It's the last day, so it'll be terribly exciting.'

'And Eva?' Dawn laid her head against his lapel, reaching for another prawn.

'Oh, dear, yes. I know – say you want her to choose *you* a dress in London. The flattery is irresistible. I think a lot of suburban women get rid of awkward wives for the afternoon that way. It's why you can never squeeze into Harrods.'

They jumped apart as the telephone rang.

'Auntie Florrie!' Pip called a moment later across the

lawn. 'Urgent call from St Sepulchre's. The boilers have blown up.'

'Oh, dear!' She emerged from the arbour. 'I thought there was an ominous rumbling from the boiler-house as I drove past.'

'Enjoy your dinner first,' Sir Lancelot commanded, following. 'You've got to let the fire brigade have their fun.'

'Out of the question.' She drained her last drop of sherry. 'I've been in the front row for every disaster at St Sepulchre's during the past year. Everything from the consultants' loo overflowing to the oil-tanker in gynaecology out-patients'. I don't intend to miss the big one.'

'You *must* be there, Auntie Florrie,' Pip urged. 'Otherwise, it would be like the burning deck without its boy.'

'Or D-Day without Eisenhower,' added Freddie, who had emerged through the bead curtain with Eva.

'Exactly,' the matron agreed. 'Duty comes first with every nurse, however outdated an attitude it seems today.'

'Personally, I think these two are trying to get rid of you,' said Sir Lancelot. 'Let me escort you to your Mini. I haven't finished telling you about the arrangements for my protest meeting.'

'Dawn—' Freddie pulled out his wallet as the door shut. 'Why not nip up to Harrods tomorrow afternoon and buy yourself a new dress?' He thrust several notes at her. 'You'll want something decent, if we're to spend a whole month in a gossipy place like Spratt's Bottom.' He pushed over another handful. 'Have some more.'

'Oh, Freddie! How thoughtful, how generous. But you know I've disastrous dress-sense. You always tell me it's worse than my cooking. Now, Eva dresses like a duchess. I'd ever so much rather she went up to Harrods and chose one for me.' Dawn pressed the notes into Eva's fingers.

'It's a dreadful responsibility, choosing a dress for another woman,' cried Eva in alarm. 'Like bearing her baby.'

'But you're so efficient in everything, Eva,' said Dawn. 'I bet you'll get your own pregnancy finished in four-and-a-half months.'

'Freddie,' said Pip. 'I know how much this game of cricket means to you. I don't mind in the least, my dear old chap, putting myself out tomorrow and doing your surgery, so you can go and enjoy yourself.'

'Didn't you hear the score?' asked Freddie in surprise. 'Jowler took so many Aussie wickets, England need only twenty runs to win. It'll be over well before lunch. Now, why don't *I* take surgery, and you have a nice game of golf? I know how you want to iron out that wobble at the top of your swing.'

'I've pulled my back.'

'Dawn can take you upstairs and give you some massage. You'll be right as rain in the morning. If you don't want a dress, Dawn, why not go to Harrods and buy something useful? A bicycle, a pair of skis, say?'

'No more of this nonsense.' Eva stamped her foot. 'Freddie and I have rediscovered each other.'

'So have I and Dawn,' said Pip. 'That's why I wanted to get Freddie to the Test match.'

Freddie looked shocked. 'Wouldn't it make you feel pretty rotten, as an Englishman, committing adultery with a chap's wife while he's watching cricket?'

Dawn started to giggle. They were all laughing as Sir Lancelot returned. 'What's the joke?' he asked. 'I'll take the Turnhorns' third bedroom tonight, next to the airing cupboard. Though I believe that I shall have to share with a skeleton.'

They all stopped. 'You're staying, sir?' asked Pip.

'Of course. Where I dines I sleeps, and where I sleeps I breakfasts. Don't you know your Surtees? No one in his right mind would drive home after drinking as much as this.'

'But that's no trouble at all,' said Freddie. 'You go and sleep with the skeleton, sir. Pip and Dawn will bed down overlooking the garden, and Eva and I facing Apricot Avenue. Though which has which is really quite immaterial.'

Eva yawned. 'I'm so tired.'

Freddie grasped her hungrily.

'Oh, for my bed!' Dawn stretched voluptuously as Pip gripped her tightly. 'I can hardly wait.'

Sir Lancelot stared at the two embracing couples. A minute went by. He coughed loudly. He finished his whisky. He poked Pip hard in the ribs. 'I don't know about you, Chipps, but I want my dinner.'

'Dinner,' murmured Dawn. 'Haven't we had it?'

'Dinner!' Sir Lancelot pummelled Freddie with his fist. 'Din-dins. I'm ravenous.'

'We don't want any,' Freddie gasped. 'We're going to bed.'

'What is this? An outbreak of sleeping sickness?'

'The air at Spratt's Bottom,' Pip explained. 'Very strong.'

'I'm ready to drop,' said Eva, jerking Freddie towards the stairs beyond the bead curtain.

'I suppose I've got to spend the evening dying slowly of starvation?' Sir Lancelot objected crossly.

'Your dinner is in the oven,' Dawn told him from the archway.

'And half a dozen bottles of claret, sir,' Pip added. 'Should be enough to see you through.'

'Good night, Sir Lancelot!' they all called. He was alone.

He grunted. He scratched his beard. He supposed that was how young married couples behaved these days. Well, perhaps it was healthier to air their intimate life in

97

the public gaze, as they aired their intimate garments on the washing-line. He took off his jacket. He picked up a folded copy of that morning's newspaper and a pencil. He went on to the patio and lit the gas candles. He poured himself a glass of wine, and while slowly nibbling prawns with his left hand he deftly changed Maud's gran into a guardsman and Cathay into a yacht. Like many Englishmen in the highest positions of military command or government, he found in moments of testing confusion *The Times* crossword an unfailing solace.

IO

IT is a truth universally acknowledged, Sir Lancelot paraphrased Jane Austen at seven-thirty the following Thursday morning, that a widower in possession of a good fortune must be in want of a wife.

He drew back the kitchen curtain, looking into his walled garden. It was another lovely June day. He noticed the floor aswill with dirty water. Sir Lancelot possessed a dish-washing machine, but not the technique of using it. He lit the gas for his breakfast coffee. He remembered he was out of bread, but he would have Bath olivers and marmalade instead. As there was no marmalade in the cupboard, he substituted a jar of mixed pickles. He munched at the kitchen table, while dipping a wooden spoon into a tin of pineapple cubes discovered at the back of the fridge. He was dressed in his last clean shirt, and presumed he must appear at St Swithin's the following morning in the striped jersey he wore thirty years before while winning the hospital's rugby cup.

He poured a little treacle into the tin of pineapple. The telephone rang in the hall.

'Lancelot? Did I get you out of that kingly bed? How are you this morning?'

'I am already enjoying my breakfast, Amelia. Last night I presided at the annual dinner of the St Swithin's Hospital chess club.'

'Sounds sober enough.'

'I fear that the annual dinner of any St Swithin's student club would have aroused public notice even in ancient Babylon. With the possible exception of the

99

Student Christian Movement, and even there I gather the fruit cup is a whited sepulchre.'

'Talking of sepulchres – are we due back there this morning?'

'No. The builders have called off their strike, but unfortunately there has been a strike for some months in the factory which makes the special electric wiring. I had another little expedition in mind. I do not see why you and I should not strike for the day, too.'

'Good idea. Nobody healthy should be inside a hospital on a morning like this.'

'May I pick you up at Bunter's about nine?'

The breeze outside tickled his nose like the bubbles from a morning glass of fruit-salts. It was heartening to find the weather so kindly for a day of such aggravating decision. He drove his old Rolls towards Mayfair, thinking about Amelia. She was a forceful woman, certainly. As jealous of her rights as Mrs Pankhurst, and as suspicious of supposed slights as Becky Sharp. But she amused him, and she stretched his intellect on her fingers like a rubber band.

He thought of the matron. She had looked disturbingly attractive in the laurel arbour at Apricot Avenue. She would have kept his house as clean as his operating theatre, and fed him with the care of a gastric patient. But she had the likelihood of continually telling him to open his bowels, wipe his nose and wear wool next to his skin.

He thought of his first wife. How much more lightly a man tripped through life, before suffering the progressive arthritis of habits. She had been the staff-nurse on night-duty, he the houseman, which coupled them as predictably as the siblings of the Pharaohs. He sighed deeply. To lose one's wife in middle-life was not only a tragedy, but an inconvenience.

'Has the fair maid of Perth returned to you?' Amelia

asked, climbing into the car. He shook his head. 'I thought she might have found herself out of birdseed.'

'Admittedly, I have never heard of such affection between a woman and a feathered beast since Leda and the swan.'

'Where are we going?' She looked mystified as he turned northward. 'That cricket game must surely be over by now?'

'I thought you might care to see a place I have not visited these twenty-odd years, but which I shall find exactly the same.'

'You sound confident.'

'Only because it has not changed substantially over the past seven hundred and fifty. By the way,' he added generously. 'Do smoke if you wish.'

'I've given it up,' she told him proudly.

'Good. Much less dangerous. People these days do seem to possess only the courage of their addictions.'

'I gave it up because I respect your opinions.'

He looked gratified. 'My opinions would cost you hard cash in Harley Street.'

'That's immaterial. Every doctor I meet watches me light up as if I was about to disembowel myself. But I respect *you*.'

The enterprise was starting excellently, thought Sir Lancelot. 'I suppose it is vanity and not curiosity which impels me to ask why?'

'It's the way you admire an original painting, but give only a pleased glance to its reproductions.'

'I fear you think of me less as Rembrandt's anatomist than one of Delacroix's fierce Assyrians.'

Amelia laughed. 'I imagined at first you were just another over-bearing egotist,' she added pleasantly. 'Typical of many successful doctors, and other men who go through life without the remotest chance of being con-tradicted. I had to pick through the pachyderm to find the kindness, consideration, sensitivity.' Sir Lancelot squared his shoulders. 'You've a splendidly robust personality, that's all. Do you know something? However much we complain, we women like being told exactly what to do by men. But most men are such hopeless ditherers, they couldn't tell a cat how to lap milk. Where *are* we going?' she asked, as they passed the Post Office Tower.

'Compose yourself, Amelia. The journey is about sixty miles, but the countryside is pleasant.'

He parked near Addenbrooke's Hospital. He took her first to King's College Chapel.

'I have seen the wonders of the world,' said Amelia admiringly, neck craned at the fan-vaulting. 'The Acropolis, the pyramids, the Taj. ... but nothing with such casual perfection as this. That carving's like giant, petrified fronds, left over from the mesozoic era.'

'It has been advised to lie during the services on the floor, with one's head on a hassock, admiring the roof.'

'It's so purely beautiful, yet so unaffected. Like your English women.'

'Thank you,' said Sir Lancelot.

'When was it built?'

'It was started in 1446, but took some little time. About a century.'

They went into the court, spreading like a vast green carpet towards the river. Amelia wore a bright cotton dress, Sir Lancelot his usual sober suit with his cricketing boater. It was shortly after the end of the Easter Term, and the academics had retreated briskly before an occupation army of tourists. 'Were you a Cambridge student?'

'I was once an undergraduate at Audley.'

'Where is the University?'

'You cannot find it. The colleges are all little kingdoms. You eat and sleep in them, and go out for lectures. It is necessary to have a bicycle.'

'What's the matter?' she cried, as he grabbed her.

'You stepped on the grass. That is the most jealously guarded privilege of the College Fellows.'

'I can't think of you as a student. Just as you can never think of some men as boys.'

'I was smooth-cheeked and bun-faced, wore a long scarf in winter and a bright blazer in summer, did as little work as possible and was on good terms with far too many barmaids.'

They strolled along the river-bank. 'You must have lots of romantic memories,' Amelia said dreamily.

'Oddly enough, all I can recall is awaking after a May Ball in a punt, in some remote creek at Grantchester, with a cow licking my face. I thought it was my partner, becoming amorous. But she had dropped off somewhere on the way.'

Amelia looked alarmed. 'Don't you know what happened to her?'

'Perhaps she suffered the same fate as Ophelia?' Sir Lancelot said casually. 'There is a sufficiency of willows growing aslant the Cam.'

They leant on the stone parapet of the bridge, gazing upstream. 'That is Queens' College, with Erasmus' wooden bridge. His old rooms by the river are so chilly, it explains why every portrait you see of the holy gentleman shows him in a furry overcoat. I thought we might take the opposite direction, for luncheon at a pub whose beer I can guarantee.'

She seemed puzzled. 'Why did you ask me to join you on a sentimental journey?'

'Yes, it *is* a sentimental journey. But not for the reason you think.'

She smiled. 'You're not in the slightest sentimental about anything, Lancelot.'

'My profession is not conducive to it. Early in our training, we learn to drop a fireproof safety-curtain between feeling and thinking. Do you know what would happen, if we became emotionally involved with our patients? Or if we responded emotionally to anything they told us? They would die, rather than come and see us. As it is, a man or a woman can say absolutely anything to their doctor, however outrageous, perverted or simply ridiculous, without risking the slightest censure, or even surprise.'

'And that is the doctor's advantage over us frail humans?'

'It is also our blind-spot. We just cannot see how powerfully, if stupidly and self-destructively, people are swayed by their emotions. That is why few doctors get far in politics. One excludes Dr Clemenceau and Dr Jean Paul Marat.'

They started to amble away from the river towards King's Parade. 'Talking of emotions—' Amelia paused. 'Why didn't you try getting into bed with me?'

Sir Lancelot looked alarmed. 'Did you expect me too?'

'Well, I hadn't come for surgery.'

'I suppose it didn't occur to me.'

'That's not very flattering.'

'I must be careful in my personal life. I have the opinions of my colleagues to respect. The dominant position which I enjoy at St Swithin's depends largely on my being regarded as superhuman – not only in surgery.'

'Your colleagues' ideas must be twenty years out of date.'

'Isn't that the customary distance at which everyone keeps the morals of others behind their own? The dean was perfectly right. The students are mischievous monkeys with their noses on the scent of scandal. The last time such rumours went round, they wrote a ribald song for their Christmas pantomime which brought the house down. He was a psychiatrist, too – from whom such conduct might be expected. It even reached *Private Eye*.' Sir Lancelot shuddered at the two words which terrorize the notables of Queen Elizabeth II as 'Star Chamber' those of Queen Elizabeth I. 'I hope you didn't think me unappreciative?' he added hastily.

'No, for the first time I thought you extraordinary. And how do we reach this pub of the nectarean beer?'

'By punt.'

'Am I dressed for a punt?' she exclaimed.

'A punt is a craft which can make any woman look as languidly arousing as Garbo at her best,' he assured her.

They hired a punt at Silver Street Bridge, which bears across the Cam each morning the earnestly-pedalling contents of Newnham. 'I have not propelled a punt for some years,' confessed Sir Lancelot, removing his dark jacket to expose his scarlet braces and rolling up the sleeves of his white shirt. He retained his boater. 'Though doubtless, the knack is never lost. Like bicycling. I shall punt you down the backs.'

'Backs of what?' asked Amelia, settling herself on the cushions at his feet.

'Backs of the colleges. They turn their kindest faces to the river. We shall pass Trinity, where Newton formulated the Law of Gravity. I cannot describe to you the beauty of the Great Court there, because its beauty is indescribable.'

He fell easily into the rhythm of the punt-pole. The green years sprouted on gnarled bark. He began to feel that he had simply cut another morning's lecture in the Cambridge anatomy school.

'But you're an expert,' said Amelia admiringly, letting her fingers trail in the water.

'It's remarkably simple. So long as one does not foolishly impale the pole in the mud.'

'There's only one thing spoils the atmosphere.'

'Yes?' he asked, mystified.

'As a good American, I smell effete privilege.'

'Your nose misleads you. The son or daughter of any British home can get here.' They slid under Garret Hostel Bridge.

'They need the money.'

'No. They need the brains. Which is a far more difficult commodity to acquire. By the by, the atom was first split about half a mile from here.'

'I thought that was in Los Alamos? Really?' Sir Lancelot skilfully avoided a head-on collision, raising his boater to the passing punter. 'Tell me, what's the difference between Cambridge and Oxford?'

Sir Lancelot adopted a pained, distant expression, like Mr Quelch in similar pleasant circumstances reminded of the Remove and Billy Bunter at Greyfriars. 'Oxford provides the prime ministers – Eden, Macmillan, Home, Heath, Wilson. Cambridge the technocrats – Darwin, Rutherford, Kelvin, Crick of the double helix, Keynes.'

'And Churchill?'

'Sir Winston enjoyed the supreme advantage among this country's top persons of being almost entirely untainted by its education. Oxford has a High Street so jammed with traffic that the only safe – indeed, feasible – way of crossing it is by breeches-buoy. It has the stone heads of Roman emperors which broke into sweat over Zuleika Dobson. It has All Souls College, which does not even bother to take students, but is a tank that has been thinking since the fifteenth century. By the by, penicillin was first used there at the Radcliffe Infirmary. And this,' he said fondly, as they swept gently towards a pretty garden with willows washing their hair in the stream, 'is Audley.'

It struck Sir Lancelot that the backs of his old college was exactly the place for the consummation of his painstaking scheme. He glanced down at Amelia, her eyes closed, as delicately reposeful as a muslined Edwardian

maiden. An upsetting thought struck him. Was it something that one asked a lady before lunch?

'Amelia—' He slowed the punt.

'Yes, Lancelot?' she murmured.

'Do you think of me as ... old?'

'Don't be stupid.'

'Perhaps the sands are running out,' he admitted. 'And
I rather like playing on the sands.' They were directly
opposite Audley gardens. He stopped, holding the pole
vertical.

'Amelia—'

She murmured again, 'Yes, Lancelot?'

He hesitated. He felt like Caliban pressing his advances
on Prospero's daughter Miranda. And he remembered the
amount of trouble that caused.

'Amelia, I have something to ask you.'

'Yes, Lancelot?'

'I am about to take the plunge—'

He found himself grasping a punt-pole, surrounded by
the river Cam.

'Oh!' She was on her knees, hand to her mouth, drifting
slowly away. 'What shall I do?'

'Grab my blasted boater from the water,' he shouted
irately. 'They're damn difficult to buy.'

'Do you want any help?'

'Not in the slightest. I intend to remain in this position
all afternoon, as a means of avoiding the overcrowded
streets.'

'You needn't be so rude.'

'I believe there is no social necessity to say "please"
when requesting a life-buoy?'

'I'll paddle with my hands.'

'Not with your bloody hands, you stupid woman.
There's a perfectly good paddle provided in the stern.'

'Now you're being damn well offensive,' she
snapped.

'All right. You come and hang on to this blasted pole, and I'll sit in the punt and blow you kisses.'

'Mum!' came a shout from the bank. 'Here quick, watch this bloke fall in the water.'

The banks at Audley College had a moment before been deserted. They now appeared to Sir Lancelot lined as thickly as the rails at Tattenham Corner on Derby Day.

'Try doing the pole vault, mate,' someone suggested helpfully.

'Look at the poor old thing. Reminds me of those toys we had as children, monkey up a stick.'

'Shall we send for the Fire Brigade?'

'It's a commercial, dear, we'll see it on the telly.'

'Caught any fish yet?'

'This position is not only dangerous and uncomfortable, but ostentatious,' commented Sir Lancelot, as the punt swung in a lazy circle. 'Can't you put some beef into it?'

Amelia told him irritably, 'I haven't used a paddle since I was at children's summer camp in Maine.'

'While simultaneously sinking into the mud and losing my equilibrium, I am not in the frame of mind to enjoy reminiscences of your childhood.'

'You're not helping, are you?' she said furiously.

'That is the most asinine remark since Stanley greeted Livingstone.'

'What the hell do you expect me to do instead?' The punt jammed against the bank. 'Send someone to that college, and have Newton repeal the Law of Gravity?'

'Push yourself off with the bloody boathook. *Not like that*!' She hit another punt. 'You're about as much use on water as a pregnant camel.'

Amelia stood up, hands on hips. 'Well, I'm more use than you – stuck there like a lighthouse-keeper trying to walk to work.'

'Don't *stand*, you fool,' he shouted urgently. 'You'll fall in.'

With a splash like a bag of cement, Sir Lancelot disappeared from view.

'Lancelot!' Amelia was alarmed. 'Can you swim?'

'Don't ask so many questions,' he replied, spouting water.

'Excuse me, sir,' a brisk voice called. 'No bathing, sir. Strictly forbidden. College rules.'

'Shut up, you blithering fool Crumphole.'

'Well, well, well! If it isn't young Mr Spratt,' said the wizened, bowler-hatted, dark-suited college porter. 'And how are you getting along, sir? Went to be a doctor, as far as I recall.'

'Here—' Amelia leant from the punt with the boathook. 'Grab this.'

Sir Lancelot did, and pulled her in.

'Come along, now,' Crumphole directed the jumping spectators sternly. 'Visitors must conduct themselves with proper decorum. College rules.'

'Crumphole! Would you kindly afford priority to extracting us from this surprisingly insanitary river?'

'Yes, sir. Certainly, sir. At once, sir.' He looked up and down. 'How do you suggest I do it, sir?'

'I can only recommend that you invite the young lady and gentleman in jeans to secure your ankles, and extend us a helping hand.'

'Soon have you ashore, sir. Hardly look a day older, sir, if I may say so. In the pink, I'm sure. Got a beard there under the water, I see, sir.'

To the excited applause of the audience, Sir Lancelot and Amelia were hauled up the grass bank. She was still grasping his boater. She handed it to him silently. He tipped out the water and donned it.

'Your wife, sir?'

'A passing acquaintance.'

'You *are* wet, sir,' said Crumphole in surprise. 'You'll catch your death. Come along to my lodge, and I'll see if one of the bedders can find you a change of clothes and cup of tea.'

'And what about me?' demanded Amelia, dripping and shivering.

'Oh, yes, madam, we have lady undergraduates now. Though I hardly think the sort of thing they wear will be entirely suitable for a lady of riper years.' He chuckled, turning twinkling eyes back to Sir Lancelot. 'Remember that milkman's horse? The one you put in the chaplain's bedroom? Ate his straw hat. The chaplain doesn't know to this day who did it.'

Sir Lancelot walked with dignity towards the college buildings. 'I beg your pardon?' he remarked to Amelia.

'I said nothing. It was my teeth chattering.'

'And that young lady from the Petty Cury flower shop, sir. When I was your gyp, and you tried to hide her in the morning under the laundry. The things that goes on in Audley now, sir, you'd be surprised.' Crumphole shook his head sadly. 'No fun in life any more, sir, I always say. When everything's permitted, nobody can enjoy feeling naughty.'

'What were you about to ask me?' enquired Amelia sourly.

'Nothing of importance,' Sir Lancelot responded.

II

'You've got a brand-new Rolls,' exclaimed Sir Lancelot to the dean. He stood glaring at it in the roadway at Lazar Row.

'Yes and no.' The dean's eyebrows cavorted delightedly. 'It certainly *is* the brand-new model. Airconditioning, stereo sound, and all that. And I certainly have the *use* of it.'

'I don't follow?' said Sir Lancelot aggressively.

'I have it on permanent loan. Like some of the masterpieces which hang in the National Gallery,' he said airily. 'From the Tosker Organization.'

It was just after nine o'clock the following Saturday morning. The fine weather had vanished overnight, and a layer of cloud stretched unbrokenly across the sky, bulging with rain like water-filled paper bags.

'Care to sit inside?' the dean insisted. 'It's unbelievably comfortable.'

From curiosity, Sir Lancelot climbed beside the dean. 'You seem to have feathered your nest with a peacock's tail.'

'You just don't understand the business world, Lancelot,' the dean told him condescendingly. 'Appearances are everything. You can't expect me to meet some bunch of wogs – I mean, our Arabian customers – in the sort of car which these days is run by a Birmingham machine-minder.' Heavy drops of rain began to smack the pavements. 'Strange, isn't it? How I, an ordinary St Swithin's student, from an ordinary lowly home, rose to be the trusted confidant of rich and powerful men? Admittedly, it has its advantages. I am obliged to take my wife on a business trip to Rio de Janeiro this August, instead of our usual Swanage. And the expense-account is useful for stocking the cellar – just in case I have someone to entertain. But my greatest reward is doing something for the country's export drive,' he ended smugly.

'And are these brand-new hospitals already arising from the desert sand, like shimmering white mirages?'

'Such things take time, of course.'

'Not half so long as putting a new ceiling on my operating theatre at St Sepulchre's.'

'At least you've got the walls,' the dean pointed out. 'Our khaki friends have no hospitals at all. They have to fly to the private beds at St Swithin's and suchlike, if they get anything nasty. Or shoot each other, which they seem to do with curious frequency.'

'It nevertheless strikes me as unfortunate that we cannot have a hospital equipped with the latest body-scanners, ultrasonics, hypobaric radiotherapy, computers and all that bag of clinical tricks, a little nearer the Thames than the Tigris.'

'It's only because of the oil money, which the sheiks are screwing out of you and me.' The dean switched on and off the windscreen-wipers. 'One day it's going to dawn on the population of the world that you don't get medical treatment unless you pay for it. Out of your own pocket, or the Government's. And as it is difficult to identify clever research workers early enough to strangle them at birth, the cost of health care is as unlimited as the cost of a really decent war.'

'I've seen that for years, dean,' Sir Lancelot agreed gloomily. 'It's all very well, surgeons and patients complaining that by the time they can get together for a hip-repair operation, one of them will be dead. But that's going to be normal, unless everyone hands us their wage-packet every week, which I doubt would be popular. We'll have treatment of acute diseases only. I suppose it's better to have prompt efficiency when your life's at stake, rather than neither for anything.'

The dean switched on and off the headlights. 'Which is why the Government has to economize by blocking financial drains like St Sepulchre's.'

'Like most things with most governments, their intentions are admirable and their execution disastrous. Clinical palaces like St Swithin's were all built the wrong size in the wrong places. The music-hall and the film industry made exactly the same mistake. People prefer to be ill within sight of their own chimney-pots.'

'Nevertheless, St Sepulchre's will close.'

Sir Lancelot glared. 'St Sepulchre's will *not* close. You were at the Area Health Authority meeting yourself.'

The dean said calmly, 'You know perfectly well, the Minister can overturn that decision between two sips of his morning coffee.'

'Then he will be one surgeon the less, because I shall countenance it over my dead body. I am driving to Spratt's Bottom this very afternoon, to lead a mass demonstration of militant workers from ACHE up the High Street.' The dean looked shocked. 'Misery acquaints a man with strange bedfellows, and I am extremely miserable indeed. It is lunacy running a health service from general headquarters like the army. A hospital should be a local possession, instead of a clinical outpost garrisoned by an odd-looking bunch of troops.'

The dean tooted the horn a couple of times. 'While you're in the High Street, you might confirm the arrangements for Hamilton Tosker's lunch on Tuesday at the Spratt's Arms. He's a very simple man, you know. His father was a scrap dealer, going round with a cart and handbell. As Hamilton says, "Lady Luck's given me a fair squirt with her beer-gun. I'm an Aussie okker," he says, "reared among the middies and moggies of the Western suburbs." By which he describes himself as uncontaminated with pretentious sophistication. His dinkum tucker, by the way, is lambs' fry and a foaming Fosters.'

Sir Lancelot grunted 'I regret that I shall be unable to share your feast of sheeps' entrails, as I am never in Spratt's Bottom on Tuesdays.'

The dean adjusted the dashboard clock. 'I must get along to St James's Square. Meeting of the College of Therapeutics. We're deciding who wins this year's James Lind Medal.'

Sir Lancelot screwed up his eyes. 'Lind? Edinburgh man, wasn't he? Naval surgeon. Published his *Treatise of the Scurvy* in – let me see – 1753?'

The dean nodded, starting the engine. 'He knew nothing of vitamins, of course. They hadn't been invented, as it were. He abolished scurvy at sea by the simple expedient of feeding the sailors lemon-juice, and seeing that it worked.'

'Like all the most useful discoveries in medicine,' Sir Lancelot concurred.

'The medal goes for the best contribution to world nutrition during the year. It always seems to be won by Norwegians. Perhaps because they're interested in nutrition rather than food, as you soon discover when dining out at Oslo.'

'You can give me a lift to Jermyn Street. I have to buy two dozen new shirts.'

The dean looked at him sideways. 'What happened to your American lady-friend?'

'I fear I damped her ardour.'

It rained all morning with the persistence of a leaky tap. It was still raining at two o'clock, when Sir Lancelot picked his way through the pot-hole of corridors beneath St Sepulchre's, reaching the basement. This was long, grimy and brick-walled, ill-lit by strip lights from a roof of tangled pipes, its stone floor littered with forgotten crates and cartons, abandoned trolleys and stretchers, disused refrigerators and tea-urns, and a pile of anonymous green metal containers stencilled, ARP – TO BE KEPT IN WARDEN'S POST.

'Afternoon, Sapworth,' said Sir Lancelot from the door. 'Hope I'm not late?' He picked his way across the room. 'Not much of a day for our demo, is it?'

'It ain't exactly a scorcher.' The shop-steward was sitting in a broken wheelchair, with two of his workmates on boxes. 'Still, my raspberries need it. Right, brothers, this mass meeting of ACHE is hereby convened. If you can't spell "convened", Abdul,' he directed to the one with the minute book, 'put "kicked off".'

'Where are the others?' Sir Lancelot demanded, looking round.

'Yeah, well, um,' said Harold awkwardly 'Seen any of the lads hanging about, Francisco?' he asked the other member. 'I suppose we four is enough to express the anger of the workers, eh, Ron?'

Sir Lancelot noticed Ron Cherrymore in his jeans, flowered shirt and beads, leaning against a dusty stack of patients' case-notes. 'I didn't know you were a member of ACHE?'

'Fully paid-up. To be a Labour MP, you have to be a member of a trade union, of course. I'm a real worker now,' Ron said proudly. 'A porter in the hospital dispensary.'

'OK Abdul, first item on the agenda,' Harold directed. 'All right, put "list". We are assembled at this moment of time to discuss industrial action over Brother O'Riley. He was taken queer at his work in the mortuary, and cracked his head on a coffin. Sent to casualty. Bleeding, all down his cardie. No one goes near him, except a nurse asking name, address, religion, none of which Brother O'Riley can remember. No doctor, not for half an hour.'

'Good God, Sapworth,' interrupted Sir Lancelot, 'at St

Sepulchre's, members of the general public wait all day in casualty, when the doctor's busy.'

Abdul looked up. 'We don't care a monkey's what happens to the bleeding public. Only to members of ACHE. OK?'

'Anyway, Brother O'Riley was pissed,' said Francisco.

'Got to make allowances on that sort of job, pushing stiffs in and out all day,' said Harold. 'Can get on a bloke's nerves.'

'So what?' asked Abdul truculently. 'We want a good excuse for a strike—'

'Industrial action,' Harold corrected him.

'To put the bastards running this hospital in their place—'

'Establish good industrial relations,' interrupted Harold. 'Let's move to the patients' breakfasts. Them in the office is trying to start what they calls a "Continental breakfast". Just a bit of bread and cuppa coffee. Which the lads in the kitchens will not stand. Because they knows the patients wants a proper bacon and egg to start the day, whatever the doctors say.'

'I am distressed and disgusted,' declaimed Ron Cherrymore, striding to the centre of the basement. 'To find my fellow-workers obliged to discuss such trivia as injuries from coffins and the patients' corn-flakes. This should be a forum for topics near all our hearts – the provision of proper treatment for all free of charge, and particularly for those we socialists care for most in the community, the poor, the aged, the single-parent family, the exploited and the handicapped.'

'Ron, I saw your Aunt Lucinda last week,' Sir Lancelot remarked mildly. 'Who is flat broke, aged eighty and crippled with arthritis. She wishes you would come and see her some time. Or possibly send her a small cheque for Christmas. You did not give up the family fortune, as I recall, along with the title. As Aunt Lucinda is a patient of mine – on the National Health, naturally – I cannot speak more about her.'

Ron turned pink. 'Aunt Lucinda is a....' he stammered.

'As irrelevant as all poor relations, doubtless. By the way, you might visit your sister. She's getting depressed that you're ashamed of your mongol niece.'

Ron slunk back to his pile of case-notes.

'Let's get to the big one,' said Harold.

'Closure of St Sepulchre's. Well, just look at it, lads. The past ten years has seen a nice, healthy increase of thirty per cent in hospital staff. Hospitals, you might say, was one of our growth industries. Now the government wants to shut St Sepulchre's and lose us our jobs. With a million and a half unemployed, they need their heads examining. Mind, we're prepared to talk to anyone about redundancies, once they've got sensible suggestions to lay on the table. Otherwise, we put the old boot in, if we don't get all our own way. Anything to say, Sir Lancelot?'

'I am reserving my remarks for the Market Place. I have taken much trouble preparing a speech to suit this suburb, with its estimably high level of education. But I hope I shall have a few more followers?' he added anxiously.

Harold Sapworth scratched his chin. 'Could be dodgy, squire. See, this afternoon's the European Cup Final, direct from Munich.'

'But surely, your members would put securing their livelihood before watching a football match?'

'Oh, yes, sure, but ... well, they reckon somebody else can do the securing, while they do the watching. Might as well go and see if the rain's stopped, I suppose?'

Clasping his umbrella like a Guard's officer his sword, Sir Lancelot headed through the rain from the St Sepulchre's forecourt up the High Street. Behind came Ron, in yellow plastic raincoat and sou'wester, bearing a placard which started by saying SAVE ST SEPUL-CHRE'S but soon ran into soggy incomprehensibility. Next marched Harold and his two companions, hands in pockets and shoulders hunched. Their rearguard was four policemen.

The thin, scurrying, damp crowd of shoppers on the pavements took no notice. The demonstrators were splashed by buses, barked at by dogs, cursed by motorists. Sir Lancelot strode unfalteringly. At the top, by the town hall, the High Street disintegrated at a large traffic roundabout. Sir Lancelot led his party on to the central grass island. Harold produced from his streaming rain-coat an electric loud-hailer.

'I borrowed it off of the hospital fire-fighting equip-ment,' he explained. 'It's not likely to go up in flames before we get back. And if it does, in this weather it doesn't matter, does it?'

Ron holding the umbrella over his head, Sir Lancelot took several pages of foolscap from his inside pocket.

'Sorry, sir,' said the sergeant in charge of the policemen. He was a sharp-faced man with bulging green eyes, a short black moustache and a crooked mouth. 'You can't loiter here. Against the Road Traffic Act.'

'Then where *can* I go?' he demanded shortly, rain running down his neck.

'Over there in the square by the War Memorial, sir. Usual spot for demos. Not that we get many in a respect-able place like Spratt's Bottom.'

'But on Saturday afternoons it's a car-park,' Sir Lancelot objected.

'Can't help that, sir.'

He remustered his soggy band a hundred yards away. Cars ground and squelched all round them. He had the feeling that his protest march was not being entirely a success. He mounted the steps of the war memorial.

'Excuse me, sir,' said the police sergeant.

'Yes?' snapped Sir Lancelot.

'Can't stand there, sir. Religious monument. Likely to provoke a breach of the peace.'

Sir Lancelot stepped down.

He switched on the loud-hailer. 'Fellow citizens,' he began. He peered at his notes through half-moon glasses. The rain had got at them, the first paragraph was unreadable. 'Unlimited power is apt to corrupt the minds of those who possess it,' he said.

'Excuse me, sir—'

'What the devil is it now?'

'I think it might be salutary if I reminded you about the law of seditious libel. Vilifying the Constitution and promoting insurrection.'

'I didn't say that. William Pitt said it. You could take it up with him, but he doesn't happen to be here.'

'Oh, I know that, sir.' The sergeant gave a crooked smile. 'William Pitt the elder, Earl of Chatham. But we have to be careful. Might be misinterpreted. Don't want to stir up unnecessary trouble, do we? Everyone thought the Blasphemy Act was as dead as Bishop Sacheverell, when hey presto! It was back in court.'

'I'll start again.'

'I think that's best, sir.'

'Fellow citizens—'

'Comrade Spratt,' said Ron, close behind him.

'Who? Yes? What is it?'

'Why don't you hold the umbrella and I'll make the speech? I've had a lot of experience in outdoor oratory. Some parts of Spratt's Bottom know me as a regular rabble-rouser.'

'I do not wish to rouse the rabble. And please hold that umbrella straight. I can tolerate the rain penetrating my collar to my vertebral column or my sternum, but I do not see why I should suffer both.'

It had started raining more heavily. 'Fellow citizens,'

Sir Lancelot began again. He began to feel that his adult life had been spent immersed in water. 'Freedom which in no other land will thrive, Freedom an English subject's sole prerogative—'

'Excuse me, sir,' said the police-sergeant.

Sir Lancelot barked 'John Milton said that, and he's not here either.'

'Just want to let these cars out, sir. Give you more room.'

The sergeant stood waving his arms. One of the drivers leant from his window, shouting at Sir Lancelot, 'Try doing a day's work for a change, you lazy hairy Marxist parasite.' A woman with rain dripping from her plastic hat asked him the way to the loo.

'Right ho, sir, carry on,' said the sergeant brightly. 'Though mind you don't get run over.'

Sir Lancelot asked him with curiosity, 'How do you keep so cheerful?'

'Oh, I'm paid to stand here. I'd be off my head doing so otherwise, wouldn't I? And if you'll forgive me, sir. It wasn't Milton who said that about freedom. It was Dryden. It comes in *Threnodia Augustalis*.'

Sir Lancelot's damp beard elevated. 'You seem singularly well-informed, Sergeant.'

'One of my subjects, sir. Open University. Please continue, sir.'

'I'm pissing off,' said Abdul. 'I do not really give a fart if St Sepulchre's stays open or not. Anyway, I've got a job all lined up on the buses.'

'I'm going too,' said the shivering Francisco. 'If there's going to be a revolution, I want it on a nice day.'

'Sapworth,' barked Sir Lancelot. 'Is this the sort of loyalty you exact from your members? If I *am* acquainted with strange bedfellows, I do not expect them to leap out and leave me in the cold. Where's your working-class solidarity?'

'Oh, with them two the solidarity starts above the neck.' Harold squinted at the teeming sky. 'Bit of a wash-out, ain't it? Let's go home. Might catch the end of the Cup Final.'

Sir Lancelot became furious. 'I will *not* go home. I set myself to break the self-discipline of a lifetime, and riot in the streets. I will not retreat at the first whiff of grapeshot.'

'Nobody finds us worth aiming at,' said Ron. 'I'm going, too.'

'No, you're bloody not! Who's going to hold my umbrella?'

'Look, Comrade Spratt, the whole protest is a flop, just like Kornilov's against Kerensky in 1917—'

'If you want quick results, squire, get yourself arrested,' suggested Harold.

'What an utterly outrageous suggestion, Sapworth.'

'No, it ain't. I've been on these demos since I was a kid. Good way to meet your mates and get a bit of open-air exercise. Mind, I'm cheesed off with them now, you don't meet the same sort of blokes. They take themselves too bloody seriously, I suppose because the middle-class gets involved.' He glared at Ron, invisible between oilskin collar and hat-brim.

'But look what them M Ps, and that, does. Sit on their arses drinking Scotch and watching the telly, while poor sods like us are soaking on the picket-lines. Then to show they've got the interests of the workers almost as much to heart as their own, they takes their car, jabs a policeman on the third button down, and becomes a martyr.'

'I am not going to embark upon a criminal career at my age, particularly on such an unpleasant afternoon.'

'Nothing to it, if you ask me. By the time they let you out on bail, the rain might have stopped,' he added helpfully.

'Come on, Comrade Sapworth,' said Ron. 'If we shift, we'll catch the bus.'

Harold started after him, turned and thrust a damp scrap of paper into Sir Lancelot's wet palm. 'Something red hot from my brother for Kempton Park.'

Sir Lancelot was alone with four policemen.

He looked at his notes. The first soaked page was unreadable. He still had the loud-hailer, but decided to trust the power of the human voice.

'Fellow citizens,' he tried again on page two, umbrella in hand. 'The late Bertrand Russell describes pragmatism in essence as a practical as opposed to the theoretical school, to which our great systems of philosophy belong. Aristotle, Hume, Berkeley, Kant and so on. The pragmatists, originating with the ideas of the American John Dewey, consider pure knowledge a mere instrument in the hands of man – Yes? What is it?' he rasped at the police-sergeant, standing in front of him, helmet streaming.

'In the first place, sir, if I may take the liberty, Dr John Dewey was not the originator of the pragmatic school of philosophy. He was, if I may say so, merely its propagandist. Its father might be described as William James – 1842 to 1910 – of Harvard University. A psychologist, sir—'

'I know that,' snapped Sir Lancelot.

'I'm sure you do, sir. This is one of my subjects at the Open University. As you will know, William James attributed the basic principles of pragmatism to C. S. Peirce—'

'Do you mind greatly if I get on with my speech? Thank you,' said Sir Lancelot cuttingly, peering through rain-smeared glasses. 'In the immortal words of the philosopher, Jeremy Bentham, "That action is best, which procures the greatest happiness for the greatest numbers—" What the bloody hell do you want now?'

'It's funny, sir, but a misplaced quotation sends shivers up and down my spine. An understandable mistake, sir,' he admitted generously, 'because the doctrine of utility is the principle which pervades all Bentham's writings. But if you'll recall, sir, it's your second in ten minutes.'

'I too went to a university,' Sir Lancelot said icily. 'As a Master of Surgery at Cambridge, I do not care to stand in pouring rain suffering repeated correction by a prospective BA (Ope.).'

The sergeant eyed him less amiably. 'Very well. You look down on us people who have to dig knowledge from the academic gravelpits with our fingers?'

'I despise only people who pedantically correct others on grammar, dates or quotations, because their minds are generally as small as the original slips. May I have the floor? As Jeremy Bentham repeatedly said—'

'It was, sir, Francis Hutcheson, 1694 to 1747.'

'Can't you flaming well shut up?' roared Sir Lancelot, crumpling the pages of his speech and hurling them in the sergeant's face.

'That's assaulting a police-officer,' said the sergeant. 'Right. Come along with me.'

12

'WHAT's for dinner, darling?' Freddie Bisham came into the lounge at Apricot Avenue, throwing his white coat over the straw donkey. It was the following Monday, and he had just finished his evening surgery.

'I'm giving you my *goulash à l'hongroise*, lovey,' said Eva.

'Oh, great. Your stews were always delicious.' Freddie kissed his finger-tips. 'The ultimate in savoury glutinosity.'

'How kind you always are,' Eva smiled.

'How long do you suppose it's going to take us, getting rid of one hundred thousand "Save St Sepulchre's" car stickers?' he asked doubtfully, kicking the brown paper packets piled in front of the indoor plants.

'And a quarter of a million leaflets in the garage,' she recalled.

'Hello, darling,' Freddie said, as Dawn pushed through the beads in the Moorish arch.

'Hello, dear. How was surgery?'

'Bloody. The whole of Spratt's Bottom suffers from only three diseases. Indigestion, headaches and sexual fantasies. Oh, and enlarged prostates. There was a programme about it on TV last night. This morning, everyone had it. It was particularly rife among the women.'

'Remember that documentary on VD last Friday?' Pip followed Freddie through the surgery door, throwing his white coat on the plastic-topped coffee-table. 'You'd have been surprised on Saturday morning at the number of ladies, of high respectability and even of advanced age, who sat down in the surgery, leaned across the desk and started in guilty whispers.' He broke off to Eva, 'What's for dinner, dear?'

'Goulash, dear. What's the matter?' she asked, seeing him wrinkle his nose.

'Too much like Dawn's moussaka.' Pip threw himself on the black plastic recliner.

'What's wrong with my moussaka, darling?' Dawn asked, sounding hurt.

'I never really liked it.'

'And you never told me!'

'I suppose I was afraid you might produce something worse.' Pip reached for that morning's *Times*.

'This time round, darling, I'll make quite certain you'll never even *smell* moussaka. I think I'll try turning myself into a good cook. You'll give me some lessons, Eva dear, won't you?'

'Of course I will, Dawn dear.'

'Suburban general practice!' Freddie had been busy at the repro-Jacobean cabinet. 'It has as little connexion with medicine as a parish jumble-sale to religion.'

'Perhaps it's our fault?' Pip suggested thoughtfully. 'We keen young doctors. We do rather view our patients as a do-it-yourself assembly kit of human organs. I suppose that only about . . . what? One patient in six, goes to their GP because they're ill.'

'The others go for the reassurance that they're not,' agreed Freddie, adding to four gin-and-tonics ice from a plastic pineapple. 'I always say, "There's a lot of it about this time of the year". Which is very comforting whether you've got tenesmus or tetanus.'

'If everyone in Spratt's Bottom was as ill as they thought they were,' observed Pip turning the pages of the paper, 'it would make the Black Death look like a flu epidemic.'

'But think of all those lonely old ladies,' said Dawn charitably, sitting next to Eva on a pink pouffe and taking a glass from Freddie's tray with the hunting scenes. 'They've absolutely no one in the world with the patience to listen to them, except the milkman and the doctor.'

'Those frustrated mums,' murmured Eva, sipping her drink.

Freddie nodded. 'Blaming every disappointment in their life on some boisterous little toddler, who's wrecking the surgery in a perfectly normal manner.'

'And the cries for help,' added Pip. 'Neuralgia means a nagging wife, stomach ache a straying husband.'

'You can always tell the really sick ones.' Freddie stared pensively at a Venus statuette in a circular curtain of constantly dripping water. 'They take the chair behind the waiting-room door, and they apologize profusely for wasting the doctor's valuable time.'

Pip agreed. 'When you examine a patient and say he's got absolutely nothing wrong with him, and he seizes both your hands to thank you with tears in his eyes, then rip off his clothes again and take another look. That's what I've learnt from just one week in general practice.'

'I think we've all learned rather a lot from just one week in general practice,' observed Eva quietly.

'I suppose some time we should sort ourselves out?' Freddie sat on the cut moquette. 'It's all so socially untidy. Perhaps get a couple of divorces? Though it seems a shame, as we're all such good friends.'

'What are we to do in three weeks' time, when this locum is up?' asked Eva. 'Though I never thought of Spratt's Bottom as the ideal place for a package honeymoon.'

'We must find another rich suburb, darling,' Freddie told her. 'To support us both until Sir Lancelot lands me that St Swithin's consultant job.'

'You know I utterly hate the beastly suburbs, Freddie.'

'Do you?' he asked in surprise. 'I rather like them. The

countryside's far too noisy, with all those mooing cows and farmers' Aston Martins.'

'Unless Sir Lancelot lands me a substantial grant for nutritional research,' Pip intervened, 'at the end of the month I'm back in Kenya. Do you suppose you could be happy there, Dawn?'

'Oh, I could be happy anywhere, dear,' she said dreamily. 'It's all in the mind, isn't it? Some people are happy in jail. Have you noticed how miserable everyone looks, lying on the beach?'

'So it all comes down to Sir Lancelot,' said Freddie solemnly, idly picking from the repro-piecrust occasional table a highly-glazed ceramic shoe with old woman and children.

'One good thing—' Pip pointed to the newspaper. 'He's got so much on his plate, being run in for clobbering the constabulary, he's not likely to trouble us again.'

Cindy appeared at the door leading into the hall. 'Doctors, I just got that formiminoglutamate test back from the biochemistry lab,' she announced breathlessly. 'Also the 17-oxogenic steroids and the vanillylmandelic acid. All normal, Doctors, I'm pleased to say, so far as I can tell. Always a lot of clearing up after Monday surgeries,' she continued cheerfully. 'And there's another male patient outside.'

'Tell him to clear off and come back tomorrow, unless he's actually *in extremis*,' Pip directed.

'I did, Doctor, and he won't.'

'Bisham, call off your watchkitten.' Sir Lancelot pushed into the room. All four jumped up, exchanging alarmed glances. 'I'm here for the night. I'm due to face the magistrates at 10 tomorrow morning, and don't want to arrive in a flaming temper from a frustrating drive and find myself facing further charges for contempt of court. Good evening ladies. What's for dinner? Bisham, any of that single malt whisky left?'

'There's a second bottle, sir.' Freddie was already feeling in the cabinet with one hand. With the other, he was shooing Eva and Dawn urgently towards the kitchen.

'What's this?' enquired Sir Lancelot as the two females vanished. Glass in one hand, he picked up a book between Mozart and Schubert on the television set. *'Divorce by Post.* Not all falling out of the nest, are you?'

'So many of our patients have marital difficulties,' Freddie explained. 'I bought it to help them with sociological advice.'

Sir Lancelot grunted. 'Divorce seems much less of a bother than getting married these days.'

'Much, sir,' Pip assured him. 'None of that dreadful fuss about the bridesmaids' dresses.'

'Grounds for unreasonable behaviour.' Sir Lancelot read out. 'Cruelty, husband's sodomy or bestiality, wife's unnatural practice with other women, unsoundness of mind, refusal to have sexual intercourse. H'm. All rather mediaeval. Desertion seems rather more decent.' He snapped the book shut. 'Though a divorce is now regarded as a bigger revel than a wedding, and I may be as old-fashioned as a pair of bloomers, I believe that a man should make the reasonable attempt, or at least pretence, of cleaving to his wife.'

He stood sipping whisky with his back to the peacock-ironwork fire-guard in front of the electric logs.

'Marriage is an easy ride for you two,' he declared generously, 'with your delightful and well-suited spouses. But marriage is not simply a matter of mutual trust between man and wife. It is an institution which affects the entire community. That is why the suburban practice of wife-swapping earns my intense disapproval. Not only is it insanitary, but once men start exchanging their wives it weakens the structure of society. As well as being very confusing at cocktail-parties.'

'There's a lot of it about this time of the year,' said Freddie uneasily.

'Though why anyone bothers to swap wives in a place like Spratt's Bottom is beyond me,' Sir Lancelot continued. 'All the women are so alike in outlook and conversation, they are probably as indistinguishable on the bed as on the telephone.'

'Another drink, sir?' asked Pip pressingly.

'Thank you.'

Pip went to refill the glasses of all three. Freddie started talking to Sir Lancelot about cricket. His mind was busy reconnoitring the pitfalls of the evening. No trouble at all, he decided. The four of them were now paired as firmly as Sir Lancelot thought. The last two years were being rewritten in their minds like Orwellian history. He was already convinced that his life with Eva was one continuous performance. She had not changed in the time, not even to her coat of nail-varnish, he reflected contentedly as she appeared from the Moorish arch, carrying a tray loaded with glasses and cutlery.

'It's such a lovely evening, Sir Lancelot, I thought we'd dine by gas candlelight on the patio. I'm offering my goulash. I hope you can take paprika?'

'The Emperor Elagabalus himself never gloated over so delightful a cuisine as provided by this lady,' announced Sir Lancelot mellowly. 'It amazes me, my dear,' he added, as Pip proffered his glass, 'how your husband and yourself manage to preserve such enviably trim figures.'

Smiling, Pip told him, 'Talking of Eva's figure, I must confess to one little worry. Her appendix is not – shall we say, Sir Lancelot, one of your greatest masterpieces? I mean, even Leonardo da Vinci had his off days. We can't expect a Mona Lisa every afternoon.'

Sir Lancelot frowned. 'What *are* you talking about?'

'About Eva's appendix scar.' Pip gave a waggish look, wondering how far he dare bait the bear. 'May I say, sir, you ploughed a lonely furrow, rather than sewed a fine seam?'

'My dear Chipps, you do go through the world in a chronic confusional state, don't you? I most certainly never removed that lady's appendix.'

'Doesn't the possibility ever occur to you, sir,' asked Pip more firmly, 'that you conceivably might be wrong?'

'No. Because I so seldom am.'

'Indeed, sir?' Pip eyed him severely. 'One of the very first things Eva ever said to me was that you removed her appendix. In the Clinic. As a private patient. You say you never forget a face or an abdomen?' Sir Lancelot nodded. 'Then let me refresh your memory. Look.'

Planting his glass on Eva's tray, Pip whisked up her skirt with one hand, slipped down her pants with the other, and said, 'See what I mean? Rather a long incision for an appendicectomy, oh my God.'

He dropped Eva's skirt. He stood with drooping shoulders in the middle of the orange tufted acrilan. He assumed a twisted smile, slowly rubbing his hands and turning bright pink.

'Have you seen this Spanish wine-flask, sir?' enquired Freddie, picking it from the plastic marble of the coffee-table. 'Did you know, the Spaniards can pour the wine directly into their mouths, without a drop touching their lips?'

'Really, Chipps——!' Sir Lancelot stood holding his glass and glaring. 'I know the St Swithin's students go about like a pack of stoats on heat. But I should not have expected such blatant familiarity with Bisham's wife under his very nose.'

'That's all right, sir.' Freddie gave a desperate smile. 'Perfectly all right. You see, Pip's her doctor.'

'Doctor?' exclaimed Sir Lancelot. 'But the man met her for the first time only last Monday morning.'

'Exactly, sir,' Freddie agreed. 'Last Monday morning.

Very wise of us, not to waste time, don't you think? I mean, we'd just moved into Spratt's Bottom, and obviously had to get Eva registered as a temporary resident with a National Health practitioner. Didn't we, darling? You know the hazards of the home well enough, sir? The most dangerous place in the world, according to the Society for the Prevention of Accidents. Housewives run bigger risks than astronauts. All sorts of things could have befallen her – tripping over the patio bird-bath, frostbite from the deep freeze, sunstroke from the bathroom solarium, drowning in the lily pond, electrocution from the cooker, suffocation in the linen cupboard. I wish all our patients were as punctilious in observing NHS regulations. Don't you, Pip? Obviously, Sir Lancelot, I couldn't look after my own wife professionally. Bad principle. Unethical, too, I should imagine.'

Pip stood looking at Freddie with the panic combined with relief of a struggling swimmer thrown a badly frayed rope. Sir Lancelot stood looking at both with the expression of Sherlock Holmes sensing that Moriarty had a twin brother. 'Be that as it may. But you don't seem to have wasted much time, Chipps, in submitting Mrs Bisham to a thorough physical examination.'

'But that's what you always told us, sir, at St Swithin's,' Pip said eagerly. 'Every new patient must be examined all over. Completely, from scalp to soles. Even if they come in with nothing more obvious than a boil on the nose.'

'I doubt if you would have shown such commendable enthusiasm had she been a portly middle-aged gent like myself. If I may be frank, I assume, Bisham, that you have considered the wisdom of allowing an old acquaintance to be your wife's medical attendant? The doctor should be a friend of the family, always. But an intimate, never. Otherwise, his clinical judgement may be seduced from the necessary severity of its detachment. Not to mention himself personally.'

'I'd trust Pip anywhere with anyone,' Freddie said heartily.

'*Would you?*' Sir Lancelot was mystified. 'I wouldn't leave him alone in the same room as a bearded lady suffering from a nasty cold.'

'The trust is mutual, sir,' Pip said stoutly. 'Freddie, I want you to doctor my wife.'

'Anything you say, Pip.'

'Take all her clothes off, examine her from top to bottom, do what you like.'

'Very much obliged, Pip.'

'I think I want another drink,' decided Sir Lancelot.

'Just a minute—' Pip stood scratching his chin. 'One small thing. Exactly who *did* take out your appendix, Eva?'

She stood immobile with her tray, staring blankly across the lounge at the birds cavorting in their bath on the patio. 'Er—I can't remember.'

Pip stepped closer. He looked keenly at her across the cutlery. 'But you *told* me it was Sir Lancelot.'

'What, when you stripped her to the chassis almost as soon as setting eyes on her?' exclaimed Sir Lancelot. 'Obviously, my dear Eva, it couldn't possibly have been me. Everyone I operate on remembers it for life.'

Pip was no longer listening. He continued menacingly, 'Yes, Eva, who performed this extraordinary appendicectomy?'

'It was removed by the greatest surgeon in the world.' Smiling and proud, changed into a loose, flame-coloured dress, Dawn appeared through the beads of the Moorish arch.

13

'I JUST said it *wasn't* me,' Sir Lancelot told Dawn crossly.

'Some of the Spaniards can pour the wine on to their foreheads and down their noses, so that it runs into their mouths,' said Freddie, picking up the flask again and demonstrating.

'Then I must take care not inviting them to my club,' snapped Sir Lancelot. 'All this seems to me as confusing as trying to play snooker on a ship. I agree, plenty of people walk this earth in ignorance of who their fathers were. But most can put their finger on the man who removed their internal organs.'

Dawn languidly stretched out an arm to encircle her husband's neck. '*You* did it, didn't you, Freddie?'

'You!' Pip advanced, opening and closing his fists. 'No wonder the scar looks like a relief map of the Grand Canyon.'

'I'm sorry, Pip.' Freddie looked pathetic. 'But I did my best. It was my very first.'

'And he's still got it, Pip. Look—' Dawn admiringly held up the bottle from the coffee-table.

'That's ... that's Eva's?' Pip turned pink again and began to splutter. 'Give it me at once.'

Freddie produced a weak grin. 'It's just a little keep-sake, old man.'

'I will not have bits of Eva displayed as your hunting trophies.'

'Now I come to think of it,' Dawn reflected, turning the bottle, 'it's not much to stare at on a mantelpiece. Personally, as a decoration I'd prefer a bowl of goldfish.'

'Look at it!' Pip snatched the bottle from Dawn. 'It isn't

even inflamed. The greenest medical student could tell you it's a perfectly normal appendix. There's nothing wrong with it at all. You made the wrong diagnosis,' he told Freddie witheringly.

'Pip, I can only be open with you.' Freddie looked at him entreatingly. 'That is something I've had to live with. Quite literally. Far greater surgeons than me have misdiagnosed an acute appendix. It could have been a whole heap of things. You know as well as I do, how the symptoms fit other conditions. Flatulence. Constipation. A spanner in the gynaecological works. Maybe glandular fever. There was a lot of it about that time of the year,' he recalled.

'You always had an itchy twitch at the end of your knife,' Pip accused him.

'But surely you agree, Pip, that suspected appendicitis, of all conditions, merits the first principle of surgery – If in doubt cut it out.'

'So you made a mistake?' The two turned in surprise, as Eva slammed down the tray with a rattle on the coffee-table. 'You made a complete error in my diagnosis. And never once did you so much as mention it. Really Freddie! That is utterly disgraceful. And I think the most atrocious manners.'

'I didn't want to upset you, that's all,' Freddie apologized. 'You were a rather difficult patient.'

'You used me for practice,' she told him savagely.

'Of course I didn't use you for practice. No more than I'd have used Dawn for practice.'

'Oh, you know what surgeons are,' said Dawn lazily. 'They've no faith in curing anything, only in putting it somewhere different.'

'Would one of you doctors explain to me what appears a singularly difficult case?' invited Sir Lancelot Spratt.

All four stared at him. They had forgotten him, as the tumbling young forget the headmaster with the cane.

'A very simple case, as a matter of fact.' Freddie assumed his professional voice. 'I operated on Eva late one night at St Sepulchre's.'

Sir Lancelot was shocked. 'On your wife?'

'She wasn't. I mean, she wasn't then.'

'And you see, sir,' Pip continued quickly, 'Eva was so ashamed of the scar, and not wishing to detract from the surgical skill of her husband, the morning that I examined her, as her new doctor, she used the name of the first surgeon who came into her head. And your name, sir, would be the first into anyone's head, surely?'

Sir Lancelot looked slightly mollified. He asked, 'But why all the fuss about the specimen in the bottle?'

'May I explain, Sir Lancelot?' Eva smiled sweetly. 'Freddie and I had it at home, and I thought it was just some old appendix. I mean, doctors have all sorts of things in bottles hanging about. Liver, gallbladders, kidneys, two-headed babies. He never told me it was my own, because . . . because . . . ' She looked appealingly at Freddie.

'Why, because it was normal,' Freddie said promptly. 'No man likes to be faced with his past mistakes.'

'Like running into his former wife,' agreed Pip.

'Exactly.' Eva clasped the bottle to her bosom. 'I feel like a mother reunited with her long-lost baby.'

'I've never in my life before heard of anyone growing sentimental over their appendix,' muttered Sir Lancelot. 'I need yet another drink.'

'Don't we all,' said Freddie, striding to the cabinet.

'Either I'm getting senile or mentally dimmed, or something extremely fishy is going on,' said Sir Lancelot.

'Nothing in the slightest piscine, sir,' Pip assured him airily. 'You just see two ordinary couples – Eva and Freddie, Dawn and myself – sorting out a trivial little misunderstanding buried in the past. I expect we'll all have a good laugh about it, before the day is out.'

The doorbell chimed.

'That'll be the matron,' remarked Sir Lancelot. 'She seemed possessed with an urgent desire to see me, and here seemed as uncompromising a venue as any.'

The four stared at each other again.

Cindy threw open the door. 'The matron of St Sepulchre's Hospital,' she announced, as though producing her from a top hat.

'Hello, Pip. Hello, Eva. And there you are, Lancelot,' the matron began distractedly, hurrying into the lounge. 'I can't tell you how shocked I was, seeing the news of your arrest on television. Though I've always said – haven't I? – that explosive temper of yours would land you in serious trouble one fine day. I'm sure that unfortunate policeman was only doing his duty. I hope you've briefed a top-class QC to defend you? You mustn't take any risks with these things, you know, no more than consulting a second-rate surgeon to remove your stomach. But I expect he'll get you off. People seem to get away with murder these days. What's the matter?' she demanded, puzzled. 'Why are the four of you staring at me like that? I haven't just dropped in from outer space, you know.'

'Sherry, Auntie Florrie?' asked Pip falteringly.

'No. Tonight I'm going to try Lancelot's tipple of whisky. The possibility of twelve months at St Sepulchre's driving me to drink has finally materialized itself.' She collapsed on the purple cut moquette.

'Tell us exactly what happened,' said Freddie compellingly. 'I'm sure we'd all like to know, particularly Sir Lancelot. Take your time over it.'

'I've just had the most horrible day of my life.' She took a glass of whisky from Pip. 'Not only must I tolerate, humour and even suck up to that appalling Harold Sapworth from ACHE every day. Now I must do exactly the same to an equally awful man, who ought to know better. Ronnie Cherrymore, if you please. He thinks he shouldn't be a member of ACHE but of the Organization for Unqualified Co-operatives in Health, as he works in the dispensary with dangerous drugs. Apparently, it's a superior sort of union for white-collar workers, though if you ask me, they behave these days just as disgracefully as the miners. Of course he shouldn't be a worker at all, he went to Eton. ACHE and OUCH being deadly enemies, and this man Sapworth making so much fuss, both unions are calling a strike tomorrow morning. My hospital is coming to a halt, not because the faces of the workers are being ground, but because they won't look at each other. You don't seem very interested,' she complained abruptly.

'Oh! Yes, we are, very,' Freddie assured her. 'It's like play being stopped by the supporters of both sides invading the pitch.'

'That's exactly the trouble with the world today.' She swigged half the whisky. 'Everyone keeps invading the pitch everywhere. That's why you get all this hi-jacking. I'd never dream of going through a door marked, "Pilots Only". But people don't know their place any longer. You're very silent, Lancelot?' she observed.

He was standing beside the brass lampstand, slowly stroking his beard. 'I was just working something out.'

'Not only is my life sickened by the pest Sapworth, but a dreadful psychopath in central sterile supply called Arbuckle, a leading light in the General Ancillary Services Personnel, had his home raided by detectives and was found to have half the hospital stores. GASP is of course claiming they're only useless bits and pieces, no good to anybody, but I know for a fact he has sufficient bandages and dressings for a battle, enough syringes for every drug-addict in the country and crutches numerous enough for an entire ski season in the Alps. GASP is going on strike tomorrow, too, because of harassment by the police. Just like the loaders at London Airport, when one of them's discovered with his pockets sagging with bullion. No wonder there's no law and order. Now I know what it was like, living during the Wars of the Roses. I think I'll have another,' she told Pip, gulping the whisky and thrusting out her empty glass. 'Lancelot, don't you intend speaking to me at all tonight?'

'I'm still working something out.'

'I hope the domestic arrangements have operated well this past week?' the Matron asked more cheerfully, taking her whisky from Pip. 'They say that two women cannot exist sharing the same kitchen, but I'm sure you and Dawn get along splendidly, Eva.'

'We've a lot in common,' agreed Dawn.

'That Pip and Freddie are firm chums, I think goes without saying. Pip, you *are* looking glum this evening.' She stared at him keenly. 'That dhobie itch from Kenya isn't troubling him in the groin again, is it Eva?'

'Oh, no, it's absolutely healed up.'

Sir Lancelot glared at Freddie. 'How does she know about Chipps' groin?'

'I told you, sir. He's her doctor.'

'Good God, does the medical attendant remove all his clothes, too, when performing an examination?'

'Here's something to cheer you up,' the matron said brightly. She opened her handbag. 'Pip, I've found some dreadfully funny snaps of your wedding.'

Eva leapt up. 'The goulash! It's burning.'

The matron wrinkled her nose. 'I can't smell anything. Somebody's garden bonfire, I expect. Lancelot, just take a look at these – Pip!'

He snatched the handful of photographs. 'Forgive me, Auntie. It's very embarrassing. One looks such a fool on one's wedding-day.'

'I thought you looked most distinguished. Ask Sir Lancelot's opinion.'

Freddie gave a loud sniff. 'I'm sure that goulash is

burning, if not actually in flames. Let's have a look, Pip. Let's *all* have a look. Let your Auntie Florrie have a look.'

'Me? Why? But I'm just relaxing with a drink.'

'Take it with you.' Freddie grabbed her wrist. 'You're just the one for an emergency. Remember the St Sepulchre's boilers?'

He pulled her through the bead curtain.

Sir Lancelot found himself alone. He grunted. He slowly stepped through the sliding glass doors on to the sunlit patio. He was shortly aware of sharing it with another.

'Excuse me—' Cindy smiled coyly. 'Are you the famous Sir Lancelot Spratt, what operates on pop singers, and that?'

'I have a varied practice, certainly,' agreed Sir Lancelot, looking down sternly at her tiny white form.

'I thought I recognized you from your picture in the papers. You know, after you did that copper last Saturday. Mind, the Doctors Turnhorn are always talking about you,' she continued flatteringly. 'They say that your opinion of a surgical case is almost as important as your opinion of yourself.'

'H'm,' said Sir Lancelot.

She continued complimenting him, 'You must have more experience of nurses than Paul Raymond has of nudes.'

'Possibly.'

'Tell me, Sir Lancelot – I mean, be frank – do you think I'm a good nurse?'

'Well, you look the part.'

'I've always wanted to be a proper nurse, and do really exciting things to people.' Cindy clasped her hands below her bosom and gazed at him starry-eyed. 'In the operating theatre.'

'You might find it rather confusing. There's a lot of cutlery.'

'But I'm ever so good at picking things up,' she told him eagerly. 'I'm sure I should soon be doing operations, all on my tod. I'd start with something simple – a herniorraphy or a thyroidectomy – but I might work up to a pancreatectomy or a mitral valvotomy.'

He frowned. 'Where *do* you learn these long words?'

'I take Dr Turnhorn's books home. They make a good read before I go to sleep.'

He told her not unkindly, 'I'm afraid that surgery is not taught on the principle of sitting with Nellie.'

'Now, my boy-friend – he really *should* be a doctor. He's got such lovely soft hands. Such a gentle touch. He's already started in medicine, you know. Really. But at the bottom. Perhaps you could give him a helping hand?'

'I am always ready to encourage the ambitions of the young – so long as they do not conflict with my own. But perhaps you would first help *me*? Tell me, what exactly is the domestic situation in this house?'

'Oh, dear, it's got me properly confused, I must say. I don't think the doctors know themselves half the time. There's Mrs Chipps and Mrs Bisham, but I don't know which is which. They started off with the tall blonde one married to Dr Chipps, but they didn't seem able to keep it up.'

'Eva *married* to Dr Chipps?'

'Oh, yes. She had jet lag from the plane. Can't you see how suntanned she is? The little fat one was married to Dr Bisham. He's a lovely feller, isn't he? Reminds me sometimes of my boyfriend – he works in the Spratt's Bottom crematorium, by the way. Pushing round the customers. You've got to get your knees under the table somewhere, haven't you? Well, I must be getting along home. It was ever so nice having a chat with you, Sir Lancelot. My boy-friend won't half be impressed. Though come to think of it, he's probably handled a good bit of your work already.'

As Cindy disappeared towards the hall, Sir Lancelot noticed Pip and Freddie gingerly edging through the Moorish arch.

'Chipps! Bisham! You have been deceiving me.'

'Deceiving you, sir?' Pip looked amazed. 'But I'd as soon try to take a banana from an orang-utan with gout than deceive you, sir.'

'I don't give a damn about your squalid sexual arrangements. But I *do* care about your trying to pull the wool over my eyes. The sooner you return to your jungle, Chipps, the better. As for you, Bisham, I would never countenance so untrustworthy a colleague on the St Swithin's consultant staff.'

Freddie replied with a gust of laughter. 'But don't you see, sir? It was all a great joke. Wasn't it, Pip?'

'Just a bit of a giggle, sir. To liven up this dull suburb.'

'We are not amused,' Sir Lancelot roared at them.

'What are you shouting about now?' asked the matron, appearing through the beads. 'Pip, I think I'll have another of those drinks. Very comforting. I was already under severe tension, before you all seemed to confuse your dinner with an incendiary bomb. Thank you.' She took the glass. 'Now you'd better go back to your wives, who for some reason seem suddenly reduced to a state of inexplicable hysteria. Perhaps it's something to do with the pollen count. I have anyway an important matter to discuss with Sir Lancelot.'

'I have just discovered that Chipps is married to Eva and Bisham to Dawn,' said Sir Lancelot fiercely, as Freddie and Pip shot gratefully through the bead curtain.

'Took you rather long, didn't it?' She patted the cut moquette beside her. 'Come and sit here, Lancelot.'

'I will not sit anywhere. I am far too disturbed for chit-chat.'

'You really must try going through life unlike Alice's Duchess. Pip and Freddie are two perfectly pleasant young men, and you keep wanting to cut off their heads. People suffer far less from their own shortcomings than do the other people who take them so seriously. You'll soon be a psychological disaster area. Come and sit down,' she insisted.

Sir Lancelot sighed heavily and obeyed.

'Close beside me, Lancelot. God, this stuff makes me feel sexy. Does it have the same effect on you?'

'With me, its side effects are limited to laughing immoderately at other people's jokes.' He folded his arms and stared dully into the brick fireplace.

She twisted on the yellow satin cushion, staring closely into his face. 'Every time you walk into St Sepulchre's, you turn me on like a surgical cautery.'

He pulled his left ear. 'I did not appreciate my stirring your emotions to that extent.'

'Don't you understand what a tragic life I lead?' To Sir Lancelot's concern she again sounded tearful. 'What is my home? Two horrible chintzy rooms in that ramshackle lazar house of St Sepulchre's. What is my life? Dedicated to caring for the sick, and I have to spend all day battling with bloody-minded trade-unionists. They're so selfish, they'll hardly pass the salt in the canteen. They're so lazy, someone had to invent sliced bread. I need a man to lean on,' she said, leaning on him.

'Florence, I—'

'Yes?' She looked at him expectantly.

'I am not in the mood.'

'Are you ever? Do you always bite the hand which caresses you? But I suppose all surgeons are sadists.'

'You overlook that tomorrow morning I am to stand arraigned in the dock.'

'You're being too dramatic. I expect you've done much worse undetected things to the Inland Revenue, like all the other consultants in Harley Street. Can't you at least stop stamping your feet on Pip for the rest of the evening?'

'Very well, very well,' he said wearily. 'I shall be perfectly charming to everyone. We can all six enjoy a good dinner. I really don't care who's married to whom, so long as the claret's the right temperature.'

He had been aware while speaking of voices rising in the kitchen. The bead curtain rattled violently as Dawn swept through, hands on hips. 'I'm cross. I'm really cross. It doesn't happen often, I know. But I am now. Very cross.'

'But Dawn, darling,' Freddie expostulated, following her. 'You haven't got it in context.'

'You called me an old banger. Eva just told me.'

'I meant it affectionately.'

'Oh, charming. Next time try calling me an ancient monument.'

'I am leaving this house at once.' Eva appeared through the beads, eyes blazing. 'The stress has been utterly unbearable for a week. Now I find that my own husband has been uttering filthy innuendos behind my back. I am on the point of suffering a cruel nervous breakdown.'

'But it was a compliment, dear,' Pip protested, appearing behind her. 'It's a wonderful, inspired piece of music, revered by the whole civilized world. Not many women get compared to Beethoven's Ninth Symphony.'

'Possibly. Dawn told me that your description was more technical. The climax was all right, but you had to wait an awful long time till you got there.'

'Well, yes,' Pip admitted awkwardly. He stood scratching his chin. 'Don't take it to heart, Eva. I merely said that ... well, sex should be fun, but you took it rather more seriously—'

'Like a visit to the British Museum. *I* know. *She* told me.' Eva pointed quiveringly at Dawn.

'No woman's perfect,' said Freddie defensively. 'Even the Venus de Milo has no arms.'

'As for you, Freddie—' Eva turned on him furiously. 'You haven't a fraction of Pip's brains. You only got where you are through brazenness and craftiness. They said at St Swithin's you were the only one who always pulled strings rather than his weight.'

'Who said?' Freddie demanded.

'Pip did,' Eva said, pointing again.

'You did, did you?' Freddie scowled at him. 'Well, do you know what Eva said about being married to you, Pip? It was like being a Siamese twin, with the other half under an anaesthetic.'

'Oh, the remorse!' Eva clutched her forehead. 'The guilt. I am an exploited woman.'

'You're not,' said Freddie. 'You're a member of a wide-spread modern movement. The Society for Making Uplifting Gestures. SMUG.'

'Why, you—' Eva grasped the Spanish wine-flask.

'Eva!' shrieked the matron, jumping up and grabbing her wrist. 'For God's sake don't give him a fractured skull. All the neurosurgical instruments are away for repair.'

Eva dropped it on the table. 'I'm going,' she announced.

'Where?' asked Pip.

She looked round, lost. 'Back to mother.'

'But that went out with P G Wodehouse,' Pip told her.

'Mother is running a seminar this week on Ethics at the University. I think I shall find it most interesting.'

'I'm coming with you,' declared Dawn.

'Surely you're not *that* angry with me?' objected Freddie.

She shivered. 'No. But this place is beginning to give me the creeps.'

'And I'm leaving too,' said the matron. 'I don't know what's going on. It's quite beyond me. But I am in a very delicate emotional state. Never did I imagine that I should find St Sepulchre's preferable to anywhere. But at least a pesthouse is quieter than a madhouse. We can continue our conversation, Lancelot, when you have overcome your little legal difficulties. Perhaps you should get the Consultants' Guild in Harley Street to call a strike on your behalf, like GASP and your fellow-criminal Arbuckle.'

'Good-bye,' said Eva, glaring at Pip and Freddie impartially. 'For ever.'

'Good-bye,' sighed Dawn. 'I think I'll go back to Llanfihangel-yng-ngwynfa. I'd rather spend my holiday watching Wimbledon on the telly. At least the men in the mixed doubles don't run down their partners' performances.'

'And that,' muttered Freddie sarcastically, 'is the crack of Dawn.'

The door to the hall slammed. They heard the matron's Mini and Eva's Rover fade away in Apricot Avenue. Pip and Freddie leant silently against the fireplace. Sir Lancelot sat on the sofa calmly sipping his whisky.

'The novelist Trollope—' he announced suddenly. The other two jumped. 'Whose works I have been enjoying in bed, since my poor wife died, once said, "Of all hatreds that the world produces a wife's hatred of her husband, when she does hate him, is the strongest."'

All three relapsed into silence for some minutes.

'We're better off without them,' Freddie decided. 'You can't do a proper job of doctoring, when the house smells of sex like mice.'

'Perhaps we should have been more tactful,' said Pip ruefully. 'But I suppose one switches off one's inhibitions with the bedroom light.'

'You have learnt a pair of useful truths,' Sir Lancelot told them. 'One, that intimate confidences imparted to irregular bedmates are razor-sharp boomerangs. And two, that it is considerably less trouble to be fond of your own wife than someone else's.'

Freddie shrugged his shoulders. 'What do you suppose we should do?' he asked Pip.

'Go out and get stewed.'

'We can't. I'm on call.'

'You are not.' They both stared again at Sir Lancelot. 'I assume that, as a surgeon, I am competent to make some sort of stab at the emergencies which arise in general practice? Don't thank me,' he cut them short. 'I am not being generous. Nor am I being forgiving. You will now have to rise in the profession, if you do, by your own efforts. Though doubtless, with the ingenuity which you have used to befool me, you will rapidly become rich by applying the same treatment to your patients. But to suffer the company of you two for the rest of the evening, particularly with Bisham cold sober, is unthinkable.'

Five minutes later, Sir Lancelot was lighting the gas candles and sitting alone at the table on the patio. The matron was quite right, he reflected. He must apply more conscientiously his doctrine of humorous resignation, in a world of broken reeds shading weaker vessels. It would be beneficial for his arterial pressure. He opened the casserole of steaming goulash. Absently ladling a portion on his plate, he opened that morning's *Times* and reminded himself of the cricket scores. He turned as usual to the Court page. 'Nobody interesting died,' he murmured. 'They never do on a Monday.'

He folded the newspaper, and slowly eating goulash with one hand, with the other he swiftly turned Arundel into launder and a Cowes rest-cure into Worcester Sauce.

14

THE Spratt's Bottom magistrates' court and police
station, which shared the same square, shabby brick
building with the town hall, stood at the top of the High
Street by the traffic roundabout. Opposite was the war
memorial, scene of the crime. Sir Lancelot had expected
the reporters, photographers and television crews jostling
outside. Spratt's Bottom seemed to share, in the nation's
news, the tedious contentiousness of central Africa
or the Middle East. He left the Rolls at a meter and
strode through the crowd with jutting beard, saying, 'I
have no comment, ladies and gentlemen, no comment
whatever.'

The courtroom was through a lobby with mustard-
coloured walls and two massive benches back-to-back
in the middle of the pock-marked flooring. The only
decorations were police notices inviting help with their
unsolved murders. It reminded Sir Lancelot of St
Sepulchre's. He stood in one corner, fastidiously separat-
ing himself from the small knot of silent men and women
who shared the room, and who from their looks he was
sure had perpetrated the most repulsive and heartless
villainy.

'Spratt, L?' enquired a mild-looking police sergeant,
without his helmet and carrying a clip-board.

Sir Lancelot drew himself up. 'Present,' he said, with
the look of a defiant aristocrat at the final, creaking,
opening of the door in the Conciergerie.

'Your case is being taken first, sir. All the others are
traffic offences.'

The sergeant led him through a small opening in the
corner. They descended stone steps to the basement. Sir

Lancelot fancied he could hear the clank of manacles and fetters. They reached a small room with whitewashed brick walls, containing a table and chairs and smelling strongly of disinfectant.

'You're a doctor, aren't you, sir?' enquired the sergeant.

'That is correct. I might add, never in my professional career did I anticipate finding myself in this position.'

'I wonder if you'd take a look at my knee?' The sergeant pulled up his uniform trouser-leg. 'I gave it a nasty wrench last Sunday, tying up my bean stalks in the garden. Very convenient, your being with us this morning. You have to wait such an age, down at the doctor's, before he can see you.'

Sir Lancelot nodded towards the table. 'Up there. *Both* trouser-legs, please.' He felt the knees. 'H'm. No fluid present. Rest as much as you can. Should be better in a week or two.'

'Very kind of you, sir,' said the sergeant, stepping down again.

'Morning, Sir Lancelot.' A cheerful young policeman in rolled-up shirt-sleeves entered with another clip-board. 'Remember me at St Sepulchre's?'

'Yes. Prolapsed piles.'

'That's right, sir. You did me the world of good.' He laughed. 'Well, I'm in charge of *you* today.'

'It's just occurred to me, officer. This experience, like many others wholly unexpected in life, is worthily salutary. Now I know exactly how a patient feels, arriving nervously in hospital. All the doctors and nurses, busily proceeding with their everyday tasks, seem indifferent towards the greatest crisis which has occurred in his whole existence.'

'Oh, don't take it too much to heart,' the young policeman advised. 'Practically everyone's up in court these days. There's so many laws, you can hardly avoid breaking a few.'

'What are the beaks like?' asked Sir Lancelot more practically.

'Mrs Widmore's chairman this morning.' The policeman pursed his lips. 'She has her good days and her bad.'

'What exactly do you mean? The students say that about me.'

'Well, she can be a bit of a terror. Other times, if you couldn't get away with murder you might with speeding. She's very fair, though, very fair.'

'That's reassuring. Though I suppose being fair is the lady's job, as it is mine to scrub-up properly.' He became aware of a scuffling above.

'Here we go, then,' said the policeman.

Sir Lancelot preceded him up a short and narrow flight of steps, with the expression of Socrates calculating the toxic dose of hemlock.

He blinked in the strong sunlight through the windows. He was in the dock. Five or six yards away, his judges faced him from high-backed chairs below the Royal Arms. On the left, was a red-faced white-haired man with the air of a retired officer. On the right, a pale, thin, bespectacled one with a small moustache, whose expression of weary peevishness made Sir Lancelot suspect him a schoolmaster. Between, stiffly upright, hands clasped on the fumed oak bench, sat a pale, handsome woman in her mid-thirties, dark hair drawn severely back from a smooth brow and an expression of judicial composure.

'Lancelot Lister Spratt,' came a voice with the flat disinterestedness of a railway-station announcement. 'You are charged that, on June the twenty-fourth last, in the Market Square in the Borough of Spratt's Bottom, you did assault Sergeant Alfred Stevenson of the Metropolitan Police Q/R Division, while in the execution of his duty, by striking him in the face with a sheaf of papers, contrary to the Public Order Act, 1936. Do you plead Guilty or Not Guilty?'

'Not guilty,' said Sir Lancelot, in the voice used by Charles the First in 1649.

He found himself addressing a ferrety, gingery man in a dark suit, sitting below the magistrates at a desk loaded with documents, who continued, 'Are you represented by a solicitor?'

'No, sir.'

'You are áware that you have the right to be?'

'That is the right of every Englishman in my position,' Sir Lancelot told him, with the dignity of Warren Hastings at the bar of the House of Lords.

'Then why haven't you taken it?'

'Because my inborn distrust of the legal profession has been reinforced by my occasional experiences in their hands.'

'I am, of course, as Clerk of the Court, a qualified solicitor,' the man told him. He picked up a document, and appeared to lose further interest in the fate of so benighted a blackguard.

The sergeant was already taking the oath.

'At two-thirty on the afternoon of June twenty-fourth,' he sang out, while handing the Testament back to the usher, 'I proceeded on duty to St Sepulchre's Hospital to observe a demonstration of which we were previously advised. This was led by the defendant. I had occasion to warn him three times. First, for trespassing on the central grass area of the High Street traffic roundabout. Second, for attempting to climb the borough war memorial. Third, for obstructing the free passage of vehicles out of the Market Square car park.'

'Was he lying on the ground?' asked the chairman. She had a soft, low, carefully modulated voice. She reminded Sir Lancelot of a prima donna he had once treated for laryngitis. He glared round him as defiant as Adolf Hitler on trial for high treason in Munich. Between him and the bench, a foot or so lower, were half a dozen seats like pews, at which two men and a fat woman in a black dress sat reading typewritten documents. To his right were the reporters, who mostly struck him as adolescent. On his left, two dozen helmetless policemen squatted on long benches with their feet stuck out, waiting to give evidence instead of suppressing the crime of Spratt's Bottom. Sir Lancelot noticed the variety of socks below their uniform trousers. No one except the scribbling reporters seemed in the slightest concerned with him.

'No, he did not go so far as to lie on the ground at that time, Your Worship.'

Mrs Widmore fixed on Sir Lancelot two large, brown, severe, eyes. 'I wanted to clear that point, because it is a favourite tactic among demonstrators.'

'The defendant thereupon commenced his address to the public, during which he struck me in the face with several sheets of paper. I then took him into custody.'

'He gave no more trouble?'

'No, Your Worship.'

Her censorious gaze returned to Sir Lancelot. 'Have you any questions for the witness?'

'None.'

'Then you agree with his version of the events?'

'I agree with the events. But not with his version of them.'

She adjusted some papers. 'I must allow that subtlety to pass over my head.' She nodded. The sergeant left the witness-box. 'I will accept, Spratt, that you are of previous good character—'

'I wish to conceal nothing. I have committed one felony.' Mrs Widmore looked alarmed. 'I once stole a horse. Some years ago, in Cambridge. I was fined five pounds.'

She shrugged her neat shoulders. 'I think the Court can overlook some drunken escapade following a football match.'

He corrected her severely. 'Following a first class in the Natural Science Tripos.'

'That is immaterial.'

'It is certainly not at all immaterial,' Sir Lancelot barked. 'The one is a mindless diversion. The other an academic exploit doubtless beyond the ability of anyone in this Court.'

'Will you kindly remain silent?' she asked coldly. 'Might I remind you that I am in charge here?'

'Then you might try to create some semblance to a court of justice. If I ran my operating theatre as haphazardly, there'd be corpses all the way from St Sepulchre's to that sergeant's beastly roundabout. His account of the facts was as twisted as a skewer through a shish kebab. He tried to present me as some sort of thug, which is downright perjury.'

'*That* is downright contempt of court,' she told him sternly. 'I shall however overlook it. This once. I invited you to question the sergeant. If you thought silence more prudent, the bench can only draw its own conclusions. But I should like to know exactly what motives you had in assaulting the officer?'

Sir Lancelot calmed down. 'We differed whether John Dewey or William James was the originator of the philosophy of pragmatism.'

'Please do not waste the time of the Court,' she said briefly. 'You struck a police officer in the face—'

'Yes, I did. But hardly with a knuckle-duster.'

'If you continue to interrupt me, I shall have you taken below to the cells while I hear all the remaining cases,' she said, with the smoothness of a sharp icicle. 'All assaults upon the police, however feeble in execution, are taken most seriously by the bench. What today might be a rolled-up sheet of paper, tomorrow all too easily becomes a brickbat. We have observed this frequently with the children of Spratt's Bottom Comprehensive. In times like ours, when the police are assaulted daily in every country of the world, it is our duty to preserve, as best we can, our own unarmed officers from such attacks. We therefore pass exemplary sentences, to deter those who might otherwise be encouraged to use violence in achieving their own criminal ends, or to escape the consequences thereof. I understand you to be a distinguished citizen, Spratt. But that is all the more reason for you to set a good example to the young, and to others who, like yourself, find difficulty in controlling their passions.' She whispered briefly to the other pair. All three nodded. 'We find you Guilty, Spratt. You are fined £150 with £100 costs.'

Sir Lancelot glared as though she were Pontius Pilate sending for the wash-basin. Thoughts tumbled in his brain. That would be the takings for a hydrocele on a visiting sheik, but before tax. The young policeman touched his elbow. 'Come on, sir. Got to give the others a chance,' he whispered cheerfully. 'Hope you've brought your cheque book? We don't take no credit cards here.'

Sir Lancelot drove his Rolls down the High Street towards St Sepulchre's, in a flaming temper – but stopping punctiliously at all the zebra crossings and amber lights. However disgraced, however defamed, his work as a healer must go on. He would use his unexpected day at Spratt's Bottom to see a few patients, and investigate how far his operating theatre had been repaired. He drove into the forecourt, to notice the dean climbing from his Rolls accompanied by a midget. Sir Lancelot backed, deciding to use the goods entrance. It was galling enough, being submitted to the most disgraceful miscarriage of justice since Captain Dreyfus. To endure the dean's comments upon it would be psychological hanging, drawing and quartering.

He could do with a drink. He wondered if he dare first slip into the Spratt's Arms. Then he recalled that the dean was displaying Spratt's Bottom that morning to his new chum and paymaster.

Hamilton Tosker was five feet tall, bandy-legged, sparse-haired and leathery-faced, resembling the jockeys who had brought him the worship of his native land. His wife Pearl, leaving the Rolls after him, was tall and angular, in a flower print dress, a wide white hat and long white gloves. She came from Melbourne.

'So this is the end of the trail?' Hamilton asked with dreadnought Australian cheerfulness, as the dean led him into the crowded lobby. 'Christ! Is this a hospital? I wouldn't use it as an abattoir for saltbush weaners.'

'The National Health Service suffers from a degree of financial anaemia,' the dean told him blandly. 'But I assure you, Hamilton, that we— er, Poms, rather specialize in making the best of bad jobs. After all, remember Dunkirk.'

'Kick the wall, Lionel,' Hamilton directed. 'It needs the rest of the roof to fall in.'

'As you know, the hospital will shortly be closed down completely,' the dean continued apologetically. 'And will doubtless become a multi-storey car park, like every other bit of spare land in the suburb.'

'Where's some service?' Hamilton stared round. 'Come on, cobber, don't stand there like a boiled chook. Go and boot someone up the jaxie. I'm as busy today as weevil borers in ripe bananas.'

'I'll fetch the matron,' the dean responded with a smile. 'I'm sure we can locate the young lady in question with little trouble.'

'You're not to come the raw prawn with the matron, Hamilton,' his wife warned him sharply, twitching the tops of her gloves.

'And don't you come the bludger with me, darl. I just want to see the kid, then I'll be off quicker than whore's drawers.'

The dean crossed the lobby to the matron's office, his eyebrows as flat as a pair of hairy caterpillars hit by an Australian fly-swat. He felt it galling, a proud Englishman submitting to the peremptory orders of the immutable Colonials. Worse still, he could barely comprehend them. Perhaps the Australians were a nation of natural, if complex, poets.

The three had spent the morning in Balaclava Road, beyond Spratt's Bottom station. There Hamilton Tosker's father had been born, and plied his inoffensive, useful trade, before emigrating to New South Wales after learning in the Spratt's Arms, if erroneously, that it offered gold nuggets for the stooping. The road had been rebuilt with semi-detached council houses, the inhabitants of which responded suspiciously, or bewilderedly, to enthusiastic enquiries after kin, uttered in an accent as characteristic as the thunder of surf on Bondi beach.

Finally, a white-haired lady in carpet-slippers, drawn from her front door by curiosity at the Rolls, remembered a Mr and Mrs Tosker. They had lived on the corner, respectable persons, he had worked for the council in a suit. They had retired to Littlehampton because of the air, but their daughter had gone to be a nurse in the hospital.

Hamilton Tosker became excited. He remembered his cousin Jack, a no hoper who pushed a pen for those ning nongs in the town hall. They'd sent him a photo of their little sheila one Christmas, and a real beaut she was.

'How remarkably convenient,' the dean had said, delighted at the prospect of a swift return to central London and his own mastery. 'My influence at St Sepulchre's is, of course, considerable, if not overwhelming.'

The dean returned across the lobby with the matron. He introduced her to Hamilton and Pearl, then turned to ask her, 'You say you have a Nurse Tosker in the wards?'

'Elaine Tosker. Certainly. She's in casualty.'

'Mr Tosker would like to see her.'

'Out of the question.' The matron was in an uncompromising mood from frustrated passion and a hangover. 'You'll have to wait till she comes off duty.'

'But she's a distant relative of Mr Tosker's,' said the dean anxiously.

'There are plenty of people employed by the hospital who imagine they can give me orders. I see no reason for encouraging outsiders.'

Hamilton fixed the dean with an eye like a Watson's Bay oyster with a cold gale blowing through Sydney Heads. 'See here, you constipated pee-wit, I either meet my filly or you shift your bloody boots out of my Organization.'

'Hamilton!' exclaimed his wife. 'Stop behaving like a Wooloomooloo larrikin.'

'And you,' he returned the geographical sarcasm, 'stop acting like the Yarra Park blue-rinse brigade.'

'I'm quite sure it can be arranged perfectly easily,' said the dean, eyebrows cavorting nervously. He drew the matron urgently aside. 'Please help me,' he implored in a whisper. 'My whole existence is bound up with this man. He has a heart of gold – being Australian – if inclined to somewhat lurid expressions and volatile moods.'

The matron thought for a second. 'Tell me – where will Sir Lancelot Spratt be tonight?'

'At home,' the dean said readily. 'We're attending the annual dinner of the St Swithin's rugby club. I suppose he'll be back in Lazar Row about elevenish.'

The matron nodded. 'Perhaps I can make an exception. After all, Mr Tosker is no stranger to hospital wards. When the National Health Service finally crushes my spirit, I may go out myself and administer to the sheiks of Araby, even if it means no booze and wearing a yashmak.'

The three followed the matron down the dim, smelly main corridor towards the casualty department. 'This a hospital?' repeated Hamilton with disgust. 'Makes you want to chunder.'

Nurse Tosker appeared nervously through the door of casualty. She had been summoned by the matron. Her head whirred painfully with possible misdemeanours.

'That's my girl,' exclaimed Hamilton, his mood suddenly as bright as the waters of Port Jackson on a January morning. 'Hasn't changed since I got her photo, except for developing a full house in the balcony. I'm your uncle Hamilton, darl. Give us a big kiss.'

She gasped. 'Uncle Hamilton? Who dad always called the Henry Ford of the mutton chop?'

'Yeah, I'm big in sheepmeat.' He beamed at the compliment. 'But now I reckon I've a lot of other tucker boiling in my billycan.' He embraced her ardently. 'My oath, but you're as sweet as a raspberry pavlova.'

'Oh, thank you.' She looked doubtful. 'You're not a bit what I expected, Uncle.'

'Oh?' His eye congealed, as though the oyster had been dipped in vinegar.

'I mean, you're just not what I thought millionaires were like. I imagined they were all surrounded by armed bodyguards and wore dark glasses. You seem to be nothing but an ordinary sort of feller.'

'That's my moll!' He grinned wider. 'I am just an ordinary sort of bloke, too right, who likes a few schooners and a game of swy on a Saturday afto before going home and wiring into his steak-and-eggs tea. There's no bloody class about me, is there, matey?' he asked the dean.

'Precisely, Hamilton,' the dean assured him eagerly. 'You exemplify the great Australian ideal, that every man thinks himself as good as the next.'

'The great Australian ideal is that every man thinks himself twice as good as the next,' Hamilton corrected him. 'What do you reckon of Australia?' he asked Nurse Tosker.

'I ... I think it must be a lovely country.'

'It is *not* a lovely country. It is a *bloody* lovely country. Gum trees, the Southern Cross, and empty beer cans thick as daisies. A man's country. Or it would be,' he admitted handsomely, 'if we got rid of all the wombat-headed, magpie-legged, splay-footed, rotten, mongrel, commie, poofter bastards sitting on their arses in Canberra.'

'Don't rubbish the Government,' said Pearl severely.

'Stop whinging like a mug copper. I don't know a politician the world over who couldn't hide behind a corkscrew,' he told her confidently. 'Come out and live with us, over the bridge in the Northern Suburbs,' he invited generously.

'But I couldn't do that, uncle.'

'What's the matter?' he demanded shortly. 'Strilia not good enough for you? We're not all Abos and roos and the duck-billed platypus, you know. We've got the Opera House open now,' he said proudly.

'Oh, no, uncle, I'm sure it would be Heaven upon earth. But I've got my career.' She glanced at the matron shyly. 'I just want to go on nursing. Here at St Sepulchre's. Because I think it's here that I'm most needed.'

'What a darl!' said Hamilton warmly. 'Would you find such devotion among them ratbags in Canberra, Pearl?' He planted his bandy legs impressively. 'I've got an idea. How'd you like your own hospital?' Nurse Tosker looked startled. 'Lionel—.'

'Hamilton?'

'You know the sort of bloke people say I am?'

'Exactly, Hamilton. Straight as a billiard-cue, transparent as a beer-mug, as open as a pub at lunchtime,' the dean quoted dutifully.

'When I take a liking to a bloke or a sheila, nothing's too good for them. Remember what you told me, Lionel – how you could do, here in London, with one of the hospitals I'm building all the way from the Red Sea to Afghanistan?' The dean nodded. 'Well, you shall have it, cobber. Here in Spratt's Bottom. Free as the bloody air. The Tosker Organization will build it. Lionel, you'll run it. And you, moll, can run the nurses.' He slapped the matron cheerfully on her seat.

'There'll be private beds for everyone who wants to pay for them,' he outlined. 'Free beds for everyone who can't. Same standard throughout, whether for your heart transplant or your tucker. Private treatment for the workers! We won't even have to put the bloody operating theatre facing Mecca. What do you think?' he asked enthusiastically.

The dean looked at the matron in confusion. 'Various technical problems might arise. I mean, objections at the Ministry, from senior Civil Servants—'

'Don't talk to me about Pom Civil Servants,' Hamilton said contemptuously. 'They're like the kippers they eat for breakfast – two-faced, no backbone and they smell.'

'Of course, I know you enjoy influence in high places,' the dean said hastily. 'But where would you find the building-land in Spratt's Bottom?'

'Details, details.' He waved them aside. ' "The Elaine Tosker Hospital." Beaut.' He kissed his fingers. 'Perpetuating for ever the name of Spratt's Bottom's first family. Can't go wrong. My impulses have a habit of being profitable, eh, Lionel? Maybe I've solved the problems of the entire Pom Health Service.' He glanced at his watch. 'Just in time for the morning papers back home.' He nodded towards the wall telephone. 'Pearl, gimme Sinney aniline. Then let's all go out and celebrate with a few handles. Fix it, Lionel. No point in paying a wet-nurse, if you're left swinging on a dry tit.'

'Mr Tosker,' said the matron more amiably. 'Though I appreciate your offer of employment – and I cannot think you will find anyone better than myself – I cannot let my staff drink on duty.'

'Aw, don't be a wowser,' he urged, slapping her again.
'There's nothing I'd like just now more than a Fosters
from the esky and a meat pie.' The philanthropist's eyes
glazed at recollection of his country's national dish, with
its blotting-paper pastry, its unidentifiable interior, its
decoration of shiny scarlet sauce like hot floor-polish –
Hamilton poured tomato sauce on everything, including
Camembert, roast grouse and caviar – and its squirting,
oily juice which covered chin, tie and toe-caps. 'I'm so
starving, I could eat witchetty grubs. Or kangaroo. Ever
tasted kangaroo, matron?'

'It is not included in the usual hospital diet.'

'You boil it with your boots. When your boots are
tender, the roo's ready to eat.' He laughed. 'You do a
cockatoo the same, but instead of your boots you use an
axe-head. I feel a real box of birds, because I've done my
good deed for the day,' he announced smugly. 'But my
oath, I'll do another.' He took a folded square of paper
from his top pocket and handed it to the dean. 'A hot tip
for Ascot this afto. Read it out, Lionel.'

The dean opened the paper. Horses *did* have peculiar
names, he reflected. He declared, 'Hoof Hearted.'

'Not me,' said Hamilton. 'Must be the matron.'

He continued laughing all the way down the main
corridor. The matron followed with the expression of a
Botany Bay governor calculating whether two or three
hundred lashes was the punishment to fit the crime.

15

'Not a bad dinner at all,' the dean was saying that evening. 'Very jolly, in fact. Thank you for asking me, Lancelot, as the President's guest.' They both sat dinner-jacketed in the back of the dean's Rolls, driving away from a Soho restaurant. 'I must say, there *did* seem rather a lot of verses to the rugby club song. Still, I suppose it's gratifying to know that the boys have remembered so much anatomy. They all disappeared rather early, didn't they?'

'They were going to a film.'

'At this hour? But the last performance will have started.'

'Not the particular performance they were going to watch.'

'Oh, that sort of film. I hope the place doesn't get raided,' the dean said sternly. 'St Swithin's has suffered enough disgrace for one day.'

'Dean, you are becoming a bore. This morning's experience was the most humiliating of my life.'

'I must confess to feeling slightly disturbed at a colleague from St Swithin's being run in for beating up a copper. You don't object to friendly candour?'

'Not at all. It is the most civilized way of delivering insults.'

'Fortunately, most of the consultants at St Swithin's attribute the episode to your reasonably harmless eccentricity, which we have had to tolerate for years. I sincerely hope for your sake that the General Medical Council will think the same. The convictions of all medical men are reported to them automatically, of course.'

'Hadn't we better turn right here, if we're going to St Swithin's and not to the Zoo?'

'Oh, yes, quite correct. Chauffeur, that way, please,' the dean directed. 'So convenient of Hamilton Tosker to supply a driver, isn't it? It does allow one to enjoy one's dinner without the possibility of having to pee into test-tubes for policemen.' He laughed. 'Not that I suppose it would worry you, Lancelot, as a hardened criminal.'

Sir Lancelot grunted.

'There's one item on the credit side for the hospital today,' the dean continued jauntily. 'The College of Therapeutics had decided on awarding the James Lind medal to a St Swithin's man. A great honour for us. The only trouble is, I can't find him. Very hush-hush, you understand,' he added warningly.

'That sort of medicine is hardly in my line. I looked into St Sepulchre's this morning, to see how my operating theatre was proceeding – with luck, it should be open for business in another ten days. I noticed you in the distance with Tosker.'

'I was with him when he hit on the great idea,' said the dean proudly. 'Amazing, işn't it, how he makes decisions involving millions of pounds as easily as you or I would decide to send a letter by first- or second-class post? He's certainly made a splash. Front-page headlines in the evening papers, half of the television news bulletins ... Hamilton may affect one like an emery-paper undervest, but he knows how to make the generous, impulsive gesture.'

'I am not too sure about either of those adjectives.' Sir Lancelot stroked his beard. 'I looked into the club for a quick one before the dinner, and ran into Charles from the Ministry. Tosker's had this idea of a workers' luxury hospital for months. He's already got the site at Spratt's Bottom.'

'Impossible,' objected the dean.

'He bought the golf course.'

The dean whistled. 'He's as crafty as a cockatoo in a cornpatch,' he said, falling into the idiom of his taskmaster. 'The sort of bludger who'd play you two-up with a three-headed coin.'

'Tosker's little plan is to make a fat profit from building a hundred of these hospitals for the NHS.'

'And what's the Ministry think?'

'According to Charles, they're in a bit of a stew. It would betray the great Bevan ideal of a free health service, run almost entirely from taxes. On the other hand, Nye Bevan would have assuredly updated his vision – long before anyone else even glimpsed it – to a health service run as a participation deal. You know, among various bodies with an interest in the public's health. The Government, the unions, the Confederation of British Industry, the insurance companies, philanthropic societies, pharmaceutical industry, and so on. And of course us. Otherwise, the cash won't stretch, as I mentioned last Saturday morning.'

'Tosker's idea might be a back-door for the Government getting the idea accepted?'

'Exactly. No Government would use any institution's front door, which is effectively draught-proofed against the winds of change. The Ministry is going to keep an open mind, whether to close St Sepulchre's as planned, accept the new offer as Tosker's loss-leader, or keep St Sepulchre's open, in dutiful acceptance of the Area Health Authority's resolution at our meeting.'

'I don't much care for "Tosker Hospital,"' said the dean. 'That little nurse didn't have quite the inspiring presence of Miss Nightingale or even the matron.'

'He can call it St Mickey Mouse Hospital, as far as I'm concerned, so long as the operating theatre roofs don't fall in. I am now, of course, throwing my publicity campaign into reverse. I am advertising St Sepulchre's as a blot on the clinical landscape, which urgently needs clearing up. According to my public relations chappie, it is perfectly easy to make the public believe that black is white, even after you've been telling them it's yellow.'

'First on the right here,' the dean directed, as they drove past the brightly-lit St Swithin's casualty entrance.

'The Government's thinking is somewhat deranged at the moment by the imminence of a General Election,' reflected Sir Lancelot. 'More than the most nervous patient by the imminence of an operation. But I suppose its chance of survival is less.'

The dean looked sly, eyebrows rising on their tails and kissing each other. 'I am perhaps the most powerful person in the country today. Next to the Queen,' he conceded gallantly. 'You know how slender is the Government's majority? Well, it's all lying in my care, in there.' He jerked a thumb towards St Swithin's. 'Two cardiac cases, a nasty pancreas and two ... well, I haven't quite decided yet. Private wing, of course. Even the most egalitarian MP should not be forced to sit on a bedpan in full view of his voters. Or perhaps otherwise,' he reflected. 'The fate of the Prime Minister depends on my getting them fit enough for the lobbies. Terrible responsibility. Quite frightening. Still, there are compensations. What do you think of Ponder's End as a name?'

'It suggests someone contemplating suicide.'

'It's where my family comes from.' The dean twinkled. 'It might well be my name after the next Honours List. Life peerage, you know. So nice for my wife. She'll become *The* Lady, instead of common Lady. Such a difference a definite article can make. Here we are, Lancelot. You'll forgive me if I don't invite you in for a nightcap? I've an unbelievable amount of case-notes to wade through.'

The dean dismissed the Rolls and let himself into his front door. Sir Lancelot turned towards his own. He paused, pulling the end of his black bow tie. A light gleamed. Burglars? He contemplated following the dean and dialling Scotland Yard, but decided that he had seen enough policemen for one day. He felt for his key. Waiting in the hallway was Miss MacNish.

'Sir Lancelot!' She gave a tearful gasp. 'He's dead.'

Sir Lancelot's brain for once spun out of control. 'Who? Hamilton Tosker?'

'No.' She took a clean folded handkerchief from the pocket of her green overall. 'Rob Roy.'

Sir Lancelot frowned. 'I believe that is reasonably common knowledge?'

'My budgie.'

'Oh. Yes. I'm sorry.' She began to sniff. 'I know how you loved him,' he consoled her stiffly.

'Thank you, Sir Lancelot,' she said humbly. 'I expected you'd say that. It is so typical of your nature. It was a terrible shock. But it brought me to my senses. You see, I have come hame,' she said simply. 'Though my heart's in the Highlands, my heart is not here, my heart's in the Highlands, Sir Lancelot, a-chasing the deer ... this is my ain hame.'

Sir Lancelot nodded briefly. 'And what did it die of?'

'The puir, wee tim'rous beastie burst.'

'That must have been somewhat alarming,' he observed. 'With much noise?'

'My sister in Putney put pop-corn in his seed-tray,' she explained tragically. 'I suspect deliberately. She had no sympathetic feelings towards Rob Roy. In fact, I think she developed persecution mania about him. Nor was she very accommodating about the use of hot water and cooking facilities, and she watched all the wrong programmes on the telly,' Miss MacNish revealed bitterly. She dropped her eyes. 'And all the time, Sir Lancelot, I knew you were thinking, will ye no come back again? Better lo'ed ye canna be, will ye no come back again? I've done the washing-up, and I've put your shirts in the machine and I've made the porridge ready for your breakfast.'

The gyroscope of Sir Lancelot's thoughts regained its balance. He supposed that he was pleased to see Miss MacNish back, particularly as Rob Roy had flown into the great granary of birdseed in the sky. He would be able to concentrate on his patients rather than his pots and pans. And his bills for new shirts were growing alarming. But the circumstances of her departure could no more be overlooked than those of the tempestuous Carmen from her slighted Corporal José.

'It has not escaped my memory that you were somewhat uncivil to my overnight guest.'

Miss MacNish crushed her handkerchief. 'I have been guilty of a sin. Uncharitableness, even hypocrisy. I do not condone fornication, Sir Lancelot. Do not think that of me. But I can open my heart to the occasional lapse.' She gulped. 'One Burns' Night, I was unwisely walking alone down Sauchiehall Street—'

'Let us both be spared such painful reminiscences.'

'Very well, Sir Lancelot. We live in a wicked world, and I have decided in future to shut my eyes against it.'

'I am sure you are right to apply a protective dressing to a soul of such sensitivity.'

'I have laid out the lady's nightdress on your bed.'

'Nightdress? What nightdress? What lady?'

She turned on him a look of sickly coyness. 'The one hanging behind the door of my bathroom. Your American lady mentioned it when she telephoned a little earlier. She said that she would be arriving rather late, as she was attending a Lord Mayor's Banquet at the Mansion House. As I expect you're tired, you can sit comfy against the pillows and wait.'

'My dear Miss MacNish! You have grasped the wrong end of the bed-post—'

'No need to protest too much,' she reassured him with a

166

winsome smile. 'I could not live so near you, Sir Lancelot, for so long, without knowing you so well. You are a man of healthy desires. I shall now withdraw, and leave you to your paramour. Please knock on my door if she wants any cocoa.'

Miss MacNish ascended the stairs. Sir Lancelot stood in the hall. He heard the door of her flat slam, the bolts shoot, the chain rattle. He followed slowly to his first-floor bedroom overlooking the back garden. The four-poster was turned down on both sides. Across one fold were his striped pyjamas, neatly arranged with their arms raised in the position of surrender. Across the other lay Amelia's forgotten nightie, short, transparent, smoke-blue. On his bedside table was a silver bowl crammed with roses, on his chest-of-drawers, on his bookcase of soporific reading, were crystal vases filled with a display of delphiniums and lupins. 'Like a royal bloody bridal chamber,' muttered Sir Lancelot.

He reached for the nightie. He rolled it up, looking round for some wrapping. He would hand it through the door to Amelia. She need not even abandon her taxi. He had torn a couple of sheets from the *Lancet*, when he paused. He lowered his nose and sniffed the flimsy material. He straightened up.

'H'm,' said Sir Lancelot.

He turned to the dressing-table mirror. Miss MacNish was right. He *was* a man of healthy desires. Why should such junior members of the profession as Chipps and Bisham get all the fun? His thoughts picked up speed, and all the lights ahead were green. There was only one snag. The last he had seen of Amelia, she was dressed in a pair of teenager's jeans and a striped Audley College football shirt, slamming the door of his Rolls outside Bunter's in an abrasive temper.

The doorbell rang.

Sir Lancelot carefully rearranged the nightie. He

smoothed hair, beard and the wings of his black tie. Surely his charm would sink the punting incident from her mind? He descended the stairs full of unsurgical thoughts.

The bell rang again. He opened the front door.

'Lancelot! I must have a word with you before another night has passed,' said the matron, pushing into the hall.

'Er ... good evening,' he said politely.

'I know that I could not sleep a wink, unless I did.'

'Ah! Dear me.'

'So I said to myself – what's the matter?' she broke off. 'You look as though I was a terrorist armed to the teeth.'

'It's just that the pleasure of your company is somewhat unexpected,' he said lamely, shutting the front door. 'I'm just back from the rugger club dinner, with the dean.'

'Yes, I know that. You're rather early, aren't you? I've just been to the annual reunion dinner of my nursing year. In the sisters' dining-room at St Swithin's.' He noticed that she was arrayed in a flowing, orange tule dinner-dress, cut low between the breasts. Her hair and make-up seemed to have enjoyed much attention.

'I hope it was an enjoyable occasion?'

'No, of course it wasn't enjoyable,' she told him impatiently. 'How could I enjoy anything, when I'm boiling inside? I could hardly keep my mind on the speeches. I'm in a turmoil. Can I have a whisky? Ever since I tried it at Pip's place last night, I've thought how comforting it is.'

16

SIR Lancelot shut the door of his front sitting-room behind the pair of them. The matron sat on the leather sofa, her back straight, hands clasped tensely on her lap. Sir Lancelot opened his lead-lined celarette for a bottle of malt whisky, and poured it into two glasses in silence.

He applied to the circumstances a brain which could decide calmly the correct succession to clip off a dozen unexpectedly spurting arteries. He had himself attended Lord Mayors' Banquets, heady and voluble feasts which continued till eleven. He had ten minutes to stand under the deluge of the matron's emotional outpouring. Then he would firmly turn her out. Otherwise, she would be likely to suffer an attack of acute hysteria, which could bring Miss MacNish from upstairs, and even the dean from next door.

'Lovely.' She gulped the glassful. 'I think I'll have another. That reunion dinner was dreadful. All the nurses who turned out failures were trying to pretend that we were exactly like we were in the old days. With all the ones who were successes firmly indicating that we were not. What was your dinner like?'

'Rowdy, but it is a privilege to be accepted by the young as a friend. They are heartlessly choosy.' He handed her a second drink.

'Come and sit here.' She patted the hard, shiny leather. 'Lancelot, you are a very, very strange man.'

'I always imagine I strike others as monotonously normal.'

'Of course you think nothing of the kind. You cultivate more eccentricities than did Harold Macmillan. Look at this dreadfully uncomfortable sofa. Like so many things about you, it is quite aggressively old-fashioned.'

'I am a traditionalist,' he said simply, sneaking a glance at his watch. 'I inherited it. Apart from the expense, my life is too full to go about choosing sofas.'

She seized his hand, twining her fingers round his. 'Now, don't edge away. That's right, you're a traditionalist. That's your trouble. The way you treat women would do credit to Jane Austen.'

'Our profession teaches us to hide our feelings.'

'What hypocrisy. Most doctors are randy exhibitionists. Why not come out with it, Lancelot? I know you love me.'

'Do I?'

'Of course you do,' she informed him ardently. 'And you want to marry me. I know that, too. I knew it the very first day we met. I'd barely arrived at St Swithin's, I was terrified of the sisters, the surgeons, the patients. It was my first morning as junior theatre nurse. I stood there, all dressed up in mask and gown, frightened to death that I'd faint or be sick or touch something sterile or otherwise disgrace myself. I tried to hide behind the anaesthetic trolley. Then suddenly – I saw your own eyes above the patient, seeking my own. It inspired me with determination, with courage. I can never forget it.' She sighed deeply. 'It was the most wonderful moment of my life.'

'As I recall, I had noticed you standing on the oxygen pipe-line.'

'Typical! Typical!' She squeezed his hand fiercely. 'You're always trying to present yourself as unromantic as a concrete-mixer. Of course, you'd noticed a new girl in the theatre. All the surgeons look at the nurses before the patient. Not that we'd much to show, those gowns do as much for your figure as a paper bag for a couple of oranges. But fortunately my eyes are my most attractive feature.' She squeezed his hand again. 'Had I not received a glance from those Jove-like orbs of yours, I might have fled from the operating theatre, the hospital, my talents lost to the sick for ever.'

'I am glad that I could further your career with so little trouble to myself.' He wondered how he could draw so personal a conversation swiftly to its close. It was so easy in the consulting-room, you shoved a thermometer in their mouths.

She sighed again, breasts quivering gently, like the froth on overfilled glasses of Guinness. 'Since then, Lancelot, we've been through a lot together, haven't we? At St Swithin's, I rose to be your theatre staff-nurse and then your ward sister. We shared the same work, the same patients. With all the intense gratification, all the bitter humiliation, which they can bring.'

'It is true that medicine, as much as marriage, can bind a man and a woman in the steely cobweb of shared experiences,' he agreed. 'But I think, Florence, you are being somewhat dramatic. You often were so in the wards. God knows how many times you called me from my bed for an acute abdomen when it was wind.'

She smirked. 'Perhaps I just wanted to see you? I used to get terribly lonely on night-duty, and the housemen all seemed to be newly married. *You* went to my wedding.'

'Yes, I gave you an umbrella-stand.'

'I think both of us knew that day, equally well, that my marriage was an unwise one,' she said tragically. 'It was you I really loved. I tried to express it, but you interpreted my attitude merely as that of a competent ward sister.'

'I don't think a man gets full efficiency from any woman unless she is to some extent in love with him. But you overlook that at the time I was happily married myself.'

'I haven't overlooked it. I'm speaking of our past together only with relevance to our future together.' She pressed close. She felt him quiver. '*Your* marriage ended in tragedy, Lancelot. Mine petered out with pointlessness.'

'It's interesting – fewer marriages are broken up now than fifty years ago. Divorce has gone up, but death has gone down. I always think it irritating that our professional moralists never look on the bright side. But I suppose moralists are gloomy by nature.'

'Shut up!' She sat bolt upright. 'That's another of your dodges, Lancelot. Generalizing, philosophizing. Anything, so you can keep your emotions in the deep-freeze and sit firmly on the lid.'

'How can I be romantic, after a lifetime regarding women as loosely-filled bags of organs washed by hormones and moved by neuroses?'

'Surely you can appreciate the glorious joy of sex?' she asked, flopping back on the sofa and sticking out her high-heeled shoes.

'Not when I recall the mother's vomit coming up and the baby coming down.'

'All right. Very well. Have it your own way. Let's sterilize every microbe of romance from the air around us. If we don't marry each other, who else is going to marry either of us?'

'Perhaps I don't want to marry again?'

'Of course you do,' she assured him. 'What should a wife be? A young man's mistress. A middle-aged man's companion. An old man's nurse. So the older you grow, the more suitable I'll be. I think I'll have another whisky,' she said, holding out her glass.

'Surely not?' Sir Lancelot looked anxiously at his watch. 'I mean, if you're shortly driving back to Spratt's Bottom—'

'I'll take the last train. If I go home at all,' she said, lying down on the sofa, looking at him open-mouthed and pulling her skirt up her thighs. The doorbell rang.

She jumped up. 'Who's that?'

'Er—Miss MacNish.'

'But she left!'

'She came back. This afternoon. Her sister in Putney clearly found her as intolerable in twelve days as I have in twelve months. She has been in a taxi to collect her belongings. I must help her upstairs with them. You stay here. Mustn't let her know you're in the house, must we? You know what a scandalmonger she is. It would be all over St Swithin's by lunchtime. Keep as quiet as a mouse. The whisky is at your elbow.'

Sir Lancelot carefully shut the sitting-room door behind him. He again smoothed his bow tie. He opened the door to the street.

'Hi!' exclaimed Amelia. She was dressed in a long, crimson formal gown, diamonds glittering at ears and cleavage. He put a finger urgently to his lips.

'Miss MacNish ... the utmost quiet.'

Amelia nodded conspiratorially, stepping into the hall. 'I escaped early from the Lord Mayor,' she said in his ear. Sir Lancelot replied by pointing dumbly upstairs. He could retreat and somehow get rid of the matron. She raised her eyebrows, smiled, and started tiptoeing upwards. He let her into the bedroom.

She said to him softly, 'You certainly seem sure of yourself.'

'The stage-management is Miss MacNish's,' he told her hoarsely. 'It appears that the sentimentality poured upon her budgie is now flowing in my direction.'

'I heard every detail of the death over the phone. It sounded a perfectly horrible end. Just what the thing deserved. I'm sorry I was so angry at Cambridge.' Amelia laid a hand softly on the lapel of his dinner-jacket. 'But even the crew of the *Bounty* didn't end up in the water.'

'It was an unfortunate accident in more than one sense. I was about to ask you to marry me.'

'Well ...' murmured Amelia in surprise. She placed a hand on his other lapel. Smiling tenderly, she slowly

173

linked them behind his neck. She drew his lips towards her own.

'And what do you say?' he asked.

'It's still the greatest compliment a man can pay a woman, isn't it? Even though we like to think of it as just an invitation to share the household bills.'

'Am I accepted?'

Still smiling, she slowly shook her head. 'Think.'

'I have thought. Extremely deeply. This and my birth are the only events in my life which I have experienced only once before.'

'It wouldn't work, would it? You know that, Lancelot,' she said gently. 'No more than Captain Bligh and Sarah Bernhardt. One marriage isn't big enough for our two egos.'

He frowned. 'Really, Amelia, I must say you're being somewhat pernickety.'

She laughed softly. 'See what I mean? But I shall love you always, Lancelot darling. Which is much better than merely marrying you, isn't it?'

He shrugged his shoulders. 'Perhaps you're right. Were you not such a sensible woman, I should never have asked you, anyway.'

'Kiss me again.'

She drew down his head. The matron appeared in the bedroom doorway, with her dress over her arm.

'Ah, yes,' said Sir Lancelot. He could not recall the feeling since an oil sheik's kidney came away in his hand. 'I believe that you two ladies have met?'

'*What* is this American person doing in your bedroom?'

'She came to collect her nightie.'

'Lancelot—!' The matron's bare arm grasped the door-post. 'My God! You're behaving like an old goat that's been browsing among the jumping beans.'

'And here it is, Amelia,' indicated Sir Lancelot politely. 'Would you like me to wrap it for you in the *Lancet*?'

'I was prepared to bestow my favours, kind sir,' said Amelia pleasantly. 'But I didn't expect having to stand in line for it. Or is it part of the industrial problem you have here – overmanning?'

'I will not tolerate for one moment your treating me in this disgusting manner,' cried the matron.

'Well, I won't tolerate for much longer your walking round my house half-naked,' said Sir Lancelot briskly.

'If I may make a suggestion,' began Amelia.

'No, you may not.' He rounded on her, 'The situation does not call for suggestions, comment, hysterics or other idiocies. It is nothing but a highly unfortunate combination of circumstances, from which the sooner we extract ourselves the better.'

'Aye, aye, Captain Bligh,' she said resignedly. 'I'll hove me from the quarterdeck and go home.'

'I know what you were doing.' The matron's eyes blazed. 'You were organizing an *orgy.*'

'May I have my nightdress back?' Amelia asked him mildly. 'Before you twist it in two.'

'One woman's body isn't enough to satisfy you. Oh, no. Your lusts demand two. You always were a greedy beast. You never gave me a box of chocolates without eating half of them.'

'Shhhhh!' He pointed in panic at Miss MacNish's door.

'I am going back to St Sepulchre's,' said the matron, recovering her dignity and starting downstairs. 'I have suffered enough contamination for one evening.'

'Don't forget to put your dress on, sweetie,' Amelia called. She patted Sir Lancelot's cheek. 'Bye, darling. Call me at the hotel before I leave early Saturday. Maybe we can complete our unfinished business? Though I do advise you to buy a pocket diary.'

Deep in an armchair in his sitting-room next door, snifter of brandy in one hand, eyes half-closed, head full of pleasant visions of addressing the House of Lords, the dean heard Sir Lancelot's front door slam. Habitual keen curiosity over his neighbour's movements drew him instantly to his feet and the open bay window. He observed in the street-lamp a woman hurriedly leaving Sir Lancelot's house, still putting on her dress. A second glance identified her as the matron of St Sepulchre's. A moment later appeared another, holding up her night-dress and inspecting it for rents. He observed this to be the American lady of letters. The dean's eyebrows danced to the successive pounding rhythms of amazement, horror and wonderous admiration.

'By God, one must hand it to him,' he muttered. 'What a man! At his age, too. Testicles obviously thrumming like turbines. All the same, these surgeons,' he added to himself, 'all guts and gonads.'

Sir Lancelot was still standing in his bedroom doorway, breathing heavily, hands deep in pockets. He was recalled to reality by the sounds of slipping bolts, rattling chain, scraping key. He groaned. Before he could mop up the emotional tempest, he would be sweating in the blaze of his housekeeper's indignation. He pulled himself together.

'I must apologize instantly and sincerely,' he began, as the door opened, 'for the rowdy behaviour of my two guests, who have now left the premises. They had, I think, dined too well.'

He stopped. Miss MacNish was coming through the door towards him, staring blankly. She was barefoot in a long flannel nightgown, her dark hair in two plaits with bows of tartan ribbon. She must be sleepwalking. His mind became filled with alarming tales of instant death from shock on awakening from such a state.

'Miss MacNish—' he said softly.

'Sir Lancelot! I have come to you.'

'To me? What for?'

'Sir Lancelot, I heard it all. Every word. You have been in the hands of two wicked women. But you have cleansed

176

yourself of them.' She was close against him. He noticed her breasts under her nightdress, like the head of Highland horned cattle. 'Sir Lancelot, I can bear it no longer,' she said intensely. 'For twelve long months have I lain up there burning with desire. But you appeared to take no notice, Sir Lancelot. My passion went unrequited. *Then* you struck me to the heart. You entertained that harpy—' Her fingers indicated the front door. 'My pride would not allow me to stay under the same roof. But every moment I was away in Putney seemed longer, seemed more tragic, than the exile of the Stuarts. I can understand, Sir Lancelot, a man of your lusty parts taking fleeting pleasure from some flighty female. But what you need is the love of a guid woman—'

Half-asleep again in his chair, the dean jumped as the doorbell rang. 'All right, all right,' he called. 'You're not sounding a ruddy fire-alarm. I thought you were in bed,' he complained crossly to Sir Lancelot. 'Or so I assumed, from the traffic through your front door.'

'Shut up, and give me a drink.' Sir Lancelot snatched the brandy bottle and a tumbler.

'Hey, go easy,' said the dean. 'That stuff's thirty years old.'

'So I see. Not the cooking brandy you give your guests.' Sir Lancelot took a large mouthful.

'What do you mean, bursting into my house like this?'

'I'm spending the night here.'

'You certainly are not. You can't expect me to wake up my wife and tell her to prepare the spare room.'

'This sofa will do perfectly well.'

'What's wrong with your own house?'

'Miss MacNish is suffering from acute nymphomania.'

'Got a bit of an epidemic of it on your hands, haven't you?' asked the dean sourly. 'If the students get hold of this one, the rag week revue will make *Oh! Calcutta* look like *Peter Pan*.'

177

'We have known each other a long time.' Sir Lancelot eyed the dean seriously. He saw him as the spindly, spotty student who came on the tram from Ponder's End and always got the diagnosis right. 'I can confess to you a singular experience. In the space of twenty minutes this evening, I found myself with the prospect of getting into bed with three women.'

'Separately?' enquired the dean. 'Or *en masse*?'

'In the case of two, I did not realize the dangerous strength of passion I had aroused. In the other, the reverse was the case. I had gold-dust in my eyes,' he said sadly. 'Old windbag Shaw was right. Woman reduces us all to the common denominator. I forgot my profession, my position, and worst of all my age. Now I feel like a clapped out pensioner from the white-slave trade. I shall spend my remaining years in dignified solitude, my remaining energies in my work, and I would no sooner share a house with Miss MacNish than with a tigress on heat.'

'As a matter of fact, Lancelot, I was feeling pretty envious of you a few minutes ago,' the dean confessed. 'Now I'm not so sure. It's no good starting out for a round with brand-new clubs if you lose your balls in the rough.'

'Exactly, Lionel. You're a good fellow. I'm sure I'll be comfortable enough here.' He yawned. 'Don't take the brandy away. You might mention to your missus that I like a couple of eggs for my breakfast, with three or four rashers. And tomatoes, mushrooms and kidneys if she's got any. Good night.'

17

'GOOD morning, Mr Cherrymore,' Cindy greeted Ron cheerfully. It was the following Saturday morning. In her white uniform, she was opening the front door at Apricot Avenue. 'You've arrived first on the list.'

He propped his moped against the front of the mock-Tudor house. 'Dr Turnhorn's away, I hear?'

'I had a postcard this morning. From the Bahamas. I don't think they're enjoying themselves much. There's so many sick old folk aboard the cruise ship, all cadging free advice, they might as well have stayed at home.'

'What are their replacements like?' Ron removed his bicycle clips.

'They're two very clever young doctors, but they do get into such a tangle with their sex-lives.'

He stood idly swinging his beads. 'Haven't they got wives?'

'Oh, yes. To start with, one each. Then they both seemed to have two. Now they haven't got any.'

'Spratt's Bottom could do with a little less middle-class morality.'

'Would you like to go straight in?' Cindy showed him into one of the surgeries, and closed the door. 'Good morning, Miss Porter,' she greeted Jenny, as her MG crunched on the front gravel. 'You're nice and early for surgery.'

'I've a dreadfully busy day ahead.' Jenny slipped out of the car. 'I gather the doctors are on holiday? Do you suppose I'll care for the locums?'

'Oh, I'm sure. They're both white.'

Cindy showed Jenny into the other surgery. A few

moments later, Freddie Bisham hurried in to Ron, in a white coat and carrying the patient's file. 'Lord Cherrymore?' he began briskly, before sitting down.

'Ron Cherrymore. I gave up the title. Like I gave up smoking and drinking, to keep my brain clear for fighting the class war, which never ceases.'

'But Karl Marx was a terrible boozer,' responded Freddie absently, reading through the notes. 'He got locked up in Germany for drunkenness, and dropped dead from too many cigars. What's the trouble?'

'My ankle.' Ron slipped off his Jesus sandal. 'I sprained it a month ago. They strapped it at St Sepulchre's, and told me to see my own doctor for a check-up.'

Freddie manipulated ankle and foot. 'Seems fine to me. Forget it. Good morning.'

Ron stayed sitting. 'Doctor—'

'Yes?'

'I knew that ankle was perfectly OK.'

'Then what did you come for?' Freddie asked shortly. 'I've more than one patient to look after, you know.'

'Do some of them ever consult you, Doctor, about one thing, when they really want to talk about something quite different?'

'Frequently.'

Ron nodded. 'I have a problem.'

Freddie sat back with professional patience.

'It's in the mind, Doctor.' Ron tapped his smooth white forehead. 'I think I must be a unique case. But it's really shocking. Dreadfully shocking.'

'Doctors are unshockable. I'm only here to help.'

'Thank you, Doctor. Well, it's like this.' He tugged nervously at his beads. 'Why do you think I gave up my title?'

'Politics, I suppose?'

'Not at all. Not really. You see, I just didn't want anything to do with my father. When he died, I renounced his title. I renounced his money. Well, I kept it in the bank. I scorned his house, his cars, his yacht, his racehorses, his dogs, his guns, his London clubs, his political views. I *hated* my father,' he said distractedly. 'Oh, this is a terrible thing to say . . . while he was alive, I always felt somehow, deep within me, that I actually wanted to *kill* my father. And do you know what, Doctor?' he continued frenziedly, 'I wanted to marry my mother. Oh! How ghastly!'

'There's a lot of it about this time of the year,' murmured Freddie.

'But aren't you horrified at such a case? Will you still keep me as a patient?'

'Here's a book which might help you with your trouble.' Freddie scribbled on a prescription form and folded it. 'You can get it in paperback.'

'Oh, thank you, Doctor,' said Ron with immense relief. 'Is it the latest work?'

'No, it's rather an old work, actually. But things don't change much with the human race.'

'There's just one little detail.' Ron stood up, tucking the paper into the pocket of his flowered shirt. 'I'm shortly expecting to get married.'

'Congratulations.'

'I have been very deeply in love with a lady for some time. Only now do I understand why. She reminds me of my mummy.'

'Probably better than reminding you of hers.'

Jenny was meanwhile saying to Pip, 'I've come for a complete physical overhaul, Doctor.'

He raised his eyebrows. 'Why?'

'I'm getting married. I thought it was advisable.'

'Not in the slightest. Much of the world's population gets married without the chance of seeing a doctor for their whole lives.'

Jenny looked faintly irritated. 'Then while I'm here,

Doctor, perhaps you'd look at my gums? Or is that a dentist's job?'

'We are not yet sufficiently unionized in the medical profession to indulge in demarcation disputes. What's wrong with them?'

'They've started bleeding. And one of my teeth wobbles. Look. Like a clapper in a bell. I'm worried I'll look like a toothless old hag in the wedding photographs.'

'Open wide.' Pip shone a torch in her mouth. 'I say!' he exclaimed enthusiastically. 'Jolly interesting.'

'But I don't want to be an interesting case in the slightest,' she objected. 'I want to be something simple and easily curable.'

'Let's see your arms. Ah! Purpura.'

'You mean, where I bruised myself?'

'You didn't.' He grabbed a magnifying glass from the desk. 'Corkscrew hairs!' he said excitedly.

'But that sounds *dreadfully* alarming!'

'What do you eat?'

'You can't fault me there, Doctor,' she said more composedly. 'Perhaps you know that I am the prospective Tory MP for Spratt's Bottom? We Tories, of course, believe in self-help, maintaining our bodies without being a costly drain on the National Health Service, *mens sana in corpore sano*. I buy absolutely everything I eat at Ye Olde Healthe Shoppe, in the High Street. Home-baked, stoneground, compost-fed wholemeal loaf, fat-free yoghurt, ginseng—'

'Gin what?'

'It's a Korean root. It imparts health, strength, vigour and vitality, according to the leading doctors of China, which two of our Tory leaders have visited. Also sesame seeds, mung beans, carob powder, tenderized prunes, ratafia, salt from the sea, bee-collected pollen and herbal foam baths.'

'No apples and oranges? No cabbage and spuds?'

'I never eat fruit and vegetables, because I think they upset my bowels. As for potatoes – my figure!'

'Congratulations. You've got into the *British Medical Journal*. You're suffering from scurvy.'

'What! But I haven't been anywhere filthy.'

'That's scabies.' Pip slapped the desk delightedly. 'Living off freaky health foods, instead of an ordinary mixed diet, has given you vitamin C deficiency. A well-off, intelligent, young Tory politician in a fat, middle-class London suburb, suffering the nutritional deficiency disease of a half-starved African. Thank you, Miss Porter. You have restored my faith in the balance of Nature.'

'But what am I to do?' asked Jenny in distress.

'Go out and gorge yourself on strawberries and cream. Cindy!' He opened the surgery door. 'Ascorbic acid tablets, please. A thousand milligrams.'

Jenny left the front door to find Ron trying to start his moped in the sunshine. 'Hello, Councillor Cherrymore,' she said amiably. 'And what brings you to the doctor's?'

'My ankle, you know. I noticed your car. Nothing serious, I hope?'

'Just a little advice about my diet.'

'Coming to the council meeting tonight?'

'But most certainly. How could I miss it, with planning permission for the new Tosker Hospital first on the agenda?'

'You're for the hospital?'

'Decidedly not,' she told him firmly.

Ron looked shocked. 'But surely – a new hospital for Spratt's Bottom, without a penny to pay? Nobody could stand against it who'd a scrap of humanity, or a scrap of sense, either.'

'Do be your age,' she said wearily. 'Building a hospital on the *golf course*? Just think of the outcry from the club members. From their families and friends. From everyone who's struggled to get accepted for the waiting-list. Each of them a Tory voter, and an election due any month. I'd be mad, not opposing it with every public word I utter.'

'I think that's disgraceful.'

'Yes, but it's politics. Ron, you and I are professionals,' she said more kindly. 'And we're cynics, which is the same thing.'

Ron looked round quickly. A hot Saturday morning on the first day of July offered the inhabitants of Spratt's Bottom many pleasant alternatives to the commonplace diversion of seeing the doctor. They were alone. 'Jenny, you surely can't cut completely from your life the time we spent together behind the British Museum?'

She was already opening the door of her MG. 'Ron, dear ... there's a line in Thomas Hardy about Tess of the D'Urbervilles. Where she dismissed the past, she trod on it and put it out, as one treads on a coal that is smouldering and dangerous. Tess had good reason to. So have I.'

Ron looked miserable. 'You make a cruel point. But you might get a nasty burn on your foot. My offer's still open, you know. Why don't we live together again? I'm actually prepared to marry you.'

She stared in amazement. 'With the pair of us fighting the election on opposite sides? Really, Ron! Go back and have the doctor examine your sanity. It would be such a massive disaster, it might even let the Liberal in.'

'Why need we fight? You can easily stand down. You'd be much happier spending your life as my helpmeet. Politics is a first-class career only for second-class women.'

She told him angrily, 'You're being horribly selfish.'

He looked offended. 'Selfish? But that's impossible. I'm a socialist.' She was already in the car. He leant on the bonnet. 'Let's *both* give up politics. Fly away and start a new life together. I've a lot of helpful contacts in Albania.'

'No.'

'Very well. I shall make the supreme sacrifice. Go ahead, run as the Tory candidate. You'll certainly be elected, because I myself shall withdraw. Harold Sapworth's brother will stand, and hardly get a working-class vote, because in their eyes he's the most pernicious of capitalists, a bookie. I shall abandon a promising and perhaps brilliant political career,' he said, beads swinging emotionally. 'I shall play Mark Antony to your Cleopatra.'

She started the engine. 'Ron, I'm very touched. I appreciate fully the enormous value of your gesture. But it's no good. You must reconcile yourself to the fact that, like darling Clementine, I have gone for ever. Why don't you find yourself some nice girl in the Young Socialists? They always look so frightfully sexy, straining with protesting bosoms about something or other.'

'That would be bad for party discipline.'

'You mean, they're not the class of girl you're used to?' He made no reply. She put the car in gear. 'There's another reason. I'm marrying someone else.'

'But you can't,' he exclaimed desperately.

'I didn't want to tell you, because it's classified information until the election's over. But I'm officially engaged to the youth organizer at Tory HQ.'

'Arthur Bickley,' he spluttered. 'A bloody Lord.'

'I'm afraid so, Ron. I rather like the idea of being a Lady. I always think it a great pity that you aristocratically emasculated yourself. Must fly. See you at the meeting.'

She drove off between the flower-beds, braking violently at the front gate to avoid hitting head-on an ancient Rolls, which politely backed into Apricot Avenue.

'Morning, Ron.' Sir Lancelot climbed from his car at

the front door. 'Consulting the medical profession, eh? I must say, you look a bit dickey.'

Ron stood forlornly by his moped, unable to speak.

'I gather the Elaine Tosker Hospital comes before you tonight? I hope there's no miserable-minded little councillor who'll oppose planning permission on the golf course, which is anyway one of the dullest I've ever played on. The reaction to this new gift-wrapped hospital utterly astounds me, even with my mean professional opinion of human nature. The Government's turning against it from political expedience. Fleet Street's mostly against it, just to hit the Government. The Civil Service is dead anti, because it's administratively inconvenient. The construction workers are against it, because Tosker cuts labour costs. In the benefactor's own phrase, You can lead a gift horse to the water, and everyone looks up its arse.'

'Sir Lancelot—' Ron stared at him with quivering lip. 'I didn't go to the doctor about myself. I went about a friend. He's very ill.'

'I am sorry to hear it.'

'So ill that he is considering anticipating the inevitable.'

'H'm. My usual advice in these cases is Sir Winston Churchill's – "It is never necessary to commit suicide, especially when you may live to regret it."'

'I'm sure you have met some cases in your long and distinguished career, Sir Lancelot, when ... well, to disclose knowledge of the most painless means is merciful?'

'I have. And I did,' the surgeon admitted. 'A handful of barbiturate, a bottle of Scotch, and somewhere they won't find you for twelve hours. Otherwise, you will be subjected to the full rigours of resuscitation. Which is a fate worse than death. I leave it to you, whether you pass the information on.'

'Thank you, Sir Lancelot.' Ron shook his hand, giving his candid stare. 'You are a great humanitarian.'

He turned to his moped, and kicked it into life. Sir Lancelot strode into the house.

'Good morning, nurse,' he said to Cindy. 'Where are the doctors?'

'Doctoring.'

'Well, tell them to stop for a minute. I want to see them.'

18

'FROM the resemblance of this place to the corporation rubbish-tip, I assume your wïves are still on the loose,' Sir Lancelot greeted Pip and Freddie, as they appeared through the door from the surgery. He stood before the brick fireplace in the lounge. The orange carpet and furniture were littered with old newspapers, opened tins, dirty cups, plates and cutlery, glasses and empty bottles. The house plants in the corner were dying painfully of thirst. 'Why don't you telephone and ask them back? Or at least invite them for the week-end?'

'I cannot forget how Dawn treated the crisis as if created for her personal enjoyment,' said Pip stubbornly.

'You are speaking of my wife,' murmured Freddie. 'As for Eva, had she been set to music she'd have moved Covent Garden to tears.'

'Now you're speaking of mine.'

'Stop arguing, and listen to me,' commanded Sir Lancelot.

'We're both busy, you know,' Freddie told him shortly.

Pip nodded. 'Yes, I've just diagnosed a case of scurvy.'

Sir Lancelot scowled. 'Here in Spratt's Bottom? Which every day eats its way through an entire supermarket? Why do you take such pains, Chipps, continually to impress me that your intellect is as thin as a eunuch's whiskers? You are quite likely to diagnose frostbite in Timbuktu.'

'Well, *I've* just treated a patient with a dose of Sophocles,' Freddie told him.

'What I have to say affects more patients than your

own,' Sir Lancelot continued short-temperedly. 'Our campaign must be thrown into reverse.'

'What shall we do with the car-stickers filling the garage?' Pip asked.

'Burn them. A newly-worded consignment should arrive this afternoon. Our slogan is now changed to, "Raze St Sepulchre's, Raise a New One."'

'Personally, I find the St Sepulchre's saga about as gripping as *son-et-lumière* in freezing fog,' said Freddie. 'And I suspect the crusade is only part of a very boring Hundred Years War for always getting your own way.'

'How dare you speak that way to the man who taught you surgery?' demanded Sir Lancelot.

'Most of which, thank God, I have forgotten. Now it is pointless my sucking up to you for a consultant job at St Swithin's, you might benefit from a few home truths. Hasn't it ever struck you, Sir Lancelot, that in the operating theatre you are as outdated as Lister's carbolic spray? That most of the operations you perform went out with rock an' roll, if not the slow fox-trot? That with most of the others, your technique is so rusty you're like a blacksmith trying to mend a puncture?'

'Listen to me, you little faecalith—'

'May I say something?' asked Pip.

'You may. But as you have the mental capacity of a decerebrate cat, I shall take no notice.'

'I am becoming a little tired, Sir Lancelot, of your assumption that I am of inadequate intelligence. Which arose only because I allowed myself, at St Swithin's, to be frightened by the overbearing attitude which you present to anyone who is too ignorant, inarticulate, immature, or even inconsiderate, to turn and tell you what a stupid bully you are. It's really affectation. I believe you to be at heart a highly intelligent, compassionate and sensitive man.'

'You condescending little—' Sir Lancelot stopped. To

189

their surprise he continued in a crushed tone, 'Perhaps you are both right. I have known the pair of you since you first came to be interviewed for St Swithin's, with your best suits, a short haircut, three rather inferior A-levels and an air of painful servility. I believe you have simply cracked under emotional strain. Women ...' He sighed briefly. 'They can cause considerable, if unnecessary, disturbance to the best-ordered and most sage life.' He glanced to the hall telephone. He had not called Amelia, and now she would be over the Atlantic. 'By the way, if you stack these dishes in the bath and run the taps for half an hour, you'll find they'll come clean. I shall fight for the hospital alone. Good morning.'

He drove to St Sepulchre's, to find a television crew in the forecourt interviewing Nurse Tosker.

'Enjoy your fame,' he said wistfully, passing her at the front door as they broke off. 'These days, it is but a highly-coloured balloon inflated with inert gas.'

'Oh, but Sir Lancelot—' She turned on him her large green eyes. He noticed what a pretty girl she was. 'I'm frightened.'

'Come, my dear. You wouldn't be frightened by becoming Miss World at the Mecca? And how much more satisfying, having a new hospital named after you instead of a new bra.'

'I couldn't face being anything like that,' she confessed. 'I'm the shy sort, really, Sir Lancelot. All the nurses say so. I just want to get on with my work and help people, keeping out of trouble and hoping nobody notices me.'

'But surely, no one can be shy of a rich uncle?' he asked kindly.

'Uncle Hamilton's very generous, but ... well, he does seem to treat the world as though he was putting it through a sheep-dip.'

'Isn't he giving you a trip to Australia?'

'I don't want to go to Australia. I went to Benidorm last

summer, and I got terribly homesick. But of course I can't tell Uncle Hamilton,' she said pathetically. 'It would be like telling St Peter to go and stuff the pearly gates.'

'I think you will find that, despite the exuberant exaggerations of its sons, Australia is really quite a nice place, if you avoid Melbourne on Sunday.'

'Thank you, Sir Lancelot. You always put such heart in people.'

He went to the basement in search of Harold Sapworth.

'Morning, squire.' The shop steward was sitting on an unopened packing-case marked PERISHABLE, playing patience.

'Where's the rest of your ACHE membership? I thought this was a special meeting about the new hospital.'

'Dunno. It's a nice day. Probably the lads have better things to do. Abdul says that his religion doesn't let him out of the house before sunset. Care for a hand of poker?'

Sir Lancelot grunted briefly. 'All right.'

They rearranged three packing-cases. Harold shuffled the cards. 'Quid ante?'

'Very well.'

Sir Lancelot won the deal. 'What's the attitude of ACHE towards the new hospital?'

'It's a bit difficult, squire.'

'By which you mean that you are being intolerably and stupidly obstinate?'

'That's it,' Harold agreed cheerfully. 'We don't want no new hospital. We want to go on keeping St Sepulchre's as it is. I'll double. Look at it this way. If St Sepulchre's goes, every small hospital in London will go. The Ministry want to cut them down, to save the taxpayers' money. We want to keep them open, to save our jobs. Simple.'

'I'll see you.'

'Pair of aces.'

'Low straight.' Sir Lancelot swept up the banknotes. 'I

honestly cannot believe that a man as sharp-witted as you, Sapworth, can miss an obvious point. That hospitals, like every other organization, must be run efficiently. Otherwise, you'll all be out of work, because all the patients will be dead.'

'Of course I see it, squire. What have you got?'

'Threes.'

'Two kings.'

'Hard luck.'

'I know we don't need six grown men to put one frail lady on a theatre-trolley. But if anyone tells us otherwise, we might start dropping a few, just to illustrate our point. Now this new Tosker hospital is going to be fully automatic. Computerized. *Labour-saving*. Straight.'

'Flush. You lose. Sorry.'

'But we don't *want* to save labour, Sir Lancelot. There's plenty of people out to cut our throats, without us obliging them ourselves. So ACHE's calling one-day strikes, until the Government says it'll keep St Sepulchre's going, and return the other one to Mr Tosker, with thanks.'

'Have you no feelings of common humanity?'

'Of course. I always buy flags on lifeboat day.'

'Thank heaven that I am in a profession which can afford at least principles. At the risk of giving offence, Sapworth, I do not see why the organization of the Health Service should be dictated by your members. Any bloody fool can be a hospital porter.'

'Any bloody fool can win the VC, mate. We're all one team now, one happy family. The days when the doctors walked round like lords is dead and gone. I've got a full house.'

'And I've got four jacks. Rotten luck.'

'Mind you, I'd rather be bossed by the doctors than some of them birks what run the unions. Always got to push their weight around, show virility. Be big. Otherwise, they don't pick up them plum Government jobs and get on the telly. We're the poor sods what has to suffer, as well as the public.'

'A pair of nines.'

'Nothing.'

'How do you expect the country to hold together, when people like you continually set one half of it against the other?'

'I expect it will.' Harold grinned. 'I watched the telly last Sunday. *Hamlet*. I was going to switch over to the other side, when I discovered something. This Shakespeare and me speak the same language. All that didn't happen in Denmark. Nah. It happened in the Old Kent Road. Look, there's this Prince Hamlet and this Gravedigger—'

'I am familiar with the play.'

'Who are they, squire? You and me. We both know our place. You do your princeing. I'll bury you. We both respect ourselves. We both respect each other. And no bloody arse-licking, on either side. We're easygoing, we're sorry for them what's worse off, and we sees the same jokes. All that's what holds us together. Four queens.'

'There's a divinity that shapes our ends. Four aces.'

Harold swept up the cards. 'I'm skint. Should never have started playing with a crafty bugger like you.'

'*There* you are.' A crisp female voice came from the far end of the room. Sir Lancelot quivered. The matron beckoned him towards the door. 'What are you doing, hiding yourself in the basement? I've been looking for you everywhere.'

Harold resumed his patience.

'I expect you are utterly ashamed of yourself,' she assured Sir Lancelot in a low voice. 'Your behaviour last Tuesday was worse than any woman has encountered since the Boston strangler was put away. I suppose you were full of liquor after the rugby club dinner. You really must remember that you are no longer one of the students. I want you to quell the riot in the hospital forecourt.'

'What's the matter now?' he complained testily. 'If the mob's come to break the windows, all the better. They haven't been cleaned for months.'

'I don't know,' she said with sudden helplessness. 'It's all highly confusing. I telephoned the police, but they didn't seem interested. No wonder there's no law and order left in Spratt's Bottom. I shall have to rely on a few sharp words from someone in authority, like yourself, bringing them to their senses.'

Feeling a vaguely guilty obligation towards the matron, Sir Lancelot accompanied her down the long corridor to the lobby. A dozen or so patients were peering with interest through the windows. The television crew were still in the forecourt, their presence stimulating the two or three hundred men and women of all ages who overflowed on to the surrounding pavements. Some were shouting, some singing, some jumping up and down, some waved placards. The group seemed to Sir Lancelot identical with any which demonstrated everywhere in the country, against anything which for the moment attracted its displeasure.

'They look quite harmless,' he observed to the matron inside the front door.

'In that case, step outside and tell them to go away.'

'It's not the sort of action I relish. At Christmas, I ask even the waits in for a drink.'

'I will not have people treating the forecourt of St Sepulchre's as though it were the terracing of some football ground,' said the matron fiercely. 'If you're too scared, I'll set about them myself.'

'Oh, very well, very well.' Sir Lancelot had the obscure feeling that he must demonstrate his manliness to the woman who had shed her dress for him, with no more effect than sneezing over him. He opened the front door with the air of Henry V leaving to see how things were going in the breech.

'Good morning, ladies and gentlemen,' he declaimed from the steps. The demonstrators fell silent. Everyone stared at him. He wondered what to say next. 'And a jolly nice morning it is, too,' he remarked amiably.

He began to notice that the invaders of the forecourt stood in four groups. The biggest surrounded a tall, angular, wild-eyed man in a green corduroy suit, who seemed to Sir Lancelot faintly familiar. His arms flailed, his fair hair swung wildly, in animated conversation with his supporters.

'I'm sure you must all feel very strongly about something or other,' Sir Lancelot continued. 'And nobody is more open to the other chap's point of view than myself. But you must push off.'

There were shouts of, 'Why?' Two or three started singing *We Shall Not Be Moved*. 'Go back to the monkeyhouse,' he heard.

'Because I say so,' he told them.

There was ironic clapping and jeers. The man in the corduroy suit made a brief, authoritative gesture, silencing his followers instantly. Sir Lancelot became aware of a slim, young, pretty policewoman at his elbow, long blonde hair swept under her official hat.

'I'm warning you,' she said. Sir Lancelot turned to face her. 'We have received a telephone complaint from the matron of this hospital about the demonstration. If there is any repetition of the violence which accompanied your last one, I shall take you into custody without further caution.'

'My dear Miss—'

'Officer,' she corrected him sternly.

'My dear Officer, I assure you that no one respects the Law of England more than myself. Its tradition, majesty and history are embodied in your own slight frame, exactly as in the fully-robed Lord Chancellor upon the Woolsack.'

'Watch it, that's all.'

Sir Lancelot returned to his audience. 'I am perfectly prepared to engage the leaders of this outing in reasoned argument.'

'There's no argument about it,' said the man in corduroy, approaching with waving arms. 'Because this new hospital's not going to be built. As from now.'

Sir Lancelot swallowed. The policewoman's eye was on him. He gave a sickly smile. 'Indeed?' he asked mildly. 'And pray, sir, why not?'

The man gave a short, barking laugh. 'Because I'm against it. And when I'm against anything, it has a way of never happening.'

'I know you,' exclaimed Sir Lancelot hotly. 'Arthur Arrows, isn't it? The bloody protester – I mean, defender of our civil liberties.'

'Remember the Metropolitan Motorway?' Arthur Arrows tapped his own chest fiercely with a long finger. '*I* stood up to them. Remember the Channel Tunnel? Maplin? Even Stansted Airport? Who got them stopped? *I* did. Who stopped fox-hunting in half the counties of England? High-rise flats? Food adulterants? Fluoridation of water supplies? *Me!* Only two failures to date, Concorde and the Common Market, and I'm still working on them.'

'But why,' Sir Lancelot asked patiently, 'should anyone but a madman object to a brand-new hospital? Particularly,' he added, eyeing his inquisitor, 'when it comes as free as birdshit?'

'Hospitals? We've got enough hospitals,' Arthur Arrows replied, arms windmilling. 'They only encourage people to go off sick. We need homes, not hospitals. That money could be a lifeline to our fellow-citizens who are caught in the poverty trap. What happens when *they're* ill?

196

Rushed into hospital, three square meals a day, all wants satisfied, full care all round the clock. They're cured. Then what? Back to the poverty trap. Doesn't make sense, does it?'

'I have yet to find anyone who would prefer a week in hospital to one sleeping rough under newspapers on the Thames Embankment in mid-winter.'

'This isn't much of a demo today,' Arthur Arrows admitted with professional contempt, inspecting his ranks. 'You wait till next Saturday. Then we'll really hot things up. I've a couple of thousand of my flying protesters coming down by special train. They're having a week-end off from picketing the new nuclear power reactor in Scotland.'

'Sir Lancelot Spratt, isn't it?' A wizened man with a moustache which appeared permanently discoloured from tea stood at the surgeon's elbow. 'I'm Major Swiney, chairman of the local Ratepayers' League. That's my little lot, over there.' A knot of soberly dressed, middle-aged people clustered demurely under a banner reading, HANDS OFF SPRATT'S BOTTOM. 'I'm as humanitarian as the next fellow,' Major Swiney insisted quietly. 'But I'm damned if I'm going to stand by while the gentlemen in Whitehall – who, of course, always know best – plonk down an ugly new hospital amid our homes and gardens. Hospitals attract all sorts of undesirable people. And Spratt's Bottom is well known for possessing a certain tone.'

'You mean, you don't want to see your property values slump?' Sir Lancelot suggested shortly.

'Well, how would you like it,' the Major returned. 'Having a bloody great hospital at the bottom of your lawn?'

'I have. Yes?' He found himself faced by a tall, pale, elderly man with a halo of grey hair and small gold-rimmed glasses askew a sharp nose.

'I have been praying for you all night.'

'That is remarkably civil of you.'

'That you may see the light. We are *Fiat Lux*.'

Sir Lancelot groaned loudly. Everyone in the country knew *Fiat Lux*, which could make them feel filthily guilty for receiving a comic postcard from the seaside. He recalled it as an organization against such pastimes as pornography, prostitution, and pot, none of which he considered particularly enjoyable, nor sufficiently harmful to merit cauterization by the white heat of indignation in which its members warmed themselves.

'We have been praying that this new hospital will never come to pass.'

'But why pray, pray?' Sir Lancelot demanded crossly.

The man stuck a finger indignantly towards a notice which directed round a corner of the ugly building, GYNAECOLOGY.

'Well, it's an eleven-letter word,' Sir Lancelot agreed, 'which these enlightened days is used in public, and even on television.'

He hissed, 'To me, it spells "Abortions". Look at that—' His finger jabbed in another direction. '"Special Clinic." You cannot deceive *me*, you know. We of *Fiat Lux* are men and women of the world. That means 'V D', doesn't it? Go on, admit it. That's all hospitals are used for these days.' His tone seemed applicable to Auschwitz. 'Cleaning up the squalor of the permissive society. That and euthanasia, of course. We need not more hospitals but fewer, my friend. Hospitals staffed by devoted people, caring for the true suffering of the world, which is holy and purifying.'

'It's people like you in the last century who busied themselves objecting to chloroform,' Sir Lancelot told him angrily. 'They went around saying that if God had intended women to enjoy painless childbirth, He would have made the process more like shelling peas.'

'I sorrow at such unChristian sentiments from a medical man. No wonder our society is sicker than any of your patients.'

'Good God! You make Mr Pecksniff look like Long John Silver. *You* won't change the nature of human beings. That needs another million or so years of evolution.'

'I shall pray for you,' he said sorrowfully, falling on his knees at Sir Lancelot's feet. 'Ouch!'

'What's the matter?'

'I suffer from a loose body in the right knee-joint, Doctor.' His face contorted, one hand gripped the knee on the stone step. 'It locks, and is extremely painful. Always comes on suddenly, usually at awkward moments.'

Sir Lancelot's eyebrows rose. 'Loose bodies are interesting. Sometimes called "joint mice". If you step inside, I might be able to unlock you.'

He drew the evangelist to his feet by his lapels. He felt a light hand on his arm.

'I have been observing your threatening language,' said the policewoman. 'And I am warning you that I shall arrest you if you do not remove your hands from that man at once.'

'But I'm trying to get him up, not do him in,' Sir Lancelot protested.

'I'm warning you,' she repeated.

He let go. The patient struggled to his feet, groaning.

'Come along to my out-patients' next Thursday afternoon,' Sir Lancelot invited him. 'I can refer you to my orthopaedic colleague. A man of your piety must have efficient knee-joints. And who are you?' he demanded of a fat, red-faced man with a bushy ginger beard, in a worn tweed jacket with leather-patched elbows.

'We're The Environmental People,' he announced cheerfully. 'You must have heard of us? We're strong on furs, whales, atmospheric lead, all that. Well, we're against your hospital. Here at Spratt's Bottom, anyway.

All new hospitals should be built in open countryside, where the patients can hear the birds and smell the flowers.'

'That hospital has as much chance of opening in Spratt's Bottom as Marks and Spencer's in Cairo,' Arthur Arrows assured him.

'Hear, hear,' said Major Swiney gravely.

'What's that?' Sir Lancelot snapped, as the matron struggled towards him with an envelope.

'A telegram.'

He tore it open. He read,

SPRATT ST SEPULCHRES HOSPITAL SPRATTS BOTTOM EMERGENCY MEETING RESOLVED PLAN FOR PRIVATE STROKE PUBLIC HOSPITAL RASH ILLOGICAL UNWORKABLE IF YOU CONTINUE TO SUPPORT IT MUST DEMAND RESIGNATION

SECRETARY GUILD OF CONSULTANTS.

'Bah!' said Sir Lancelot contemptuously, crushing the flimsy paper and hurling it away.

It hit the policewoman in the face.

'I've warned you enough.' She took his elbow. 'Assaulting a police officer. You're under arrest.'

19

'GETTING quite an old friend,' said the cheerful police-man. He led Sir Lancelot down the steps from the dock in the Spratt's Bottom magistrates' court. It was the following Tuesday morning. 'See you again next week?'

'I doubt if I can afford it.'

'Yes, two-fifty quid and another two-fifty costs *was* going it a bit,' the policeman admitted amiably. 'She must have got out of bed the wrong side this morning.'

'That talk of sending me for psychiatric reports.' Sir Lancelot shivered.

'Oh, don't take that to heart. Believe me, you strike me as a load saner than the average prisoner,' the policeman assured him.

'That mention of prison.' Sir Lancelot shook.

'I wouldn't have worried,' the policeman said lightly. 'You wouldn't have got much of a stretch. Six months at the most.'

They reached a grille by the cell doors. Sir Lancelot felt for his chequebook. 'Sorry we can't give discounts to regular customers,' said the policeman.

He wrote a cheque for five hundred pounds in cold, impotent anger. There was no way to revenge himself on the State's gross injustice. He decided to cut all the High Court judges next time he visited his club. 'How's the knee?' he gruffly asked the mild sergeant on the other side of the grille.

'Quite recovered, thank you, Doctor. The chairman of the magistrates would like you to go round and see her.'

'Out of the question.'

'Mrs Widmore said she was missing the next two cases, particularly to speak to you, sir.'

'Is this the usual after-sales service?'

'Never known it before, all my time in the force. Usually, the Bench like to keep a few policemen between them and their day's work.'

Sir Lancelot frowned. He could express his feelings of shameful ill-usage to the damnable woman's face. He would keep his hands in his pockets. He wondered what the tariff was for assault upon magistrates.

'First door outside on the right,' said the sergeant helpfully.

A policeman showed him into a small, square dark-panelled room, with a square highly-polished table, some leather-seated chairs and a stout case full of thick books. His tormentress rose from writing.

'Sir Lancelot Spratt ...' She held out her hand. 'How delightful to meet you socially.'

He made no reply.

'Cigarette?'

He shuddered, as though offered an angry asp.

'Do sit down,' she directed with a pleasant smile.

He hesitated, but obeyed.

'I have heard so much about you, but never imagined that I should have the pleasure of actually chatting to you.'

'Any pleasure in our acquaintance, madam, I assure you is entirely one-sided.'

She made a slight dismissive gesture, with another smile. 'Did you operate upon anyone yesterday?'

'Upon several.'

'You did your duty. This morning, I did mine.'

'Had I done mine with the misjudgement of yours, there would now be a dozen extra corpses in the mortuary at St Swithin's.'

'You want me to feel guilty, or at least offended, but I

cannot. No more than you can feel the pain of your patients' stomach ache. I detach my world on the bench from my private life. And my private feelings. As I am sure you do yours at the patient's bedside. If every single case which came before me – or before you, it is surely the same thing – were afterwards dispatched to some other, highly undesirable world, we should be depriving ourselves of much civilized company. I think all my friends have been here for speeding. I live on a very straight road.'

Sir Lancelot grudgingly admitted that she had a point.

'From your remarks in court just now,' she asked him in a friendly way, 'do I gather that you have a poor opinion of my legal abilities?'

'I merely mentioned my belief that you people have no formal legal training at all.'

'Well, I *did* get a First in Law at Cambridge. Er—with distinction. I was at Newnham.'

Sir Lancelot's eyebrows briefly rose. 'I was at Audley.'

'But I did not steal a horse to celebrate the event. Stealing horses is one of the things at Newnham which even today, I believe, is still not done.'

A faint smile touched his lips, to be instantly eliminated.

'You knew my husband, Sir Lancelot.'

'I am sure that I did not.'

'The intensive care unit at St Sepulchre's. Twelve months ago. You came down from London specially, in the middle of the night. My husband had been admitted as a medical emergency, a heart condition. He was found later to have an aneurism of the abdominal aorta, which you operated upon. Unfortunately, without success. After his death, I spoke only to the physician, not to you.'

'Of course, I remember the case perfectly. I'm sorry I could do no better. If it is any consolation to either of us, he was lost before I even made my incision.'

'As you were doing the operation, Sir Lancelot, I knew that *no one* could do better.'

He began to think that she was really an attractive woman, when not behaving like Boadicea with a bad hangover.

'I am myself a widower,' he imparted.

'So I understand from the newspapers.'

'Your husband was a lawyer?'

'No, he was a banker. I was left living in an enormous house, and thought this and a seat on the council the most useful activities to fill my life. In court, you see, I had to compensate in my mind for all you did for my husband. Perhaps I did so a little too severely,' she admitted.

Sir Lancelot wondered about the chance of getting some of his five hundred quid back.

'And perhaps I did not allow sufficiently for aggravation by that awful man Arthur Arrows.'

'Dreadful feller,' he agreed heartily.

'Though I honestly believe that his followers protest against anything and everything for no better, nor worse, reason than expressing their personalities. We live in a society whose individuals are becoming increasingly anonymous. Our myriad human variations are as unpopular with governments, big business, mass entertainment, the press, the trade unions, the educators, as weeds in the Garden of Eden they have landscaped for us.'

'That is precisely my own view.' He just stopped himself from enthusiastically slapping his thigh. 'The first thing you learn in medicine is every man being of supreme importance to himself. If you forget it, you will have few patients and mistrustful ones. I have never understood why an instinct so compelling as selfishness should be such a social sin. This man Arrows is an individualist, who could have been defused in childhood with an interest in painting or pottery. He might have been a great poet, had he any talent. Or a great philosopher, had he any brains.'

She murmured, 'Self-importance is the spur that the clear spirit doth raise.'

Sir Lancelot smiled. He said graciously, 'I am pleased that here, if not next door, we hold an identity of views,' meaning that hers wisely accorded with his.

'Don't you smoke at all?' she asked, offering him another cigarette.

'The warning of its dangers which I see every day is somewhat more impressive than that printed on the packet.'

She replaced them on the table untouched.

'I am particularly interested in so controversial a local institution as St Sepulchre's,' she revealed, 'because – I am sure I can speak to you in confidence – I shall be the next mayor of Spratt's Bottom.'

'How gratifying that the office should be filled by one so intelligent.'

'You are very kind. I wondered if you might possibly offer me a visit there?'

'I should even admit you to my operating theatre next Thursday,' he said generously. 'Were you not likely to faint at the sight of blood.'

'That is rather unlikely. My father was a surgeon, Mr Bridgenorth—'

'Old Stuffy Bridgenorth?' exclaimed Sir Lancelot. 'Taught me all about the prostate.'

'Were you at St Swithin's?' she asked in surprise. The telephone rang before he could reply. 'Excuse me—Yes? It's for you.' She added, with raised eyebrows, 'From No. 10 Downing Street.'

'Hello?' said Sir Lancelot. 'Charles? Not at Lord's today? Jowler's in good form. H'm. Really? At eight this morning? And him? And *him*? Not *him*? Remarkable. Quite a swoop. Yes, I should suppose there would be. Tomorrow night? I'll pass the news on. He's down here today. Thank you. I think Jowler will clear them all up before lunch, don't you? That wicket is breaking up.' He replaced the telephone. 'A friend from my club,' he explained. 'If you would kindly excuse me, I must go to St Sepulchre's on an errand of some urgency.'

While Sir Lancelot was swinging on the scales of justice, Ron Cherrymore was striding glumly across the Spratt's Bottom golf course. In one pocket of his jeans was a plastic container of barbiturate tablets, stolen the night before from the St Sepulchre's dispensary. From the other, stuck a newly-bought paperback copy of Sophocles. In the breast-pocket of his flowered shirt was a note which said briefly, 'I renounced my title. Now I renounce life itself. Love to Jenny. Ron.' In his hand was a bottle of Scotch.

'Fore!' bellowed in his ears. A golf-ball whistled past his head. 'You fool, do you want to kill yourself?' demanded an irate man with a driver.

'Oh, sorry,' Ron apologized. 'Well, yes, I suppose.'

'God knows what the club's coming to,' declared the golfer. 'They seem to be moving the mental cases in already.'

Ron recalled a dense thicket which separated the 1st and 18th fairways. He scrambled his way painfully through the brambles and gorse to its middle. He cleared a space, and sat leaning against a pine tree. He took out the Sophocles and flicked it over idly, wondering why the doctor had recommended it. He opened his barbiturate capsules, thinking what a pretty colour they were. He unscrewed the cap of his Scotch. He gripped his beads. 'This is it,' he said. 'Good-bye, world.' He squared his shoulders. 'Look out, Dad – here I come.' He started the process of his self-destruction. He raised the bottle to his lips.

Sir Lancelot drove down the High Street blowing his horn, scattering pedestrians and jumping the lights. He braked sharply in the St Sepulchre's forecourt, where a television crew were interviewing Harold Sapworth. He noticed with relief his quarry standing on the hospital front steps. It would be unnecessary to hunt the dean in the office of Mr Clapper, who would only complicate the encounter, as he complicated everything he touched.

As he marched towards the front door, Sir Lancelot noticed with surprise that the dean was talking animatedly to Pip Chipps, still in his safari suit. Beside him stood Mrs Chipps. Or possibly Mrs Bisham. Sir Lancelot had given up caring.

'Ah, the jailbird!' exclaimed the dean heartily at the surgeon's approach. 'I thought I heard the clank of ball and chain. I say, Lancelot, you're becoming quite an old lag, aren't you?'

'Dean, I have something of the utmost importance to impart—'

'Next stop Dartmoor, I expect, eh?' The dean twinkled. 'Don't worry, I'll come and visit you. The wife's awfully fond of the West Country. Bring you a fruit cake with a saw in it.' He laughed.

'An event of some gravity has occurred this morning.'

'Of course it has,' said the dean more severely. 'For one of our consultants to appear in court, two weeks running, will provide the most disgraceful publicity for St Swithin's when you inevitably appear before the General Medical Council.'

'Will you listen to my news?' demanded Sir Lancelot impatiently.

'Will you listen to mine?' returned the dean proudly. 'One of your juniors, at least, has the good name of St Swithin's at heart. Chipps here has won the James Lind medal.'

'You?' scowled Sir Lancelot, the improbability distracting his thoughts from his mission.

'For his work on kwashiorkor in Kenya.' The dean smiled happily. 'The prize is well deserved, and will be the foundation, I am sure, of a most valuable career in the science of nutrition. Young, practical, hard-working, highly-motivated scientists like yourself, Chipps, are exactly what our unruly world needs today. Fat bellies hold no fire,' he pointed out.

'But the man's a half-wit,' objected Sir Lancelot angrily.

'I perhaps supply the other necessary half.' Eva eyed Sir Lancelot severely. 'I saw Pip's potential, when you did not. Which was perhaps unfortunate, as I imagined that to be your prime duty as his teacher.' She clasped Pip's hand in hers. 'However, I am in love with him, when it would seem that you are not.'

'Quite remarkable, isn't it, Chipps being here in Spratt's Bottom,' the dean continued sunnily. 'I only managed to trace him at all, because I ran into his mother-in-law yesterday at a University sherry party. He's been doing a locum for one of the local gp's,' the dean informed Sir Lancelot. 'A nice, uncomplicated rest-cure, I should think.'

'So many doors are now open to me, Sir Lancelot,' Pip told him happily, 'that I shan't have to knock on your iron-studded one for funds. I suspect that my winning the medal has only irritated you. You always regarded me as a maggot in the fruit of the tree of knowledge.'

'Your assessment of my character, Chipps, is as erroneous as was mine of yours. I offer you nothing but admiration and apologies, both unstinted.' He held out his hand. 'Kindly do not overlook that I am a St Swithin's man as much as you are. I am bloody proud of you.'

'Stay for dinner, Sir Lancelot,' Eva invited. 'I can give you my pilaff.' She looked fondly at her husband. 'Tonight, I am reunited with Pip.'

'I regret that more pressing engagements beckon – what's the matter?'

'Just my appendix scar. Itches a bit.'

'Dean, I do wish you'd listen to me—'

'What are you rabbiting on about?' he said crossly. 'I must drive my Rolls back to Town.'

Sir Lancelot became aware of a voice raucously singing *The Red Flag*. It struck him that the words were not those used at Labour Party conferences, but at St Swithin's rugby club dinners.

'Where the hell have you come from?' He demanded, as Ron Cherrymore threw his arms round his neck and sagged at the knees.

'From the dead,' he explained thickly.

'You stink like the buffet car on a Scots football special.'

'Your fault, my dear old dope-pedlar. All yours. I followed your prescription. Well, the first half. After that ... world didn't seem such a rotten old place after all. Marrofact, seemed a pretty good place, my dear old gut-rummager.'

Ron kissed him, and started to sing *The Red Flag* again.

'Great mistake, killing myself.' Ron shook his head violently. 'Great mistake. Almost as bad as giving up my title.'

Sir Lancelot hissed, 'Those TV sharks have got their camera on you.'

'Good. Always wanted to get on the box. Hello, Mummy!' He waved wildly, still clinging to the surgeon. 'It's your little Ronnie. Another mistake, calling myself Ron, my dear old body-basher. Trying to be a bloody worker. Hate the bloody workers. Bloody dimwits. If they weren't dimwits, they wouldn't be workers. Eh? Stands to reason.'

'Here—' Harold Sapworth pushed his way through the crowd which had gathered on the hospital steps. 'What are you going on about?' he demanded angrily. 'You're our Labour candidate.'

'*You're* not a dimwit,' Ron told him generously. 'You're always open to arguments, aren't you? So long as there's enough of them, and they're all printed with a picture of the Queen's head.' He roared with laughter.

'My brother will hear about this,' Harold said fiercely.

'Stuff your brother. Stuff the Labour Party. Stuff all parties. Listen. I'll explain politics. The workers have only got one virtue. There's so bloody many of them. The nobs have only got one virtue. They know which side their bloody bread's buttered. So they suck up to the workers, to get what they want. So everyone's happy. Simple. I'll start my own party. Bloody good party it'll be, too. You're invited, Sir Lancelot, my dear old crotch-chopper. I may not have a title, but I can still get as pissed as a lord. I resign my parliamentary candidature, Harold,' he said grandly. 'You microbal *mafioso*. I feel sick.'

'Nurse!' commanded Sir Lancelot. One hand supported Ron, the other prevented Harold Sapworth's assault upon him. 'Take charge of this patient before he ruins a newly dry-cleaned Savile Row waistcoat.'

'Come along, Ron. Come and have a nice lie-down,' said Nurse Tosker soothingly.

'My ministering angel,' Ron cried, transferring his weight to her. 'Minister to me. I love you.'

'I'm so glad. This way, now, Ron—'

'Ronnie. Call me Ronnie. I've half a mind to see if I can get my title back.'

'You *are* a naughty boy, aren't you? So early in the day, too. Careful. We'll go to casualty and have a little stomach wash-out, shall we?'

'What was it you kept trying to tell me?' the dean asked Sir Lancelot.

The surgeon drew him aside from Pip and Eva. 'Hamilton Tosker has been arrested. So has the Minister of Health. So have two junior ministers in other departments. The police are bringing in his other contacts by the van-load. I believe they are having to borrow vehicles from the fire brigade.'

'Oh, my God!' The dean's eyebrows appeared to take off. 'Do you suppose that I ... I ...' He made a noise like an air-lock in old plumbing.

'You know how deep you are in Australian manure, not me. Perhaps you should see that your passport's up to date. The whole thing makes that Profumo business look like postman's knock. There's an emergency debate in the House tomorrow night. The Prime Minister particularly wants you to get all five of those MPs there – your patients – somehow or other. Unless every man jack of them hobbles through the lobbies, he's sunk and there's a General Election three weeks on Thursday.'

'Oh, my God,' cried the dean again. 'But two of them ... just as I left St Swithin's ... the ones I couldn't diagnose ... turned ... as it were ... into by-elections.'

'Lloyd George was right in 1922,' reflected Sir Lancelot sombrely. 'July is a bad month for prime ministers.'

'Farewell,' cried the dean in agony heavenwards. 'Ponder's End.' He turned to Sir Lancelot, 'Could you possibly give me a lift home? I think I should prefer not to be seen for a while in that Rolls.'

20

'I'm sure you will find my first operation interesting, Celia,' said Sir Lancelot, driving Mrs Widmore into the forecourt of St Sepulchre's the following Thursday morning. 'It is the simple repair of a hernia, but I shall use it to demonstrate the basic principles of surgery.'

'I'm certain I shall be enthralled, Lancelot.' He backed his Rolls into his reserved parking space. 'By the way, I have given up smoking,' she told him. 'I thought you might be interested.'

'And gratified.'

'I gather this hospital is a somewhat trying one for the staff?' They were strolling towards the casualty entrance.

'Not to those of us who preserve an attitude of humorous resignation.'

'I wish I could,' she said feelingly. 'But perhaps it would not be an entirely correct one on the bench.'

As they pushed through the busy casualty department, he volunteered, 'I am going on holiday next week.'

'Anywhere exciting?'

'I do not care much for travelling on my own. I shall stay at home. Are you interested in cricket?'

'But I adore it! My husband used to play for Middlesex.'

'Really? Then you must come to Lord's next Thursday,' he said pressingly. 'There's a good county game. Afterwards, you might care for dinner at my club?'

'How delightful! Which one is it?'

'The Sheridan.'

'But my poor husband was on the waiting-list for years!'

'After dinner perhaps—' Sir Lancelot gave a low

chuckle. 'It might amuse you to visit some pleasant river-side public house?'

'Secretly, I love pubs.'

'We might even end in a night club?'

'Who knows?' she smiled.

'And if there is a strike at your hotel, you can come home for a nightcap.'

She looked mystified. 'But I'm not staying in a hotel. I live here.'

'Ah. Of course. Forgive me. Slight muddle. My home is anyway not fit to be seen, as I have sent my housekeeper on an extended holiday in Oban, following an unpleasant emotional experience.'

'You must find it a sad life, living alone? I do.'

'I find it sad – but hopeful.'

She stopped, looked at him and smiled more tenderly. 'I would say exactly the same.'

'Lancelot!' They had reached the crowded lobby. The matron stood in the middle, hands clasped urgently before her.

'The chairman of our local magistrates,' he introduced his companion politely.

'I am already aware that you had made each other's acquaintance. Lancelot – good-bye.' She held out her hand.

'Have a nice holiday,' he said pleasantly.

'I am going for good. As it has been officially announced that St Sepulchre's will stay open for ever and ever – now that dreadful Tosker has made the Great Train Robbers look like fare-dodgers – I have resigned. I cannot endure waiting for my next weekend off, let alone my retirement. I have taken a job with the World Health Organization, flying round the world to disaster areas. They seemed to think that I had exactly the right experience.'

'I am very relieved.'

'Why?' she asked pointedly.

'That you have congenial employment,' he insisted. 'I am sure you will find the work most rewarding. By the way, I hope that young Nurse Tosker herself is not too upset at the crash?'

'I doubt it, as she is to marry Ronnie Cherrymore on Election Day.' She glanced at Mrs Widmore. 'Can I leave you with some advice, Lancelot? As your former ward sister? All bowls and vases of flowers should be removed from the bedside at night. Good-bye.'

Sir Lancelot conducted Celia Widmore along the main corridor. Outside his operating theatre stood Freddie Bisham and Dawn.

'The hen is back in the hutch?' he asked unwelcomingly.

'Yes, sir. Our television went wrong in the middle of Wimbledon.' Freddie clasped her hand. 'No man shall ever put us asunder again.'

'Just to tell me that, you have abandoned Dr Turnhorn's patients for the entire morning?'

'No, sir. I wanted to apologize. I have behaved and spoken to you disgracefully. I am deeply sorry. Now I shall return to Apricot Avenue.'

'You won't. As you're here, you can assist me in the theatre. My houseman operates like playing the piano in boxing-gloves.'

Sir Lancelot passed Celia to the care of his theatre sister. He went to scrub-up. There was no water. He kicked the pipe behind the soiled linen bin. No response.

'Try stamping on the floor next to the transfusion stand,' Freddie suggested helpfully. 'That often does the trick.'

Sir Lancelot marched into the operating theatre, pulling on his rubber gloves.

'Perhaps you have observed, with the surgical knowledge of your upbringing,' he began to the gowned and masked Celia, 'this is an indirect inguinal hernia. I shall be making the normal incision. The case is uncomplicated, and I anticipate no difficulties whatever. All right to start, Ali? Good. Scalpel, please, Bisham. This should prove a perfectly straightforward – Bloody hell! What in the name of God? Bisham! The patient, look after the patient! You, woman, Widmore, whatever your name is, grab his feet before he goes arse over tit into the swab-bucket. Bisham! You've got a job. Here. I'm resigning. Bloody Health Service! *Grab his feet* you stupid bitch of a dimwitted magistrate! Is this the first time you've done a proper job of work in your life? Swab, sister, swab! I'm getting this hernia finished in double quick time. Bloody Lister! Bloody Pasteur! Bloody Fleming! Bloody Hippocrates, for inventing such a bloody stupid way of making a living.'

Sir Lancelot and his entourage slowly disappeared from view as the floor collapsed.